I0706057

The Arrangement

SONALI MISHRA

Copyright © Sonali Mishra 2024

All rights reserved.

No part of this book may be reproduced in any form or by any electronic or mechanical means, including information storage and retrieval systems, without written permission from the author and publisher, except for the use of brief quotations embodied in critical articles and book reviews.

This is a work of fiction.

ISBN: 978-1-963705-02-7

Cover design: Clarissa Kezen ckbookcoverdesigns.com

Published in the United States of America by Harbor Lane Books, LLC.

www.harborlanebooks.com

For my mother.

CHAPTER

One

Leather and Wood is a trendy, upscale restaurant on the corner of Clay and Polk Streets in the heart of San Francisco. It's a small building with huge, street-facing windows, through which its patrons enjoy observing passers-by during the evening cocktail hour. If you were to have passed Leather and Wood at 7:47 p.m. on January fifteenth, in a year not too far removed from this one, you might have seen a man sitting alone at a table in the center of the restaurant. This man's name was Arjun Chowdhury, and he really, *really* needed to pee.

Since arriving at the restaurant, Arjun had ordered seven glasses of water, hold the ice (he'd read once that restaurant ice machines were seldom cleaned). To the casual onlooker, this might seem an inordinately large amount to drink before eating—but Arjun had been sitting at his table alone for exactly forty-seven minutes, and he had nothing better to do.

He did not usually come to restaurants like this, where the dim overhead lighting suggested a mine shaft, and the small steel chairs had small steel arms that dug uncomfortably into his sides. He was not a fan of cocktails with such obnoxiously punny names as "Tequila Mockingbird" and "Lavender Vida

Loca", nor their inexplicable eighteen-dollar price tag. He liked least of all the other clientele, whose perfectly paired-up presence seemed to rub it in his face that he was the only single person in this entire restaurant. And this, of course, was the sole reason that Arjun had come to Leather and Wood in the first place: because it was, in the words of the *San Francisco Current*, "The perfect location for a first date."

Arjun checked his watch again. It was 7:48 now. The couple at the table next to him touched ankles and twined their feet together, like birds in a mating ritual.

The waitress came by again. She was older than the other servers in this restaurant, with various colorful pins tacked to her black apron and her gray-streaked hair spun into a messy bun. "More water?" she asked, holding up a carafe. She wore the same pitying expression she'd had the last three times she'd come by.

"I'm good for now," he said, smiling awkwardly. He felt oddly impotent in that moment, like a stray puppy dumped unceremoniously on the restaurant's doorstep, yet another problem for this poor waitress to deal with.

If she was annoyed, she didn't show it. "Of course," she replied pleasantly. "And do you know when you might be ready to order?"

"I'm still waiting on someone."

The waitress opened her mouth as if to say something—instead, she nodded dubiously and turned to leave.

"How long is too long to wait for a date, do you think?" Arjun blurted, the words tumbling out of his mouth before he could stop them.

She stopped and looked thoughtfully at him. "You've been here for an hour now?" she asked.

"Forty-nine minutes."

"And have you heard anything from this person? A call, a text—maybe even an email?" He shook his head, and the waitress smiled sympathetically. "I'm sorry to tell you, but there's a line between lateness and negligence. Your date crossed that line half an hour ago."

Arjun nodded. "That seems about right," he said miserably. He stood up, handed the waitress a twenty for her trouble, and asked her where he could find the bathroom.

The light was Arjun's favorite thing about San Francisco. It had layers here, like panes of colored glass laid one over the other. Gray fog swept over the soft yellow glow of the streetlights, and above the rolling hills soared the inky purple sky. The night was chilly, with a hint of humidity that suggested impending rain, and Arjun slipped into his blue puffer jacket and stuck his hands into his pockets.

This date had been only the latest in a string of disappointments. There had been setups with friends-of-friends and matches concocted by algorithms on dating apps. The San Francisco chapter of the Yale Alumni Association held mixers, and he had spent countless nights riding a barstool, hoping that "The One" would walk in and notice him. Of course, "The One" had never shown up—or, if she had, she'd taken one look at him and passed right by.

Arjun wondered if he'd ever find out what happened to tonight's date. Maybe she really *had* run into a problem. He pictured a variety of scenarios: a woman plummeting down a crevasse or being pursued by a hungry polar bear. Or maybe she'd gone to *another* Leather and Wood…although, to Arjun's knowledge, the only other restaurant with that name was in New York City.

No use fantasizing, he thought, resigning himself to never knowing the real answer. Of course, he could ask Kelley, his assistant, who'd set up the date—but he knew he'd be too embarrassed to tell her that he'd been stood up.

Arjun realized that he was inordinately disappointed—after all, this was just a blind date. He hadn't even known what the woman looked like, only that she was a brunette named Allison who at one point had been Kelley's roommate ("And just so you know," Kelley had qualified, "she wasn't a particularly *good* roommate, either").

So why *was* he upset, then? Arjun knew it wasn't this invisible Allison who had this power over his emotions. It was the day itself that troubled him: January fifteenth. Arjun was twenty-nine years old, and tomorrow was his thirtieth birthday.

By this time in his life, Arjun had always expected to have found his "One True Love" and to be married. He might have even been a father. And why not? His father had married his mother at twenty-eight and had Arjun at twenty-nine. And yet…here Arjun was, on the eve of the big Three-Oh, with no prospects in sight. *Incomplete*, he thought, imagining a hole tearing through his chest, a void where a vital organ should be.

Perhaps this is how it's meant to be, he mused. The realization cut like a knife. Arjun knew that some people remained alone for their entire lives…he'd just never thought *he* would be one of them. *You're still young*, he told himself—but, for the first time, that answer did not seem sufficient.

It was a short walk back to his condo in the posh Rincon Hill neighborhood beside the Embarcadero. Arjun's condo stood in a row of buildings all lined up neatly along a tree-lined avenue; up above, the tip of the Salesforce tower swirled in fog, pulsing with bright blue light.

The metal gate leading to the condos' entrance was usually locked, but a brick propped it open tonight. Arjun passed through and fished in his pocket for his keys. He wanted nothing more than to sink into the couch, flick on the television, and unplug his mind until he fell asleep. He stepped up the stoop to his front door, turned the lock, and pushed the door open.

The living room exploded with light and noise, nearly blasting him back outside. People leaped from behind the couch, trumpeting kazoos; a hail of confetti rained from the entryway closet. Arjun's kitchen island was covered in gigantic bottles of alcohol and hotel trays containing all of his favorite foods: mac and cheese from Chez Maman, brownies from Tartine—even a whole tray of bright-orange chicken tikka masala. His initial shock wore off as he recognized the people inside: his friends, practically all of them, crowded into his apartment. He felt a smile stretch across his face as he saw his best friend, Dan, leading a rendition of "Happy Birthday"—and, instantly, he forgot all about his troubles. He was content to nod along to the music, spread his arms wide, and bask in the company of his friends.

When the music finished, Dan approached Arjun and thrust a bottle of Captain Morgan into his arms. "The man of the hour!" he crowed. "Arjun and I have been friends since we were fourteen years old. And tomorrow, he's thirty—so, let's make sure he rings in the next decade with the biggest hangover of his life!"

A hearty laugh boomed from the crowd, and then Arjun's friends began chanting: "Speech, speech, speech!"

Of course, he had nothing prepared. He cleared his throat, planning to extemporize something. Instead, he just unscrewed the bottle cap. Buoyed by a tide of cheers, he began to drink.

It was two in the morning by the time the last stragglers got in their cabs to go home. Arjun's condo looked like one of those fraternity basements he'd been so careful to avoid in college. The air was redolent of spilled beer and pot smoke. The trash can overflowed with empty beer cans, and drained liquor bottles hid in strange spots all over the apartment: atop the fridge and inside the cabinets, squeezed between couch cushions, and perched on the windowsill like cats. The trays on the kitchen island were still half full, and Arjun knew he should empty them before they began to smell. *Later,* he promised himself, crashing backward onto his couch. He hadn't drunk this much since college, and his head felt like it was full of static, like an old television switched to the wrong input.

Dan slouched next to Arjun and checked his phone. "It's after midnight," he announced. "You're officially thirty."

Arjun groaned. "Don't remind me."

"Come on," coaxed Dan, punching his arm. "Thirty is a great age to be. All of this." He gestured around at Arjun's trashed apartment—"we never have to do it again, if we don't want to."

"Except for your wedding, of course."

"I should have mentioned that. Yes, we're getting sloshed that weekend."

"It *was* a great party," said Arjun. "Thank you for putting it all together."

A toilet flushed, and a set of footsteps sounded down the hallway. Dan's fiancée, Erica, strode into the living area. Her blonde hair was covered in glitter, and it shimmered as she threw it behind her shoulders. "You really think *he* put all of this together?" she asked. She sat on Dan's lap and wrapped her arms around his neck.

"I thought I would give Dan at least *some* credit," Arjun said, grinning mischievously. "Seriously, what would I do without you guys?"

She shrugged. "You'd probably never have fun again. Are you planning on cleaning any of this up?"

"Later," Arjun replied, waving his hand. He was too tired for any of Erica's suggestions now, sensible though they might be. There was practically a siren song emanating from his bedroom, calling him to sleep.

"Come on, no use in putting it off," chided Erica, getting up. "You don't want to start off your thirties in a pigsty, do you?"

He sighed. "No, I suppose not." He rose, ambled over to the kitchen, and started taking storage containers out of the cabinets.

"You guys go ahead," Dan said, yawning hugely. "I'm going to crash in the guest room."

Erica shot him a withering glance. "I meant *after* I helped you guys clean up," Dan added hastily.

The doorbell trilled. "Someone must have forgotten their phone or something," said Arjun, spooning leftover macaroni into an old yogurt tub.

"I've got it," Dan said, walking to the front door. He looked through the peephole and recoiled as if it had burned him. "*Arjun.*"

"What is it?" Arjun replied. "Not the naked homeless guy again?"

"No, dude. It's your *mom.*"

He frowned. "My mom?" he repeated. "Why would she be in San Francisco?"

"I don't know—but that's definitely her."

Arjun strode over to the door and peered through the peephole. Sure enough, his mother was standing on his doorstep, dressed in a puffy white coat and Prada sunglasses —even though the only light outside came from the security camera. There was a purple roller bag on the stoop beside her. She rang the doorbell again, thrice this time: *dingdingding.*

"Arjun?" she called, shouting in case the doorbell hadn't worked. "Aaaaarrrjuuuuuunnnn." She began ringing the doorbell even faster now, like an overzealous *Jeopardy* contestant.

"What are you going to do?" hissed Dan, his breath hot in Arjun's ear.

Arjun closed his eyes and pinched the spot between his eyebrows. Even though his mother was still on the other side of the door, he could already feel the alcohol's effects ebbing away in her presence. "You can't just leave her out there," said Dan.

"I know," Arjun replied. He turned the lock and opened the door to the hurricane standing on his stoop.

Dr. Sarita Chowdhury, MD, was not supposed to be here. She and Arjun had spoken just that afternoon, and she'd been between patients at her private practice psychiatry clinic in Des Moines. Sarita was not the type of woman to withhold details, especially when it came to her only son—but, for whatever reason, she'd kept quiet about her flight to San Francisco.

She stepped into the apartment, handing Arjun her Gucci handbag and surveying the scene. Her lips curled with distaste. "I see that the festivities have already begun," she said. She turned and noticed Arjun's friends sitting awkwardly at the kitchen island, and she beamed. "And Dan and Erica are here. Come here, you two." The pair stepped forward and allowed Sarita to embrace them. "How are you?" she asked. "When's the wedding?"

"We're still setting a date," said Dan, rubbing the back of his neck.

"Still setting a date?" Sarita shot back. "This is too much, isn't it? I mean, you've been dating since high school. I remember you two in my basement, making Arjun so uncom-fortable with all of your kissing." Arjun shot his mother a poisonous look. She only smiled, impervious to such glances from her son.

Dan chuckled uncomfortably. "Let me get your suitcase," he said, taking the opportunity to move out of Sarita's appraising gaze. He rolled the suitcase down the hallway to the guest bedroom.

"And how are you, Erica?" asked Sarita, shifting her attention to Dan's fiancée. "Are you still enjoying your residency?"

"I don't know about 'enjoying,'" Erica laughed. "But it's moving along. Thankfully, pediatrics residency is only three years."

Sarita smiled knowingly. "I always tell Arjun how proud I am of you. I always wanted him to be a doctor, you know. It makes me so happy that his good friend is pursuing it instead."

Arjun grimaced. "Yes, Mom. We're all very happy for Erica."

Dan returned from the hallway. "It was great to see you, Dr. C.," he said, rubbing his hands together. "But Erica and I should really get going."

"So soon?" asked Sarita. There was genuine disappointment in her voice.

"I'm afraid so," Dan replied, stifling a yawn for effect.

"Well, I brought some *kaju katli* for you two," Sarita said. "Erica, I remember you always used to like it." She gestured for her handbag and drew out a multicolored cardboard box. "Enjoy, dears."

"Thanks, Dr. C.," said Erica, accepting the sweets. She and Dan bade farewell to Arjun and his mother, then donned their coats and stepped outside.

Arjun turned his attention back to Sarita. "Well, this is unexpected," he said, draping the trays of food in cling wrap and sliding them into the refrigerator.

"A welcome surprise, I hope."

"I wish you would've called. I could have tidied the place up. Or gotten you a hotel."

"*Psh.* A hotel? I'm not a stranger, Arjun. And believe me, your room was much messier in high school."

Sarita kicked off her flats and sat at one of the bar stools by the kitchen island. She was a head shorter than Arjun, with a bob of shiny black hair, and once sitting, she was even shorter. Her height made her no less formidable.

"I would love something to drink, by the way," she said pointedly. "It was a long flight from Des Moines." Arjun's mother liked sparkling water, and he walked to the fridge to get some. He cursed under his breath. He'd meant to go shopping but forgot, and the fridge was empty.

"I'm out of sparkling water. But I have beer," he suggested, proffering one of the few lukewarm cans remaining on the counter.

"Do I look like a sorority girl to you?"

he sighed. "How's tap, then?"

"Do you have a filter?"

"It's San Francisco, Mom. That's not really a thing here."

"If you say so," Sarita replied dubiously. Arjun filled a glass from the sink and set it on the counter in front of her. He stood across the kitchen island, leaning his weight on both arms.

"Mom, is everything all right?" he blurted. "Are you sick?"

Sarita laughed. "Why is that always your first line of thinking? Of course, everything's all right. Can't a mother come to surprise her son on his birthday?"

"That's not really why you came, is it?" he asked, his eyes narrowing with suspicion.

Sarita rolled her eyes. "Honestly, Arjun," she purred, "you make me out to be some kind of cartoon villain. You know, I don't always have an ulterior motive."

Arjun sighed with relief. *She's just here for my birthday.* Of course, that's what it was! Thirty was a big one, wasn't it? No wonder she'd come all this way. Arjun smiled and kissed his mother on the forehead.

Sarita sipped her sparkling water. "All right, perhaps I do have an ulterior motive," she admitted. She inhaled sharply and fixed her gaze solidly on her son. "I want to find you a girl."

He frowned. "You want to find me...a girl?" he repeated. "For what?"

"For marriage, of course!" said Sarita, laughing. "I mean, don't you think it's time?"

"No," Arjun said reflexively. "For the thousandth time, Mom—I'm not getting an arranged marriage."

She grunted with exasperation and rose from her seat. "I still don't understand your hesitation, Arjun. It's not like I'd be marching you down the aisle at gunpoint. I'd simply be... making an introduction. Finding you a suitable girl, a compatible girl. Taking out all of the guesswork. Doesn't that sound better than...whatever you've been doing?" She waved vaguely at the mess.

Arjun noted the judgment in his mother's voice. Or perhaps it was frustration. After all, this wasn't the first time she'd offered to arrange a marriage for him. Her pleas had only become more frequent as he neared thirty, and each time he'd refused point-blank. *This is America,* he would explain, *and people get to find their own spouses here.*

Still, his mother was an Indian mother, and meddling in her son's life was hardwired into her DNA. "I'm not having this discussion with you," he said for the umpteenth time, crossing his arms in front of his chest.

Sarita sighed. "You've always been difficult, you know," she said. "Can't you, for once, listen to your mother?"

Arjun shook his head. "I love you, Mom...but this is the one area where I don't want your help."

"And when *will* you want my help?" she countered with sudden forcefulness. "When you're forty, and no one wants you anymore? When you're too old to play with your kids?" He didn't reply, and, sensing an opening, she pressed her advantage. "You are ready *now*," she said. "You have your looks, your health, and all the success in the world. Trust me, *beta*. I know what's best for you."

"I will *never* want an arranged marriage," he replied, trying to keep his voice steady. "Never ever. I don't know how I can make that any clearer to you."

Sarita sat down again and looked disconsolately at the floor. Arjun felt guilt flood over him—and, as always, he went to his mother. "It's fine, Mom," he said, putting his hand on her shoulder. "There's still plenty of time for me to find someone."

She brushed his hand away and looked up at him. "No," she said, and her voice was full of sadness. "You're *thirty*."

"How was your weekend, Kelley?" asked Arjun, striding into the brightly colored offices of Pay Systems, Incorporated.

"Same old, same old," his assistant replied, her beach-ball belly looking like it might burst at any moment. She bounced up and down on the exercise ball Arjun had bought for her, which he'd read would help relieve back pain during pregnancy. "Cramps, mostly. I had a really strong craving for steak, too, which is strange because I'm a vegetarian. Do you think that's weird?"

He thought about it for a moment. "I have no idea," he decided. "So, did you get your steak?"

She grinned wolfishly. "Extra bloody."

He laughed. "Now, *that's* weird."

Kelley's desk was right outside Arjun's corner office: a glass cubicle overlooking California Street, with a view of the Ferry Building in the distance. She swung herself off of the ball and waddled in after him. "So, what's on the docket today?" Arjun asked, sitting.

Kelley swiped her phone a few times. "I just emailed you your itinerary," she said. "You have a meeting with Mark

Thayer from Regulon at four. Other than that, you're pretty much free, although Jason in HR has some forms for you to fill out."

"I have them right here," said Arjun, reaching into his desk drawer for the manila folder that Jason had dropped off on Friday evening.

Kelley grimaced and clutched at her spine. "Are you sure you don't want to go home, Kelley?" he asked, rising as though he might need to catch her if she fell. "Honestly, if you need to rest—"

"I'm fine," she replied, waving her hand. She winced suddenly. "Okay, maybe I'm not totally fine. Distract me. Tell me how your date was with Allison. Did you two hit it off?"

He shifted uncomfortably in his chair. "I had to cancel, actually," he lied. "My friends threw me a surprise party, so I couldn't go."

She raised an eyebrow. "A surprise party? What for?"

He smiled sheepishly. "I turned thirty this weekend."

"Thirty?" she exclaimed, as though Arjun had announced instead that he'd spontaneously grown a tail. "Happy belated birthday! God, Arjun, I'm so sorry I forgot!"

"Really, it's no trouble," he said. "I try not to make a fuss about my birthday, anyway."

"Well, maybe any *other* birthday," she replied. "But thirty is the exception, isn't it? That's a big milestone. Huge."

"If you say so," he said, thinking briefly of his conversation with his mother. *It isn't a big deal,* he told himself. *Thirty is just a number.*

"I'm sure you can reschedule the date," Kelley said. "I can ask Allison again, if you'd like?"

"I don't think that will be necessary," Arjun replied, wanting to terminate the conversation about Allison as quickly as possible. "But thanks, anyway."

"Of course," she said, returning to her desk for a well-deserved nap.

. . .

While Kelley dozed off outside his office, Arjun opened his laptop and found the bookmarked page he'd been obsessing over for the past month. He sighed, staring longingly at the screen. *Is today the day?* he wondered, scrolling past pictures of empty storefronts. *Am I actually going to do it?*

As long as Arjun could remember, he'd wanted his own restaurant. He spent summers in India as a child and remembered going to the market with his grandfather in Hyderabad. The sun would still be rising, but the narrow alleyways were packed with people and produce. Different kinds of colorful vegetables were laid out at dozens of stalls, and vendors stood before each one, calling out to the shoppers. "Do you see this one?" his grandfather had asked, plucking a plump purple *brinjal* from a pile. "I tell you, *beta*, I have such designs for this one." The two of them would return to the house laden with produce and smelling of cardamom and asafetida. Arjun would watch his grandfather tend to a huge pot, and he eagerly awaited the meals that he would churn up.

But that was a long time ago: before Yale, before business school at Stanford, before Arjun took the high-paid startup job, and before the startup got acquired by PSI. He was thirty now—and, like it or not, his life path was narrowing from a six-lane highway to a one-way street. Now, he could hardly contemplate leaving PSI and the lifestyle it offered: stability, status, and prestige.

Still, a man could dream. As Arjun scrolled through the realty website, contemplating the various buildings for sale, his mind wandered back to his conversation with his mother.

Sarita had stayed another day in San Francisco, and Arjun had taken her to the Palace of Fine Arts, where she'd pressed her case even further. "I'm not trying to pressure you," she had said, craning her neck to stare at the massive, tawny rotunda. It was drizzling outside, and their raincoats made drip mark trails on the plaza, like monocolored Jackson Pollock paintings.

"I find that hard to believe," Arjun replied. "I mean, you literally flew out to San Francisco unannounced, and you ambushed me at my birthday party. That doesn't seem like something you'd do if you *weren't* trying to pressure me."

"Well, maybe some pressure is what you need," Sarita retorted, dropping the pretense. "I mean, to be thirty years old and unmarried! And living in San Francisco, of all places."

"What is that supposed to mean?" Arjun asked, crossing his arms.

"Nothing," she said, with a wave of her hand. "It's just that…people are starting to talk."

"What people?"

His mother fixed him with one of those telepathic glances, and all of a sudden, Arjun knew exactly who'd been wondering about his marriage prospects. "It doesn't matter," he sighed. "There are bigger things in life than the Indian Mafia of Des Moines. I mean, doesn't it ever get old? Gabbing with those nosy women like fishwives. First, it was high school gossip, but I'm thirty now. I really don't care what they think about me."

"How nice for you," Sarita snapped. "But it's not them I'm concerned about. It's you. I mean, can't you picture it? A nice Indian wife: beautiful, well-educated? And children! Oh, when you have children, I promise I'll move into your apartment and raise them for you."

The notion of his mother joining him in his apartment was almost enough to turn Arjun off from the idea of ever having kids. "I'm just too focused on my career right now," he said instead, aware of how lame and false those words sounded as they rolled off his tongue.

"Ah, yes: your career," said Sarita, smiling sarcastically. "Always, your career. When you're on your deathbed, will you have your 'career' to comfort you?"

Arjun chuckled. "I think my deathbed is a way off."

"*My* deathbed, then," she replied, exasperated. "Think of how much more easily I'd pass on with a perfect little grand-baby by my side!"

Arjun could only shake his head. "Whatever you say, Mom."

Still, her words had hit the mark. Arjun *did* want all of those things Sarita was telling him about: a wife and children, a house full of laughter, and the sound of little footsteps running across the floors. But, no matter how badly he wished for this future, he couldn't—he *wouldn't*–wrap his mind around an arranged marriage. He was steeped in a life-time of watching Nora Ephron films and chasing his own rom-com-worthy quest for true love. And true love was always serendipitous, not something you ordered like picking out a vacuum cleaner on Amazon. Having his mother find him a wife would be like surrendering, admitting that he was too broken to find true love on his own.

Arjun had driven Sarita to SoMa, where they had dinner at an Indian restaurant that she deemed "subpar." After extracting a promise that she'd call before her next visit, Arjun dropped his mother off at SFO.

Arjun alternated between the realty site and actual work until noon. When he grew hungry, he got lunch at the deli across the street, bringing back a pastrami sandwich for Kelley and setting it on her desk (where she was still sitting, sound asleep).

To Arjun's surprise, he found his boss, Adam D'Antonio, lounging behind his desk. "Arjun, my boy," Adam beamed, flashing his impossibly perfect teeth. "Did you enjoy the weekend?"

"It was all right," he replied. "My mother dropped by for a visit." He set his salad on his desk and sat down opposite Adam. "What about yours?"

"It was excellent! My kid was the fiddler in *Fiddler on the Roof*. I'd never seen it before; did you know the fiddler isn't the lead? It's some old man named Tevye." Adam let out a booming laugh that seemed to shake the office. He'd played outside linebacker at Stanford, and the years had not diminished his hulking frame in the slightest. Silhouetted against the window, he towered over Arjun like a mountain.

"So, what can I do for you, Adam?" Arjun asked. His boss usually stopped by to chat about the 49ers or, on occasion, actual work. "Are you here to prep me for my meeting with the Regulon folks? I put together a deck you can look at, if you'd like."

"Actually, I had your assistant punt that meeting to Wednesday," Adam replied. "I need you on something else today." He paused, seemingly for effect. "It's Pacific Bank. They're coming in this evening to discuss their mobile strategy for the new year. I'm going to need you to take that meeting."

Arjun raised an eyebrow. "Pacific Bank? That's one of our biggest accounts—that's *your* account. Wouldn't they want to meet with the CFO?"

"Ordinarily, yes," his boss admitted. "But I have to fly out to Seattle today. Our largest account, Crimson Financial, is considering walking away from us altogether, so I have to go personally. And, unfortunately, the Pacific Bank folks are flying in from LA and can't reschedule."

"Adam...are you sure about this?" Arjun asked. "I've pitched strategies to clients, sure, but never anyone this big. Aren't you worried that I could...I don't know, mess everything up for the company?"

Adam grinned. "Arjun, I wouldn't be asking you if I didn't know you could do it. You're not the youngest Vice President in PSI history for nothing, huh?"

Adam stood and sidled past Arjun, clapping him on the shoulder as he passed. "You'll do great!" he called over his shoulder as he sauntered down the hallway.

The presentation was scheduled for five o'clock, so Arjun didn't have much time to prepare. Adam had sent over a new slide deck, and Arjun reviewed it with Kelley in one of the conference rooms. "As you know," he said, "PSI offers state-of-the-art software infrastructure for financial institutions just like yours. I'm here to tell you about our newest product, Transfer Tech. It allows customers to transfer money between their accounts and automatically pay bills easily. Our closest competitor, Altura, charges twice as much as we do, with customer success scores that are forty percent lower than ours. Your clients deserve the best in banking technology—let the remarkable team at PSI lead the way."

Kelley yawned.

"What's wrong?" Arjun asked, his heart sinking. "I don't have Adam's charisma, do I?"

She laughed. "It's not you. It's the presentation. Is there any way to…I don't know, jazz it up a little?"

He sighed and glanced at the presentation being projected onto the conference room wall. *Was* there a way to make financial presentations more entertaining? "I mean, I guess I could change the font," he said, rubbing the back of his neck. "Would that be helpful?"

"It might be," she replied, thoughtfully stroking her chin. She and Arjun spent the next forty minutes debating the merits of serif and sans serif fonts, deciding between Avenir and Century before finally landing on Futura.

"Who are we kidding?" groaned Arjun, sinking back into

a chair. "This is the most boring pitch in history. I'll be lucky to *keep* the account, let alone expand it. I don't know what Adam was thinking. I'm a manager, not a salesman."

Kelley shrugged. "Yeah, maybe you're right. Maybe you really aren't cut out for this. Or maybe you're just acting like a scared little boy."

He sat up. "That's one hell of a pep talk."

"It wasn't supposed to be a pep talk," she replied. "Look, Arjun: Adam asked you to do this for a reason. All of the assistants have a group chat, and do you know what we talk about? First, how hot your new beard looks—but mostly about how the other VPs here can't do anything! You're the most competent person at this whole company. I believe in you."

Arjun realized that he'd been holding his breath, and exhaled deeply. He felt his anxiety subside, like a wave receding from the shore. "Thanks, Kelley," he said. He glanced at the clock; it was 4:15. "I think I'll go grab a coffee before the meeting. Do you want anything? Maybe some herbal tea?"

"No tea for me," Kelley replied, laying her hands over her stomach. "But I wouldn't say no to a chocolate chip scone. Or a dozen."

He smiled. "Of course, Kelley." He walked to the door and turned around. "Do the other assistants really think I'm hot?"

She pointed out the doorway. "Focus, Arjun. Scones!"

There was a coffee shop across the street from the PSI offices, one of those local gems that had somehow held on during the city's rapid Starbucks-ification. Delicious scents drifted through the shop: cinnamon and cloves, mocha and vanilla, and the pastries baking in the massive oven behind the counter. A Smiths song played softly from speakers hidden in the alcoves. And, because this was San Francisco, the coffee shop also doubled as an art gallery: colorful paintings hung on the walls, all available for purchase.

Arjun approached the register. "There he is!" the cashier called when he saw him approaching. "You here for your daily caffeine fix?"

Arjun smiled. "You know me too well, Ron. How's business today?"

"Can't complain," Ron replied earnestly. "Let me guess: you want your usual?" He made a face and imitated a town crier unfurling a scroll, "Iced coffee with exactly two splashes of oat milk and one packet of Splenda!"

Arjun laughed. "That's it," he said. "Oh, and a chocolate chip scone, too. I'm mixing it up today." Arjun leaned over the glass display case, considering the selection. "Actually, I'll take the lot."

"Watching your figure, I see," Ron said jokingly, sweeping the remaining scones into a white paper bag before making Arjun's coffee. "Hey, can I ask you something?" he asked, handing Arjun his drink.

"What is it?"

"You know that Vee-nee guy? Indian fellow, works in your building?"

Arjun nodded. "You mean Vinay? Yeah, he's actually another one of the Vice Presidents at PSI. What about him?"

"How's he doing? He usually stops by the shop two or three times a day, but I haven't seen him around for the past few weeks. He hasn't left the city or anything, has he?"

"As a matter of fact, he has," said Arjun. "He got married a few weeks ago. He's on his honeymoon, but he should be getting back any day now."

"That's good to hear," Ron replied, breaking into a wide grin. "That man is single-handedly putting my son through college."

Arjun laughed. "Have a good one, Ron," he said, waving

goodbye. He turned toward the door and stepped outside. It was still a bit chilly, and he hurried across the street.

A voice called out behind him. "Hey! Hey, you!"

Arjun kept moving. Having lived in San Francisco for six years, he knew it was best to ignore the homeless people who yelled at you on the street.

"Hey!" the voice called again. "Yeah, you in the blue micro puff!"

Arjun turned around, one hand on the door to his building. The woman who was yelling at him was definitely not homeless. She had dark, wavy hair that fell just past her shoulders, beneath which Arjun could discern the glint of two star-shaped earrings. Her nose was prominent and angular, and there was a small gold ring in her right nostril. The most noteworthy thing about her was her eyes: bright, piercing, and green as summer grass. Arjun had seen many Indian women, but never one with eyes like that. He felt his heart flutter as though it had been jolted by an electric paddle.

"Can I help you with something?" he asked, finding his voice.

"Yeah, you can," she said, folding her arms. There was a deep scowl etched onto her face. "Care to explain why you took all of the chocolate chip scones?"

Arjun glanced down at the paper bag in his hand. "...I wanted them."

She raised an eyebrow. "Are you trying to give yourself a heart attack?"

"They're not for *me*," he protested. "They're for my assistant. She's pregnant," he added, hoping this would convince this strange (and strangely beautiful) woman to leave him alone.

"Well, there are at least ten scones in that bag," she said. "Your assistant can't possibly eat them all."

Arjun shrugged. "I mean, maybe not. But what's the big deal, anyway? It's not like I bought all the scones in the store.

There's still cinnamon maple, peach pecan, triple chocolate, vanilla matcha—oh, and cheddar, too. You're more than welcome to any of those."

The woman scoffed. "How magnanimous," she said sarcastically.

"Look, I don't know what you want me to do here," Arjun said. "I bought the scones, fair and square. If you don't like it…well, get there earlier next time."

He swiped his key card and pushed the door open. "It was nice meeting you," he said, his voice dripping with irony.

"Screw you!" the woman shot back.

She shook her head and stormed across the street again.

CHAPTER

Three

Y*ou are an idiot*, was Arjun's first thought when he entered the club. *You are a big, dumb, stupid idiot.*

Perhaps his first indication should have been that this was the "second bachelor party" for Kevin McPherson, one of Arjun's direct reports who'd recently divorced his husband. In retrospect, a much larger clue was that the invitation, received in the office and shaped like a crowing rooster, stated that this event would take place at a Castro club called "The Cock." And, since those two hadn't been enough to jog his cognition, there were the speedo-clad male dancers gyrating atop raised platforms in the center of the dance floor.

Yes, for the first time in his life, Arjun had found himself inside a gay club.

It wasn't that he had a problem with being around gay people—this was San Francisco, after all, and back in high school, Arjun had been a card-carrying member of the Gay-Straight Alliance. But Arjun still felt…well, like his cousin's white husband, Tom, always so out of place at family weddings and his aunt's annual Diwali bash in Orlando. Arjun moved uneasily through the crowd, wending through sweaty bodies and fields of ample (and exposed) chest hair.

He spotted Kevin and the others in the VIP section, an elevated area cordoned off by red velvet ropes in the back corner of the club. A huge bouncer stood near the entrance to the section, holding a clipboard that looked comically undersized in his enormous hands. "Name?" he asked, his deep baritone booming above the thumping music.

"Uh…Arjun Chowdhury," replied Arjun, wiping away a spot of glitter that had somehow attached itself to his arm.

The bouncer scanned his list. "I don't see you," he said, shaking his massive head. "Not on the list, not going in."

"Can you ask that table of guys?" Arjun asked.

"What table of guys?"

Arjun pointed. "They're literally the only ones sitting in this section."

The bouncer frowned. "Like I said: not on the list, not going in. Move it along, man."

"It's okay," came a voice. Arjun recognized Kevin McPherson, who'd tamed his mess of curls beneath an ill-fitting fedora. Kevin was a coder at PSI who, as usual, was wearing a Hawaiian shirt. Tonight's selection was midnight-blue, with a bright-yellow parrot stitched onto the breast. The outfit was so garish that Arjun half-expected the parrot to start squawking.

The bouncer grunted, evidently frustrated that he'd lost the chance to rough someone up. Still, he moved aside. "Thanks," Arjun said, following Kevin to his booth. "I thought for sure that guy was about to pick me up and throw me out."

Kevin gave him a strange look. "I don't know if he was strong enough for that," he said. He tapped the table as they arrived. "Hey, everyone: this is Arjun. Arjun, this is everyone."

Arjun nodded awkwardly, scanning the faces around the table. He recognized only some of them: software engineers from PSI and a few people who worked at the *San Francisco*

Current, the newspaper that occupied the bottom floor of the PSI office complex. Despite being in a dance club, most of the men dressed in the typical software engineer's uniform: athleisure pants and tee shirts emblazoned with the logos of the various startups where they worked.

He sat down, only halfway planted inside the booth. "It's good to meet you all," he said, feeling very much the outsider among Kevin's friends.

"What's that?" asked one of the men, pointing to the small, gift-wrapped package that Arjun had placed on the table in front of him.

"Oh," said Arjun, staring at the box as though just now noticing it. He cleared his throat. "It's, uh…well, I wasn't sure if this was an occasion for gifts or not."

"Are you kidding me?" said another one of Kevin's friends. "*Any* occasion is an occasion for gifts." Quick as a cat, he snatched the package away and tossed it across the table to Kevin.

Kevin held the package to his ear and shook it. "What is it?" he asked, tearing away the wrapping paper.

A silence fell over the table as everyone looked at what Arjun had brought. Then, suddenly, a gale of laughter erupted.

"…bath bombs?" someone asked incredulously.

"Aren't you his boss?" cackled somebody else, choking on his drink and erupting into a fit of coughs.

Arjun reddened. He'd delegated the task of buying the gift to Kelley. Next time he saw her, he'd have to explain that the only acceptable male-male gift was alcohol or alcohol paraphernalia—certainly never something meant to be used during bath time.

Luckily, one of Kevin's friends bailed him out before he needed to explain. "Hey, at least he brought something, *Evan*," said the other man, swiping the bath bombs onto the booth beside him. "I don't know if these are Kevin's speed—but make sure he puts these to good use."

"Hopefully with a friend," purred one of the other men, wearing a shirt that flashed with sequins. He stood and clapped his hands onto Kevin's shoulders. "Come on, big man," he said, handing Kevin a wad of singles. "Let's see how many of *these* you can stuff into that gentleman's speedo."

Arjun moved out of the way and let the other men pass. He watched them parade out of the VIP section and onto the dance floor, disappearing into the crowd of bodies at once darkened and illuminated by purple strobe lights.

He sat down again in the empty booth in the middle of the empty VIP section. He glanced over at the forgotten bath bombs and briefly debated leaving the club altogether. After all, it wasn't like he really *knew* Kevin beyond their interactions at the office, and he certainly didn't know Kevin's friends. Clearly, he'd only been invited as a courtesy, and he didn't want to overstay his welcome. *What else are you going to do, though?* he asked himself. *Go home and binge Netflix?*

A waitress came by and offered Arjun a bottle of champagne, which she cheerfully informed him would cost eight hundred dollars. Instead, he left to find the bar, just below the VIP section near the edge of the dance floor. *At the very least, I can get a drink,* he thought, desperately trying to get the bartender's attention with a twenty-dollar bill.

"That won't work," said the woman beside him, standing so close that their arms pressed against one another. She was very pretty, with a button nose and a cherry-red ribbon woven into her dark curls.

"Oh, yeah?" Arjun asked. "Why not?"

"Well," she replied, "the bartender is only serving the people he thinks he has a shot at going home with. And you're so clearly straight. Which I guess might be alluring to some people here—but I wouldn't bank on it."

"What makes you think I'm straight?" asked Arjun, breaking into a sly smile.

The woman chuckled. "Take a look around," she said. "Do you see anyone else in here dressed like you are?"

He looked down at his baby blue Oxford shirt and sensible brown chinos. "What's wrong with this?"

She patted him on the shoulder. "Like I said: straight guy."

"All right," conceded Arjun. "So, what can a heterosexual like me do to get a drink in a place like this?"

The woman smiled, and her lip gloss twinkled in the club lights. "That's easy. There's one exception to the rule from before: be a hot girl." She leaned over the bar and gave a slight wave. The bartender spotted her immediately and headed right over.

"My God," said Arjun, leaning close enough to smell her perfume. "It's like a superpower."

"It really is. I'd say a display like that is worth at least a drink, don't you?"

"I'd say so. What'll you have?"

"Whiskey," she said, and he ordered the same for himself. "I'm Jamie," the woman said as the bartender plunked the shots onto the bar. "What about you, straight guy—you got a name?"

"Arjun," he said, handing the bartender his card. "Leave it open, please."

"Well, Arjun," said Jamie, nodding approvingly, "here's to me being a hot girl."

They tapped their glasses together and drank.

Three drinks later, Arjun was feeling like the club wasn't so bad after all. He was almost surprised when Jamie leaned in, her breath sweet as summer in his ear: "Want to dance?"

Arjun replied immediately: "Absolutely." Jamie extended her slender hand, and he slipped it into his. She led him to the dance floor, finding the seams between the dancers until they were squarely in the middle of the crowd. The speakers were somehow even louder here, too deafening for the usual excruciating small talk: *What do you do? Where'd you go to college? You know, I have an aunt in Milwaukee.*

The drinks had loosened Arjun up, washing away all of the self-consciousness that always prevented him from having fun in places like this. He danced with a fervor that would have mortally embarrassed his sober self: swinging his hips, throwing his hands into the air, and even doing the YMCA when it came on. He felt like he was swimming in an ocean of sound—and beside him was Jamie, moving like a sea goddess.

Their bodies drew closer.

Arjun's hands moved to her waist, the exposed stretch of skin revealed by her crop top. With one hand, she reached back and stroked the back of his head, her fingers running through his hair. Her hand tightened, pulling his head down to the crook of her neck. Then, suddenly, she turned around, and they were face to face. The sight of her belly button was almost enough to make Arjun faint.

They avoided each other's gaze, their eyes never drifting above the other's midsection. Arjun *felt* Jamie more than he saw her—like a cool breeze or the heat of the sun. And then she threw her arms around his shoulders, and he grasped her by the hips. They swayed together like sea grass, and Arjun's eyes moved up, up, up.

Her eyes were there to meet his. She didn't say anything, but her expression spoke just one word: *Yes.*

Moving slowly, purposefully, Arjun bridged the distance between them. He felt Jamie's lips against his own, soft as clouds, tasting of honey, spice, and hope.

The music pulsed loud and bright around them, and the strobe lights of the club shone a thousand different colors.

They pulled apart. Arjun could still feel Jamie's breath inside his mouth. She had an expectant look in her eyes. He almost had to shout over the music: "Do you want to get out of here?"

She grinned. "My place or yours?"

Arjun took her by the hand, and they wove through the crowd. They picked up their jackets from the coat check and stepped outside. The night air was as crisp and sweet as an apple, and the glow from the streetlights danced in the puddles of water on the sidewalk. Arjun saw the glint of sweat at the hollow of Jamie's neck, and he felt his desire for her come roaring back. He kissed her again just as their Lyft car arrived.

Their driver was an older woman, and Arjun felt too awkward to resume necking in the backseat. He and Jamie sat apart, their fingers interlaced over the hump of the middle seat. The frisson of desire hung in the space between them like a static buzz. Arjun cracked the window, and the cool breeze swept into the car, carrying the sea fog smell of San Francisco with it.

Finally, the car rolled to a stop outside Arjun's condo. Jamie followed Arjun out of the car, and he wrapped his arm around her as they walked down the sidewalk. He turned his key in the lock and let them inside.

The lights turned on automatically as they entered, illuminating the cool gray walls and the dark hardwood floor of the kitchen and living room. Thankfully, Arjun had tidied up before leaving for the club. He took off his shoes and walked to the kitchen, pulling a lavender-scented candle out of the cupboard and lighting it. "Can I make you a drink?" he asked Jamie, opening the fridge.

"Vodka," Jamie replied, peering down the short hallway that led to the bathroom and the two bedrooms. "Whatever mixer you have is fine."

Arjun filled two glasses with ice from the freezer and poured from a half-empty bottle of Svedka, one of the remnants from his birthday party. *It's funny how things change,* he thought, smiling to himself. *One week ago, I was abandoned at a restaurant. Today, I'm mixing screwdrivers.* He watched as Jamie returned from the hallway. *And who knows what tomorrow will bring?*

He stowed the orange juice back in the fridge as Jamie joined him in the kitchen. "What time does your roommate get home?" she asked, accepting the drink from Arjun.

"I don't have a roommate," he replied, sipping from his glass. The vodka went down smooth, mellowed out by the orange juice. "This whole place is ours."

She raised her eyebrows, clearly impressed. "No roommates? In a two-bedroom like this? You're not married, are you?" She clicked her tongue. "Damn, I really should have asked that before we left the club."

Arjun laughed. "I'm not married," he said, showing off his bare ring finger. He pressed a button on his phone, and the stereo system whirred to life. Belle and Sebastian's "Sleep the Clock Around" whirred over the speakers, the music soft and full of longing.

"You're not some tech billionaire, then, are you?" Jamie asked, sitting down on the large gray sectional. She folded her knees behind her and rested her elbow on the back of the couch, her face close to Arjun's.

"I wish," he replied. "If I were, I'd live in a *much* larger place."

"I'll take your word for it," she said, smiling. They sipped their drinks, listening to the music. The song changed; it was "Piazza New York Catcher," another Belle and Sebastian song. *Is this the entire playlist?* Arjun wondered, debating whether it would be too obvious to pull out his phone again and change it.

Jamie didn't seem to notice. "What's that?" she asked instead, gesturing to the large, framed poster beside the darkened flat screen. The poster depicted the cratered surface of the moon. Two orange-suited astronauts (and an orange-suited dog) crested a rise and pointed to a checkered rocket on the desolate surface. The earth spun like a bright blue marble in the inky, star dappled sky.

"It's from *Tintin*," Arjun said.

Jamie stared at him blankly.

"It's this old Belgian cartoon," he explained. "Basically, this reporter, Tintin, travels around the world with a bunch of his friends. My grandmother used to buy the comics for me whenever she visited from India. I guess *Tintin* is bigger over there than it is here." He smiled at the memory.

"Hey, do you want to hear something cool?" he continued, unprompted. "Do you see the rocket? It's standing upright. Not surprising, right? After all, that's how the Apollo rockets landed. But this comic, *Explorers on the Moon*, came out in 1952. That was almost twenty years before the first moon landing. Can you believe the imagination behind something like that?"

Jamie laughed. "That's, like, super dorky."

"Yeah, I guess you're right. But, hey, it's part of the package." Arjun finished the last of his drink, and he noticed that Jamie's glass was empty, too.

She looked up at him. Her dark eyes were mysterious and inviting, her irises dotted with little spots of brightness from the overhead lights. She raised an eyebrow, as if to ask: *Are we doing this?*

Arjun set his glass on the coffee table, and Jamie did the same. With a playful shove, she had him on his back, and she climbed on top of him, her hips straddling his. She leaned down, her hair brushing against his cheeks. He felt her breath on his face just before she kissed him—and this kiss, honeyed by the anticipation, was even sweeter than the ones that had come before.

They pulled apart. "You want to show me one of those bedrooms?" Jamie asked breathlessly, resting her hands on his chest.

"It would be my pleasure," said Arjun. He picked her up and carried her down the hallway.

Morning arrived cool and bright. Bands of light streamed through the cracks in the blinds, splashing across Arjun's face and pulling him out of his slumber.

He sat up, the sheets tangled around him. He was shirt-less, dressed only in a pair of black satin boxers. His head was pounding, and it felt like a pair of thumbs were pressing against his eyes. He rose and rummaged around the dresser for an Advil. He glanced back at the empty bed and realized he was alone in the bedroom. "Jamie?" he called, wiping the sleep from his eyes.

His dreams came rushing back to him, so vivid that they might have been memories. He and Jamie had just purchased a house together, a Victorian somewhere in the city. As they stood back on the curb and admired their new home, a little boy came bounding up to Arjun and leaped into his arms. He'd instantly recognized the boy as his son, and he was filled with a fatherly affection so deep that he was *certain* that this was his life, that Jamie was his wife—that he finally had everything he'd wanted for years.

Back in the real world, Arjun padded down the hallway and out into the kitchen. Last night's candle had burnt out, and the apartment reeked of smoke and lavender. "Jamie?" he called again. "Are you still here?"

Silence was his only answer, and it was weighty and suffo-cating. *Did she step out for a coffee?* he wondered, noticing that her heels weren't by the door anymore. *Surely, she didn't just leave.* He checked his phone for a message but realized they'd never exchanged numbers. *I don't even know her last name,* he thought despairingly.

His headache exploded into a migraine. Dreaming about

something did not make it true. Jamie was gone, and it was as though she'd never been there at all.

He sat down heavily on the couch. Had it been just last night when he'd celebrated his reversal in fortune? When he'd had the kind of meet-cute that belonged more in a romance novel than in real life? Yet, despite all those good, happy feelings: here he was again, with the same howling emptiness lodged like a boulder in his stomach.

It doesn't have to be this way, said a little voice that hid deep in the folds of his brain. *Call your mother*, it said. *Swallow your pride—because whatever an arranged marriage feels like, it can't be worse than* this.

Arjun stood. He shook his head forcefully, as though he might dislodge the voice from its hiding place and launch it out of his ear. "You're not thinking straight," he said, hoping that hearing the words spoken aloud would make them sink in further.

He went to the bathroom, brushed his teeth, and stood in the shower until the water ran cold. Stepping out of the shower, a towel wrapped around his waist, the tiredness hit him like a freight train. He glanced at the clock; it was barely eight. He stumbled back into bed, hoping that he'd be able to fall asleep again.

His phone had died while he was showering, which was a good thing. Had he seen the message on it, he would not have been able to sleep.

Four

Arjun had never been a man to answer voicemails. In fact, he'd never even *had* a voice mailbox until business school. He didn't know how to set it up, and after fifteen years of having a phone, he didn't particularly feel the need to learn.

Vicky Chang had felt differently. It was often a topic of amusement for her before she and Arjun started dating, the subject of playful teasing that he'd only later realized was flirting (as everyone knows, men are terrible at picking up signals—Arjun more so than most).

When Arjun and Vicky finally got together, she insisted on setting up a voice mailbox for him, and she'd even recorded the outgoing message: "You've reached the voice mailbox of Arjun Chowdhury. At the tone, please leave your name, number, and reason for calling, and Arjun will get back to you as soon as possible. Have a nice day!"

"You're ridiculous," Arjun had said, unable to hide his grin as he replayed the message. "It sounds weird."

"It sounds *professional*," Vicky corrected. "Like you already have a secretary."

"Well, there's no arguing with that logic," he replied. He

kept the message. After he and Vicky broke up, though, he'd re-recorded the message by himself: "This is Arjun Chowdhury. Instead of leaving a voicemail, please send me a text message at this number. Thank you."

People were generally very good about following this instruction, and it had been years since Arjun had received his last voicemail...

Until now.

The notification blazed on his phone screen like a warning beacon: NEW VOICEMAIL. UNKNOWN CALLER.

It's probably a telemarketer, he thought, setting his phone aside and shaking some cereal into a bowl. Just before he poured the milk, he had a thought: *Telemarketers don't leave messages.* Arjun retrieved his phone and pressed "Play."

"Arjun. Hey."

The voice on the other end belonged to a ghost. Arjun stopped what he was doing: eating, moving, breathing. He felt like a fly stuck in amber, the blood in his veins slowing to a trickle through his extremities. *It can't be,* he thought...but he knew that voice. *Her* voice.

"It's Vicky," said the woman. "Vicky Chang? I guess you recorded a new message, huh? It sounds good." There was a pause, as if Vicky was wondering what to say next. The silence likely only lasted a few seconds, but it felt like hours, days—centuries. "I hope you're doing well," she continued at last. "I mean, I know you are, I saw that post of yours on Facebook. At Outside Lands with Dan and Erica? Anyway, I'm going to be back in SF this weekend. For work. I was wondering...do you want to meet up? I'm in town until Sunday night, so let me know." She ended the call with her cell number—a *new* number, one that Arjun did not remember—and hung up.

Arjun sat dumbfounded, the spoon still clenched between his teeth. He still didn't believe that it had really been Vicky on the other end of that voicemail. How long had it been since they'd spoken? And why was she calling him now?

He played the message again and found himself listening intently to Vicky's voice: the way it rose and fell, stopped and started. She sounded different than he remembered. *Different how?* he wondered, listening a third time. It did not take him long to figure it out. Vicky Chang, always so confident, sounded *nervous*. In all the time he'd known her, she'd only been nervous like that once.

Don't think about that, Arjun told himself. *Just forget that she ever called.*

Dan and Erica lived in a second-floor apartment in the Mission district, sandwiched between a taqueria and an adult bookstore. Arjun hiked up the stairs to their apartment, having already been accosted by a patchouli-scented woman trying to sell him a copy of dragon-themed erotica. He knocked on the door, and Dan answered. "There he is," said Dan, pulling him in for a hug. "How are you doing, man?"

Arjun still hadn't told Dan about Vicky's call, which had happened a few days ago. He could have texted him, but he knew that was in-person news. Sitting-down news. "Can't complain," he said instead. They walked over to the couch. "Hey, have you ever heard of a book called *The Wyvern's Desire*?"

Dan scoffed. "If you can even call that a 'book,'" he said, sitting. "It's completely derivative of *Scaly Skin, Flaming Heart*."

Arjun laughed. "Well, you're the expert. I still can't believe you read that garbage. I mean, you're a product manager, not a teenage girl."

Dan shrugged. "Don't blame me—blame Erica."

"Blame me for what?" Erica asked, striding out of the bedroom while fastening one of her earrings. She was wearing a gray Patagonia fleece with "Boston University School of Medicine" stitched onto the breast.

"My love of romance novels," said Dan.

"Oh, *really*?" said Erica, crossing her arms in front of her chest. "Tell me something, Arjun: you love rom-coms, right? What makes romantic *books* different?"

Arjun smiled. After years of losing arguments with Erica, he knew better than to start a new one. "Fair enough," he said. "I'll have to borrow one of yours someday, then."

"Can I make you some tea?" Erica asked, indicating a kettle bubbling on the stove. Arjun nodded, and she brought over a steaming mug that smelled pleasantly of cinnamon.

"Hey, so something weird happened last week," said Arjun, blowing on his tea as casually as possible.

"How weird?" Dan asked. "Like, 'Erica dyeing her hair blue,' weird?"

"Shut up," Erica said, perching on the couch's arm. "I looked good with blue hair."

"If you say so," Dan replied. "So, what happened?"

"Vicky Chang called me."

Dan, who had been slouched, amoeba-like, into the couch, sprang immediately erect. "Vicky Chang?" he exclaimed. "Like, your *ex*, Vicky Chang? Like, you *proposed* to her, Vicky Chang?"

"Is there another Vicky Chang?"

"Probably," Dan replied. "I mean, there have to be at least a few of them out there."

Erica shook her head disapprovingly at Dan. "You're an idiot."

"It was my Vicky Chang," Arjun confirmed.

"Why would she call you?" Dan asked. "It's been years since you two split up."

Arjun nodded. "She's back visiting San Francisco," he explained. "Or, she *was* visiting this past weekend. She wanted to meet up."

Dan's eyes grew as wide as dinner plates. "And?" he demanded. "Did you meet her?"

"I didn't call her back."

"Seriously?" Dan said incredulously. "You dated for five years. Don't you remember how blindsided you were by your breakup?"

"No shit, Dan," said Arjun. "I was there, wasn't I?"

"Okay, and you're not even a little bit curious to see what she has to say?"

Arjun shook his head. "It was a long time ago. I've moved on." Secretly, he wished that were true.

"Good for you, Arjun," said Erica, nodding sagely. "I think that's a very mature attitude. Who knows: maybe you two can be friends again."

He laughed. "Somehow, I don't see that happening."

"You never know," she replied with a shrug. "You two might run into one another again. San Francisco is smaller than you think."

"What are you talking about?" Arjun asked. "Vicky was just visiting."

Erica pursed her lips. "Oh," she said. "You don't know."

Arjun frowned. "Know what?"

"Vicky wasn't just visiting SF," Erica said. "She was here to interview for a job at Bank of America—and she just accepted it. She's moving here."

Arjun felt like someone had dropped a piano on his head. "How…how could you possibly know that?" he stammered.

Erica gave him an apologetic look. "We're connected on LinkedIn."

"That's messed up," interjected Dan, eager as always to do combat on Arjun's behalf. "Where's your loyalty? Arjun is your best friend."

"He said he's over it, didn't he?" she retorted. "I don't see a problem. Unless…do you feel differently, Arjun?"

"It's fine," he replied, but only because he couldn't tell

Erica how betrayed he felt that she'd maintained even a tenuous connection to Vicky. The thought of Vicky moving back to San Francisco—*his* city—made him want to drive his teaspoon through his thigh.

"I'm sorry about this, Arjun," said Erica. "Really, I am. But at least you heard it from me, right?"

He nodded. "Right," he said, even though not even Mister Rogers himself could soften this news.

"This doesn't put a damper on our plans, does it?" Erica asked. "I'd understand if you wanted to cancel, considering."

Arjun shook his head. "I'll get over it," he said, rising. "Dan, are you sure we can't make you reconsider?"

Dan chuckled. "You couldn't drag me to that art fair if you tried. Enjoy your date, you two—I'm going to watch the Warriors game."

Union Square was located in the heart of San Francisco, just off Market Street. Tourists frequented the wide plaza due to its proximity to the famous cable car turnaround, located a hundred yards away, and the numerous department stores surrounding the square. In the center of the plaza rose the Dewey Monument, a soaring white column atop which Nike, the goddess of victory, stood defiant against the sun.

The scent of candied nuts drifted over the breeze, reminding Arjun that he hadn't eaten all day. "Want to get some ice cream?" he asked Erica as they walked past a family speaking loudly in German. "The guys from Tokyo Freeze are here."

"Really? Where?" Erica craned her neck over the crowd as Arjun pointed to the booth. Food stalls were set up all around the perimeter of the square today, with offerings as diverse as the city itself. There was New York-style pizza next to a Boba tea stall; there was an Indian stall next to a Vietnamese stall; there was a Chinese stall next to a Mexican stall next to a

Chinese/Mexican fusion stall. Every step forward was a different scent, each of them uniquely tantalizing.

Tokyo Freeze had a folding table under a red-and-black checkered tent. A long line snaked past several other booths, full of people eager to try the bright-purple ube ice cream, which looked like something out of a Miyazaki film. Arjun was too hungry to wait in line, so he and Erica grabbed a couple of mango lassis from the Indian cart a few stalls down. "Where do you want to start?" he asked, sucking the sweet golden drink through a paper straw.

She shrugged. "I mean, we'll see it all, right?"

Artists across all mediums packed the plaza, set up in booths in a neat grid across the square. Sculptors showed off twisted works of brass and steel, and some of the sculptures were almost as tall as Arjun. Painters displayed huge canvases splashed with bright colors, the paint rippling off the canvas like ocean waves. Graphic designers moved through the crowds, plying paperback zines.

Arjun and Erica took their time with each exhibit. Erica had taken a few semesters of art history back in college, which (according to her) made her an expert. "Your use of impasto is exquisite," she told one artist, gesturing to a confusing gray-and-brown painting that reminded Arjun of dried mud. "This says so much about society," she told a young woman displaying a collection of dollar bills stapled to various menstrual products.

"You're such a show-off," Arjun told her, leaning over to whisper as Erica ran the backs of her hands over a shiny metal statue like a rich woman stroking a fur coat.

"Hey, my parents told me I'd never use my art minor," she replied, grinning. "I have to prove them wrong somehow, don't I?" She pointed across the square. "That's her, right?"

He nodded. "Yeah, it is," he said, following Erica toward the outer edge of the plaza.

Kelley Garcia sat in a folding chair underneath a large

umbrella, her stomach rising mountainously above her lap. There was a large trellis display behind her, hung with dozens of paintings, and these Arjun could appreciate. There were mountains shrouded with clouds and meadows bursting with flowers. There were celebrities and strangers, their portraits interspersed with those of Kelley's friends and family. And there were animals, too: fish and birds, giraffes and elephants. Most striking of all was a painting of a stalking tiger, rendered so realistically that it seemed about to pounce from the canvas.

Kelley beamed when she saw Arjun and Erica approaching. "I'm so glad you could make it!" she gushed. She moved to rise, straining with effort as she pushed against the low arms of her chair.

"No need to get up," said Arjun, leaning down to embrace her. "This is my friend, Erica."

"It's great to meet you!" Kelley replied. "Arjun has told me so much about you. You two grew up together, right?"

Erica smiled. "That's right. High school in Iowa, then college out east, and back here after. My fiancé and I like to joke that Arjun's our stalker."

"Hey, you two followed *me* to San Francisco," he protested.

Erica rolled her eyes. "I love your work, by the way," she said to Kelley, examining a painting of a blue jay spreading its wings mid-flight. "It's amazing how faithfully you capture your subjects. You have a real eye for detail."

Kelley blushed. "Thanks. You know, you're the first people to stop by all day."

"People are stupid," said Arjun. "How much are your paintings going for?"

"The big ones are two hundred and fifty, and the smaller ones are a hundred apiece."

"A steal!" Erica said, prodding Arjun with her elbow.

"I know!" added a man, walking up to the booth and

putting his hand on Kelley's shoulder. He grinned, showing off a row of crooked teeth. "So, what are you waiting for, Arjun?"

Arjun smiled and shook the other man's hand. Mark Garcia was always in a great mood, with a ruff of spiky black hair and crow's feet beside his dark-brown eyes. He was a head shorter than Arjun—but he was a former Marine, and he had the grip strength to prove it.

"Mango lassi, huh?" Mark said to Arjun, pointing to the half-empty drink in Arjun's other hand (which remained, mercifully, un-crushed). "I'm surprised you didn't go with Tokyo Freeze this time. I know how much you like their ube."

"The line's too long," said Arjun, gesturing vaguely toward the checkerboard stall.

"Ah, it's never too long for me," said Mark, bounding off. "Buy something, you cheap bastard!"

"Get a cone for me!" called Kelley after her husband. "…or three."

"How far along are you?" asked Erica.

"I'm due in four days," Kelley said with a worn smile.

Erica shot an incredulous look at Arjun. "And you're still making her come into the office?" she demanded, aghast.

"Hey, don't look at me," he said, flashing his palms.

"It's not his fault. I want to work until this kid pops out of me," Kelley explained. "I can't stand being off my feet, you know?"

Erica smiled. "Of course. I'm the same way."

Kelley raised an eyebrow. "Oh! Are you…?" She patted her stomach meaningfully.

"No!" Erica said quickly. "I'm just…neurotic."

There was an awkward silence. Arjun pointed to the painting of the tiger. "Has that one been sold yet?" he asked.

• • •

Arjun meandered around the exhibition for a while longer, holding the newspaper-wrapped painting under one arm. Erica had fallen into conversation with an artist who painted portraits of politicians with his own blood, and there was no end to their discussion in sight. Erica's general friendliness was one of the things Arjun liked most about her, but he wished she'd chosen someone less bohemian to speak with. The artist reminded Arjun a bit of Charlie Manson, with wild hair and beetle-like eyes, and he spoke with an intensity that Arjun found more off-putting than intriguing. *And, besides,* he wondered, *how do we know that's really* his *blood he's painting with?*

Arjun was contemplating braving the Tokyo Freeze line again when he saw a woman standing beside a jewelry display nearby. *She looks familiar,* he thought, turning her features over in his mind like someone shifting a puzzle piece into place—then, it clicked. "Jamie!" he called, walking in her direction.

She noticed Arjun approaching, and she smiled warmly. "Hey!" she said, embracing him. It had been more than a week since their night at the club, but Arjun still remembered the sharp, floral scent of her perfume.

"What are you doing here?" he asked as they pulled away.

"What, a girl can't like art?" she replied. "How are you doing?"

"I'm doing great, all things considered. I'm glad to run into you, Jamie. It's such a nice surprise to see you again."

"SF is smaller than you think," she said, giving him the same sly grin he'd found so alluring that first night.

Arjun glanced back at Erica, who was still in animated conversation with the Charlie Manson look-alike. "You know, you're not the first person to tell me that today."

Jamie had noticed Erica, too. "Are you here with someone?" she asked, inclining her head slightly.

He shook his head. "No, she's just a friend."

She nodded. There was a pause as they wondered what to say next, the verbal equivalent of the shuffle two people do when passing one another in a narrow hallway.

"Well," Jamie said, breaking the silence, "it was nice—"

"Do you want to get coffee sometime?" Arjun blurted, cutting her off before she could finish. "I know that we only had the one night together. But I think you're great, and I'd like to get to know you better."

A small smile passed over Jamie's lips, and for a moment, hope fluttered in Arjun's chest. But he quickly recognized that pity, not affection, made up her expression. His stomach clenched. *Stupid, stupid, stupid,* he thought, mentally banging his palm against his forehead.

"You're sweet," she said, and each word was a hammer blow. "But I'm not sure we're a match."

He nodded. "All right," he said, too quickly, trying to salvage what was left of his tattered pride. He stuck his hands in his pockets and rocked back on his heels. "Well, it was nice seeing you, Jamie."

She smiled. "You too, Arthur." She gave him a quick final embrace, the sideward hug that meant Arjun was solidly in the friend zone (or the "I can't even be bothered to remember your name" zone). Jamie turned and disappeared into the crowd, leaving him alone once again.

Arjun wasn't an idiot. He knew that Jamie disappearing without leaving so much as a phone number meant that she most likely didn't want a relationship—or at least, not with him. Yes, it had been stupid to ask now, a week later. But, still, the dignity of such polite rejection, of being called the wrong name, was almost too much to bear. Like Nike on her pedestal, he felt like throwing his head back and screaming at the sky.

He felt a tap on his shoulder and saw that Erica had returned. "That girl was very pretty," she said. "Who was she?"

Arjun shook his head. "No one. Hey, tell me something: do I look like an 'Arthur' to you?"

Erica gave him a quizzical look. "Like, the cartoon? Your ears aren't that big, you know. And you haven't worn glasses in years."

Erica always knew how to make Arjun feel better. "Never mind," he said, chuckling. "Forget I asked."

"Whatever you say," she replied, shrugging. She took his arm, and they headed through the plaza to find something else to eat.

CHAPTER
Five

Monday came quickly—too quickly. Arjun had stayed up late scrolling aimlessly through the realty website, fantasizing about various locations for a new restaurant and trying to put the encounter with Jamie out of his mind. One of the storefronts in Hayes Valley had seemed promising, and he'd planned to pay it a visit in person—but he fell asleep watching TV on the couch and woke up ten minutes after his alarm had gone off.

He showed up to work bleary-eyed and exhausted. Kelley was sitting in the chair opposite his desk when he arrived. "You look like shit," she said, as diplomatic as ever.

"Don't I know it," Arjun replied, smiling weakly. "But I'll be fine. More importantly, how are *you* feeling?" Kelley's stomach looked as though it had somehow *expanded* in the day since he'd last seen her, like a balloon pumped so full that just a bit more air would explode the whole thing.

"I feel great," she replied enthusiastically. "I sold seven more pieces at the fair. Mark bought the baby all of the Harry Potter books, even though it'll be years before she can read."

Kelley gasped as though the building had shaken on its

foundations. "What is it?" asked Arjun, rushing towards her. "Are you going into labor?"

"No, you idiot," said Kelley, waving him off. "No one knows the sex yet. We've been waiting until she's born to tell people…" Her face fell again. "*Shit*. I just said it again, didn't I?"

Arjun chuckled. "Don't worry," he said. "Your secret's safe with me." He went to turn on his desktop, and he caught his reflection in the darkened monitor. Dark circles hung beneath his eyes, giving him a distinctly raccoon-like appearance. "I'm going to get a coffee before my first meeting," he announced. "Do you want anything?"

"You know the drill," Kelley replied.

The memory of the green-eyed woman from the week before flashed in Arjun's mind. "*All* the scones," he said, smiling to himself. "Got it."

There was a familiar face at the coffee shop: Arjun recognized Vinay Sampath sitting at one of the tables inside. Vinay had a ring of close-cropped hair around his scalp, and he was wearing a crisp gray blazer over jeans. A brand-new wedding band flashed on his ring finger, as golden as the sun. Fresh off his honeymoon, he seemed to be glowing.

"Congrats, man," Arjun said, taking a paper bag bursting with pastries from Ron. "How does it feel to be married?"

"The same," Vinay replied, chuckling softly to himself. "But different, somehow. Beena is great, man. I'll have to have you over for dinner sometime soon."

"I'd love that," Arjun said. He glanced meaningfully at the chair opposite Vinay.

"You want to sit?" Vinay asked, taking the hint.

"Thanks," said Arjun. "You know, I'm surprised that I haven't met Beena before. How long were you together before you tied the knot?"

"Well, we were never really 'together,'" Vinay replied, working his wedding ring around his finger. "We had an arranged marriage."

Arjun feigned a surprised expression. Of course, he knew that Vinay had gotten an arranged marriage. It had been the subject of office gossip ever since Vinay invited the whole team to his engagement ceremony a month ago (one of the software engineers had asked Vinay how much he fetched in dowry, and HR had swiftly reprimanded him).

"Wow," Arjun said, trying to play it cool. "An arranged marriage, huh? Is that very common these days?"

"Among us ABCDs?" Vinay replied, laughing. "It's more common than you think. Once people hit a certain age, they want to partner up. An arranged marriage…it's like a cheat code. It cuts through all the mess of American dating, finds you the most compatible person—financially, socially, culturally—and gets you to the altar in just a few months. And the best part? My mom loved Beena before even *I* laid eyes on her."

Arjun nodded, hating Vinay for how much sense he was making. "You didn't miss it, did you?" he asked hesitantly. "The mess, I mean."

"Like, the whole rom-com, tropey stuff?" Vinay replied. "No way, man." He leaned closer to Arjun, the coffee steaming up his wire-framed glasses. "To tell you the truth, that was my biggest hang-up about it. I thought that I was abandoning some hero's journey towards true love. Like I was the protagonist in a Nicholas Sparks movie or something. But you know what I realized?"

"What's that?" Arjun asked. He noticed that he was gripping the edge of the table very tightly, his body rigid with anticipation.

Vinay grinned. "If it works, it works. Those movies are all bullshit, anyway."

It turned out that Arjun didn't have to keep Kelley's secret for long. He received a text from her on Tuesday morning, informing him that she'd gone into labor overnight and delivered the baby not long after. The next day, Arjun told Adam D'Antonio that he'd be out of the office for the afternoon, and he made the trek up to SF General Hospital to see the new arrival.

The hospital was a maze, and it took Arjun nearly half an hour to find the Labor and Delivery ward. The admitting nurse sat alone in the nurse's station, typing furiously on a desktop. "Hi," Arjun said, drumming his fingers on the desk. "I'm looking for Kelley Garcia."

The nurse did not look up from her computer. "Garcia," Arjun repeated, in case she hadn't heard him the first time. "Spelled G-A-R—"

"Are you family?" the nurse asked, fingers still clacking rapidly over the keys.

"Uh…nope. She's my assistant. Is that okay?"

"Who am I to judge? You can have an assistant if you really need one."

"No, I mean—can I see her?"

"Sorry," the nurse replied flatly, pausing her typing for a moment to look him in the eye. "Unless you're related to the patient—"

"It's okay," came a voice. Mark Garcia walked down the hall, holding two cups of cafeteria coffee. "Come on back, Arjun." The nurse nodded and let Arjun pass, and he followed Mark to Kelley's room.

Kelley's birthing suite was a small, windowless room at the far end of the hallway. A medical bed was in the center of the room, with a small rolling crib beside it. Chairs were scattered around the room, laden with presents from friends and family: flowers and chocolates, baby clothes and stuffed animals. A giant teddy bear, nearly as tall as Arjun, was propped up in the corner.

Kelley was reclining in the bed, holding an oversized

sippy cup marked with fluid increments. She smiled wearily when Mark and Arjun entered. "Thanks for coming," she said, resting her hand on Arjun's as he stroked her shoulder.

"Are you kidding me? I wouldn't have missed it," he replied. He added his gift, a mobile featuring a variety of plush dinosaurs, to the pile. "You two are *parents*," he whispered. "How do you feel?"

"Exhausted," she said, smiling wanly. "But really, really happy."

"Is that her?" he asked, walking over to the crib. Kelley nodded, and Arjun leaned over the crib and peered inside.

The baby was swaddled in a checkered pink blanket, and she was just barely awake. She was impossibly tiny, not quite the length of Arjun's forearm. Her rosy skin was wrinkled and delicate, like a raisin. A few tufts of black hair peeked out from beneath her knit cap. Her mouth moved softly, silently, as though she was trying to say something but couldn't quite find the words.

Arjun watched her in amazement. San Francisco was a city where a passing stroller was more likely to be occupied by a cockapoo than an infant, and it had been a long time since he'd even *seen* one. He was filled with an indescribable awe, something pure and joyful. It was the feeling he when he watched the sunset or dug his feet into the sand and let the ocean lap at his toes. "Does she have a name yet?" he whispered, turning to Kelley.

She nodded. "Emmylou," she said. "You know, like Emmylou Harris."

"That's very pretty," he said, smiling and straightening. "Next time, I'll bring her a guitar."

"Would you like to hold her?" Mark asked, scooping up his daughter.

Arjun nodded eagerly. "Of course."

"You'll need to Purell," Mark said, using his chin to gesture to the bottle of hand sanitizer on the bedside table.

Arjun squirted the thin, clear liquid onto his palm and rubbed it over his hands until it evaporated. "Careful," Mark whispered, gently passing Emmylou over to Arjun. "Watch her head."

Arjun handled her like a Fabergé egg. He supported her torso in the crook of one arm, and he cupped her head with his other hand. He marveled at how small she was, how *light* she was. Emmylou stared up at Arjun with her deep, luminous eyes, and for a moment, he was transfixed. It was like he'd stepped onstage in an empty auditorium, drenched in a spotlight—as though this tiny infant's gaze had reduced the world to just the two of them.

Arjun handed the baby over to Kelley. He felt tears welling behind his eyes, and he wiped them away with his thumb before anyone could see. Kelley gave Arjun a look, but it lasted only a moment. "She's something else, you two," Arjun said, clearing his throat. "Really." Kelley smiled and gently stroked her daughter's cheek with her pointer finger.

Arjun knew, then, how far he was from his dream of having his own family. Kelley was five years younger than he was—*So, what am I doing with my life?* he wondered. His mind flashed back to his awkward parting with Jamie, to that night alone in the restaurant on the eve of his birthday, to all of those failed dates, and to the countless nights spent lying in bed and staring at the ceiling. *I know that* this *is what I want,* thought Arjun. *So, why hasn't it happened yet?*

Emmylou began to fuss. "She's hungry," said Kelley, holding her daughter close.

Arjun nodded. "Congratulations again," he said, his heart galloping. "If you need anything at all, I'm just a call away."

Arjun walked out of the room and down the hallway, and as he went, he felt his legs moving faster and faster, as though the ground were a treadmill picking up speed. He was practically running by the time he reached the stairwell, and he sprinted down the stairs of the parking garage. Adrenaline surged through his body, and his mind felt clearer than ever. *Why have I been so resistant?* he wondered. Was it Vicky Chang? Was it his pride? Was it a lifetime spent watching Hallmark Christmas specials? He thought back to his conversation with Vinay: *Those movies are all bullshit, anyway.*

He found his car, unlocked it, and threw himself into the driver's seat. He leaned back, awkwardly jiggling his butt in the air as he strained to pry his phone from his pocket. *Are you really doing this right now?* he asked himself. But, before he could further consider what he was doing, his fingers were dialing the numbers.

He held the phone to his ear. One ring, two rings…*Come on*, he thought, his leg bouncing furiously with anticipation. *Pick up. Pick up!*

The line crackled to life. "Arjun?" came the voice on the other end.

"I know what I want," he said, breathless, as though he could not wait to get the words out. "I'm ready for an arranged marriage."

CHAPTER
Six

"Um…what the hell happened here?"

Arjun stood before the door to his office, which was cordoned off by two crossed strips of red caution tape. He ducked underneath the barrier and heard a large squelch, and he leaped back before water could seep into his shoe. Peering up at the ceiling, he noticed a hugely swollen section, which had popped like a lanced boil. A steady stream of water poured from above, drizzling all over Arjun's brand-new desktop computer.

Adam D'Antonio's huge shoulders filled the doorframe behind him. "A pipe burst over the weekend. Sorry, kid."

Arjun sighed. Fortunately, he had backed up his computer to the cloud, and he quickly opened his laptop to check that he hadn't lost anything important. "It's fine," he said, moving to leave the office. "I can take a spot out in the bullpen for now."

Adam shook his head. "The bullpen?" he guffawed, as if Arjun had instead announced his intention to work from the moon. "Son, you just let go of your assistant!"

"Actually, she's on maternity leave," Arjun corrected.

"Potato, potahto," replied his boss, with a wave of his

massive hand. "The point is, I'm not going to make you lose your office, too. I've made an arrangement for you." He beckoned for Arjun to follow him through the office. They walked down the stairs, passed through the keycard-activated security gate, and crossed the lobby. Adam pushed open a door on the other side. "Welcome to Narnia," he said, leading the way into the offices of the *San Francisco Current.*

Despite working in this building for nearly three years, Arjun had never set foot inside the *Current,* which had occupied the first floor for half a century. The atmosphere inside the newspaper's headquarters was immediately different. The *Current*'s offices had a distinctly bohemian feel, which stood in contrast with the manufactured eclecticism of the PSI offices up above. There were no neatly ordered cubicles, foosball tables, or shelves packed with Catan boxes and Funko Pops here. Instead, the desks were scattered all over the bullpen like they'd been dropped there by a tornado, and no one had ever moved them back. Old newspapers—some framed, some not—covered every inch of the walls, punctuated by record covers and the occasional Pride flag. Arjun spotted a mannequin in one corner of the bullpen; someone had placed a top hat upon its head, and a sign slung across its neck designated it "Emperor Norton."

"What are we doing down here?" Arjun whispered to Adam, looking around at the people toiling away on the next edition of the weekly publication. A bespectacled man glanced up from his computer, like a prairie dog scanning for predators, before hunching over his desk again.

"All of the PSI offices upstairs are currently occupied," Adam explained, opening a side door near the receptionist's desk and leading Arjun inside. There was a narrow staircase, the ceiling so low that Arjun had to duck his head to descend. "It turns out, though, that there's a spare office here. I offered to rent it from them, and they were happy to oblige."

They came to a short hallway, which was made even

narrower by ceiling-high stacks of boxes to either side. Arjun and Adam crossed single file, disturbing large clouds of dust whenever they accidentally brushed against the boxes.

On the other end of the hallway was a scratched and dinted wooden door that might have been painted red once. Someone had taped a piece of faded yellow paper to the door: *Sprayed for mold, June 7, 1977.* "That's good, at least," Arjun muttered sarcastically.

Adam turned the handle and let them inside. "This is it," he announced, beaming. "Welcome home!"

Arjun could not imagine a worse homecoming. The room was unbearably tiny; if he wanted to, he could have stretched out his arms and touched both walls with the tips of his fingers. A harsh yellow light buzzed overhead like an incessant fly, casting the faded pop posters on the walls in jaundiced tones. The air inside the room was stale and humid, as if no one had opened the door in decades, and the cinderblock walls and lack of windows gave Arjun the distinct feeling of being inside a prison cell. There was a single desk in the center of the room, and a battered-looking desktop that looked more like a museum artifact than a functional computer. "So, what do you think?" Adam asked.

"It looks like someone's already taken up residence," Arjun replied, pointing to a still-steaming cup of coffee on the desk beside an open laptop.

"Good guess," said a voice behind them. Arjun turned around and did a double take.

It was the woman who'd accosted him in the street a few weeks ago. She wore a green cable-knit sweater, the same brilliant shade as her eyes. Arjun thought he saw a flash of recognition cross her face, and he wondered if she had any more insults to hurl his way. Instead, she folded her arms across her chest and scowled. "What are you doing here?"

Adam jumped in before Arjun had a chance to reply. "My name is Adam D'Antonio; I'm the CFO of Pay Systems, Incorporated," he said affably. "We share this building with the *San Francisco Current*. Arjun here was in need of an office. Seeing as you have a spare, Mr. Evans, the editor-in-chief of your fine publication, was happy to accommodate us."

"Well, I'm using this space," the woman replied, unimpressed. "I think that *Arjun—*" she said his name distastefully, the same way a person might say "ulcer"— "will have to find another office."

Arjun felt a funny catching feeling in his stomach, like being on a rollercoaster in the split second before it drops downhill. *She knows my name,* he thought. Then, he wondered why that even mattered in the first place.

Adam shrugged. "I'm sorry. We just submitted the paperwork to your boss this morning. For the next month, this place belongs to Arjun. Unfortunately, that means that you'll be the one to move."

The woman shot the two of them a look so venomous that Arjun actually shivered. She snatched her laptop and coffee from the table. "You can't *always* get what you want," she spat at Arjun. "This isn't over." With that, she turned on her heel and stormed off.

Adam raised an eyebrow, and he gave Arjun a look. "Do you two know each other?"

"Sort of," Arjun replied, still dazed by the interaction with the woman.

Adam clapped him on the back. "Good luck with that one, kid. And, remember, if you need anything…ask my assistant." With a mischievous wink, he left Arjun in his new office to set up his things.

In a way, being shunted off to the PSI offices was good because it allowed Arjun to sneak out of the building around three. He hurried home and tidied up his place: running a vacuum over the living room rug, arranging a bowl of fruit on the kitchen island, making sure his bed was made with military precision. He walked past the entryway mirror and fixed his hair—then, he realized that he should probably fix his entire outfit. Almost as soon as he'd changed into a fitted dress shirt and dark chinos, the doorbell rang.

His conversation with Sarita had occurred precisely three days ago, and it had been brief. Mercifully, Arjun's mother had taken her win without gloating, and she knew better than to ask any questions about how or why Arjun had arrived at his decision (though, in hindsight, she probably should have. Given Arjun's abrupt heel-face turn, an aneurysm was certainly not out of the question).

Instead, Sarita had reacted to his request by pausing, saying only, "Okay. I'll send someone over this Friday."

The woman who swept into Arjun's apartment was short and wrinkled, and she bore a marked resemblance to Yoda. Her hair was dyed a dusky red with henna, and a big scarlet *bindi* was tacked to the center of her forehead. Arjun stuck out his hand to shake—but the woman reached up and pinched his cheeks with surprising roughness. "Arjun, *beta!*" she exclaimed. "It's so fantastic to meet you. You're much trimmer than in your photos!"

Is there a good *way to respond to that?* he wondered. "Uh… thanks, I guess," he said, resisting the urge to rub his aching cheeks.

"My name is Dhanya Agarwal," the woman continued. "But you may call me Dhanya Auntie. After all, we're related, no?"

He raised an eyebrow. "We are?"

Dhanya laughed, tossing her head back. "Of course, *beta,*" she said. "I'm your mummy's cousin sister. Well, second cousin. But that makes us family!"

What's one more aunt? Arjun thought, mentally adding Dhanya to the roster. "It's very nice to meet you," he said. He gestured to the kitchen island, where there were a few stools;

just then, he became very self-conscious about not having a kitchen table. "Would you like something to drink?"

"*Shabash!*" she enthused, clapping her hands together. "Such good manners. I will have tea, if you have it, but none of that horrible English stuff. Oh, except for Tetley. Do you have Tetley?"

"I do." Arjun had prepared a spice mix for just this occasion: cinnamon, cloves, green cardamom, and star anise. He toasted the spices in a small pot before adding water and four bags of black tea. He could sense Dhanya watching him intently as he grated a knob of ginger into the tea. "It'll be a few minutes, if you don't mind," he said.

"Not at all," she replied. "Not many American boys know how to make *chai*."

Arjun smiled. "I've always loved to cook," he told her. "By the way, thank you for coming all the way to San Francisco. I know it was short notice."

"It's no trouble," said Dhanya. "With so many *desis* in this area, I'm here quite frequently. I tell you, the food down in Sunnyvale is almost as good as it is in India!"

The tea was finished steeping. Arjun poured some milk into the pot until the liquid turned a creamy brown, then poured the tea into two waiting mugs. He'd set a plate on the kitchen island, stacked high with Parle G biscuits. Dhanya was already munching on a cookie, and she took a spoonful of sugar from the ramekin Arjun had placed beside the plate. "It's excellent *chai*," she said to Arjun, beaming. "Full marks."

She spooned some more sugar into her tea. "Now, let's get down to business. You'd like an arranged marriage, correct?"

Arjun hadn't expected her to be so blunt about it. Subconsciously, he still thought of "arranged marriage" as a dirty word, something people only did when they were out of options. Hearing it so plainly, especially applied to *him,* was a shock.

He swallowed. "Yes," he said. "That's correct."

Dhanya looked him right in the eye. "And this is what you want?" she asked, her gaze unwavering.

He took a deep breath. *Moment of truth,* he told himself. *No going back now.* "Yes," he said again. "This is what I want."

She nodded, and Arjun felt the tension dissipate from his chest. "That's good. I often find that my American-born clients especially go through with arranged marriages only at their parents' urging. Unfortunately, those matches are always bad, so I refuse to do them. Both parties must be all-in, yes?"

"That seems very reasonable," he replied. Dhanya was looking at him expectantly; clearly, she wanted him to say more.

He cleared his throat. "To tell you the truth, my mother has been pushing me in this direction for a while, but the decision was mine alone. They say the definition of insanity is doing the same thing over and over again but expecting a different result. I want to be married, Auntie, and American dating hasn't worked out for me. On the other hand, arranged marriages have worked for millions of people. Heck, my parents got an arranged marriage, and they were the happiest couple I knew. So, yes, I want an arranged marriage."

That seemed enough to satisfy her. "I'm glad to hear that, *beta,*" she said. She plopped off the stool and produced a yellow legal pad from her purse. "Now, may I see your apartment?"

They proceeded with the tour. There was the kitchen with the stainless-steel appliances, the gas range, and the butcher-block kitchen island—a nice contrast with the dark hardwood floors and the cool gray walls. There was the living room that connected directly to the kitchen, with the tall bookcase, comfortable leather sectional, and large flat-screen television. He showed her the bathroom, with the rain shower and the heated floor. Then it was his bedroom, with his king-sized bed, dresser, and walk-in closet. Finally, Arjun showed her the guest room, which he also used as a home office. In addition to the queen bed, there were walls covered in bookshelves and a large table with a Mac desktop on it and another television mounted just above. Dhanya made notes on her pad at every stop, each pen stroke as sharp as a katana's slice across the paper.

"This is very impressive," she said, nodding in approval as they wrapped up the tour. "Very few of my clients in San Francisco have homes like this—except the ones who live with their parents, of course! What do you do, exactly?"

"I'm an executive at a company here in the city," said Arjun, leading her back to the kitchen. "We help other companies to process online payments."

"And before that?"

"I worked at a startup," he replied. "We also did payments processing, but PSI—my current company—acquired us three months after I started working there. I got a nice chunk of stock in PSI, so I've been there ever since."

"That's excellent to hear," she said. "It's always more stable to be working at a large company. And stable is very desirable, where arranged marriages are concerned."

Dhanya sat at the island again. "I have to say, Arjun, I think that you will be a highly desirable match. I will have no trouble finding compatible girls for you. But, first, tell me: what are *you* looking for in a wife?"

He pondered this for a moment. He'd always had an idea of the person he'd end up with, but it had always been just that, an idea. *Why is it so hard to put into words?* he wondered, feeling the weight of Dhanya's stare. "Someone kind," he said finally. "Someone smart, with a sense of humor. Oh, and if she played an instrument, that would be even better."

Dhanya smiled indulgently. "Of course, it's good to keep the personality in mind. But I was speaking more along practical lines, *beta*. Do you have preferences regarding your wife's job? Her height? Her weight? What about her family background? All of these things are important, as well."

Arjun felt like he'd just had a bucket of ice water dumped on his head. Such "practical" decisions had never even occurred to him. Most of his impressions about how love and marriage worked came from Meg Ryan movies—and how often did the leads in a rom-com talk about managing finances, or who would care for aging parents? "I haven't thought about any of that too much," he admitted. "To be honest, I'm not very familiar with this whole process."

Dhanya smiled reassuringly. "Not to worry, *beta*," she told him. "The arranged marriage process is quite simple, really. Think of it as three main steps. First, you'll tell me the kind of girl you're looking for, and I will provide you with profiles of girls who match your criteria. If you like the profile, I'll arrange a meeting for you; one or both of your families will be there. If you'd like, you can meet individually afterward— but that isn't always done. The last step is always the *roka*: your engagement ceremony, where the two families agree to the match and begin planning the wedding."

"It sounds pretty…normal," Arjun said, unsure if that was the right word. "If it's really that simple, how is this process different from being set up by a friend or an American matchmaker?"

She nodded. "For one thing: the families are involved. It's not only you who selects the girl you'll meet—her family will also select *you*. Furthermore, it's a much more expedient process than American dating. The time from the first meeting to the engagement will take one month. And the time from the engagement to the wedding will take three months."

Arjun could not hide his shock. "So…four months from meeting someone, I could be married to her?" he asked, suddenly woozy. "Is it even possible to fall in love in four months?"

She chuckled softly. "I know, it must seem very strange.

You're used to the American way of doing things, where love comes *before* marriage. Here, it's the opposite—but you'll find that this process has its own unique benefits. As I said, as a first step, I will present you with biodatas. You can tell me if you like anyone enough to meet."

He nodded. "And what exactly are biodatas?"

Dhanya pulled a thin folio from her purse and handed him a sheet of paper. "A biodata is like a resume," she explained. "But much broader. Instead of merely listing all of the jobs you've had, it sums you up as a person."

"Oh," he said. "How simple."

He scanned the biodata template that Dhanya had provided for him. It contained everything someone would need to steal his identity…or make a clone of him. There were spots to write down his date of birth, his level of education, his height and weight—even his blood type. There was a blank space where he was meant to attach a headshot. And, toward the bottom of the page, there were sections for short essays: "About," "Family Background," "Lifestyle," and "Expectations."

Dhanya patted Arjun's arm. "Relax, *beta*," she said. "This is nothing to fear. I'll leave it to you to fill out, eh? And if you have any questions at all, don't hesitate to call. Your mother has my number."

Arjun nodded. "All right. Thanks, Dhanya Auntie."

"Of course, Arjun. I'm looking forward to this journey of yours." She pinched his cheek once more and snagged the rest of the biscuits on her way back outside.

Arjun spent the rest of the afternoon filling out his biodata form. Most of the short questions were relatively simple, except for his blood type, which required him to dig out the forms from his last physical. He passed the "Family Background" section off to his mother, who returned it to him within an hour. For "About," he decided to keep it simple: "I hold a BS in Economics from Yale and an MBA from Stanford. I currently live and work in San Francisco, where I'm an executive at a mid-sized software company. In my free time, I enjoy reading and cooking." Sarita had decided that was insufficient, and she'd taken it upon herself to fill out that section, too.

The "Lifestyle" section was easy enough. Arjun didn't go out much; he was a social drinker who dabbled in pot now and again (although he wasn't a biodata expert, he knew enough to keep that last part out). He was technically a Hindu, though he only went to the temple when his mother was around. Dhanya had told Arjun to include his dietary habits, so he put down that he was generally omnivorous, with the exception of beef. *Perhaps I'm not such a bad Hindu, after all,* he mused with a smile.

The final section, "Expectations," proved to be the most difficult by far. Arjun had always envisioned his life as a husband and father: hosting Thanksgiving at his house, chasing his kids around the backyard, and watching television in bed beside his wife. *How can I condense all of that into a single paragraph?* he wondered, hoping the answer would come to him as he paced around his apartment. When pacing didn't work, Arjun decided that what he really needed was some fresh air, and so he left his apartment and took a long walk to the Ferry Building. Unfortunately, he was so distracted by the selection of food inside the marketplace that he forgot all about the biodata form.

Night had fallen by the time Arjun returned to his apartment, carrying a bag laden with pastries from Mariposa and a selection of Kashiwase plums. Some part of him had been hoping that the "Expectations" section would have been magically filled out when he returned—but, frustratingly, the section remained blank. *All right,* he told himself, sitting down with the template in front of him. *Time to buckle down and finish this.*

His phone buzzed. It was a text from Dan. *You want to hang out?*

Arjun sighed with relief. *Come over*, he replied.

Dan and Erica arrived half an hour later. "How about a movie?" asked Arjun, hurriedly stowing the biodata form inside the silverware drawer.

"We could," Dan replied. "I had another idea, though." He reached into his jacket and drew out a tiny plastic baggie. Inside were two neon-green gummy bears, dancing as Dan jiggled the baggie up and down.

Arjun raised an eyebrow. "Are those—"

"Yup," Dan replied with a self-satisfied smile. "A new dispensary opened up right across the street from my office. I tell you, Arjun, buying weed just keeps getting fancier and fancier. This place looked just like an Apple Store. I mean, it was practically begging for me to come inside and check it out."

Arjun turned to Erica. "And you approve of this?"

She shrugged. "Hey, you two are adults. And it's not like it's illegal here in California. I can be your babysitter."

"So?" cajoled Dan, opening the baggie. "Come on, when was the last time we got high together?"

Arjun sighed. It had been half a year since he'd used pot. The last time, at Outside Lands, had left him in a stupor for an entire day. Even now, he could barely recall who the headliner had been.

"Sure," he said, despite himself. "Why not?"

Dan grinned. He dropped one of the gummy bears into Arjun's palm. Arjun lifted the bear to his mouth and swallowed it. "Well," he said, "I guess we'll see how hard it hits me this time."

Dan rolled his eyes. "It'll be fine," he said. "I don't think they're that strong, anyway."

. . .

An hour later, Dan was lying on the floor of Arjun's bedroom, his arms and legs spread out like a giant starfish. "I'm floating," he said rapturously, his fingers dancing across the hardwood as he traced huge arcs with his hands.

Arjun was sitting on his bed, leaning against the headboard. The fan spun above him, and he was mesmerized by the shadow the blade cast against the ceiling. "You ever think about how weird shadows are?" he asked, reaching up toward the ceiling as if he could catch the constantly shifting dark spot.

"Whoa," said Dan. "Shadows are *totally* weird."

Arjun heard footsteps and rolled over to see Erica walking in with a huge bowl of Chex mix. "Hey, Cheech and Chong," she said, sitting on the edge of the mattress. "How's it going?"

"It couldn't be better," said Dan, grabbing a handful from the bowl and stuffing his mouth. "Honestly, babe, you should have done one with us."

Erica laughed. "I got my fill of that in college, thank you very much. You two brought weed every time you came up from Connecticut to visit me."

Arjun smiled. "We had some good times," he said wistfully, staring up at the fan as though its shadow was a projector displaying those old memories.

"Hey," said Erica. "Do you guys remember that party, freshman year?"

"How specific," Dan replied, his voice dripping with sarcasm.

"Freshman fall. The one where my roommate puked all over Arjun?"

Dan was silent for a moment, and then he began to chortle violently. "Yes, I remember!" he said, half-chewed Chex bursting from his mouth and littering the carpet. "What was her name, again?"

"Violet," Arjun said flatly. "Her name was Violet."

"That's right," said Erica. "The poor girl had anchovy pizza and seven beers. And all Arjun wanted was a dance!"

Arjun shook his head. "That's not the end of the story, you know."

"What do you mean?" asked Dan. "She threw up on you, and you had to wear Erica's John Mayer tank top until we went back to New Haven. What else could there be?"

"Well, Violet let me into their room to get a change of clothes," Arjun said. "We got to talking after we both got dressed, and we ended up hanging out for a while."

"Right," said Dan with a wink. "'*Hanging out.*'"

"Gross," Erica said. "Arjun, I love you—but I don't want to hear about you banging my freshman roommate."

"It wasn't like that. We went up to the roof of the dorm, and we just…talked. About life, all of our plans for the future. I was going to own my own restaurant. She was going to be a zoologist, like Jane Goodall." He smiled at the memory: him in the too-tight t-shirt, clutching his knees to his chest and watching the stars wink over the Boston skyline. He closed his eyes, and it was like he was back there again, with that *feeling* filling his lungs like oxygen: infinite possibilities in his life, and the beautiful girl sitting just beside him, her breath fogging in the air. "I'm going to miss that," he said softly.

Erica had caught it. "Miss what?"

"Nothing," he replied. His brain felt foggy and slow, like his synapses had been stuffed with cotton. He hadn't told Dan and Erica about Dhanya's visit, and it suddenly seemed very strange to him that they didn't know he was getting an arranged marriage. *After all,* he thought, *they* are *your best friends.*

He sat up. "Hey, guys. There's something I need to tell you. I'm getting an arr—"

His voice caught in his throat, like someone had clenched a hand around his neck. His friends looked at him expectantly. "What are you getting?" asked Dan.

"A dog," he said hastily. "I'm getting a dog."

Dan smiled. "That's great, buddy. I'm happy for you."

Arjun arrived at the PSI office on Monday to find it festooned in red and pink. He checked the calendar on his phone: February 14th. He briefly wondered why he didn't feel more upset that he was date-less on Valentine's Day. Perhaps he was beyond caring? Or, more likely, he cared very deeply but *pretended* not to, like one of those lonely spinsters who instead celebrated "Anna Howard Shaw Day" on February 14th.

No, Arjun thought, shaking his head as he ascended the stairs. *It's neither of those. This time next year, I'll have someone to celebrate Valentine's Day with.*

By instinct, Arjun found himself in front of his old office. The doorway was still taped off, but now, someone had placed a large yellow bucket beneath the dripping ceiling. "I'm sorry about this," said Adam D'Antonio, startling Arjun. For such a big man, he moved surprisingly quietly. "It turns out this is a bigger repair than we'd anticipated. We'll need to replace nearly the entire ceiling. Unfortunately, that means we'll have to postpone your homecoming for a few more weeks."

Arjun nodded. "Well, at least I have the dungeon downstairs."

"By the way," said Adam, "it's good that I have you here now. I'd like to discuss something with you. We can speak in my office, if you'd like."

Arjun felt a burst of fear rip through him. Adam usually let him be—and, besides, wasn't it always bad news when the boss asked to speak with you in private? Arjun followed Adam to his corner office, mentally counting all his infractions, however small: the days he'd ducked out early, the pilfered pens and sticky notes, and—just once—two "PSI" branded mugs from the commissary. *But, surely, two mugs aren't reason enough to fire me,* he thought, taking a seat on the opposite side of Adam's handsome oak desk. "Is everything all right?" he ventured, feeling a cold sweat beading on his brow.

"I wanted to talk to you about the Pacific Bank account," Adam began. "The one I had you sub in for me on a few weeks ago."

Arjun nodded. Had he blown the sale? Or, worse—had Pacific Bank walked away from PSI altogether? *Maybe it would be good if I got fired,* thought Arjun, his stomach tightening. *It would give me an excuse to finally buy the restaurant. Or spend all of my energy trying to get married.* Another thought occurred to him: *How would being unemployed look on a biodata?*

Adam leaned back in his chair. "I just got a call from Tom Barnes, their lead rep," he said slowly. A wide grin spread across his face. "They loved you, Arjun!" he proclaimed. "They signed a new contract this morning."

Arjun sighed with relief.

"That's a million-dollar sale!" his boss enthused. "And that's why I've called you in here. I think you have talents that I want to put to use. Specifically, as a salesman."

Arjun frowned. "A salesman?"

"That's right," said Adam. "And, now that you've proven yourself, I want to pull you up to the big leagues. That's why I'm sending you after a much bigger fish: Peacock International. You're going to India!"

"India?" Arjun repeated. "Like, the country?"

His boss laughed. "Yes, like, the country. I'm sending you to Hyderabad!"

Arjun shook his head. "Adam, I can't go to India."

"Hold that thought," Adam said. He slid open a desk

drawer and slid a check across the table to Arjun. "*That* is your commission from the Pacific Bank sale."

Arjun glanced down at the check and could hardly keep his jaw from crashing onto the desk. "Adam," he sputtered, "this is more than I make in a month."

"I know! And it's just a taste. If you close Peacock, you'll make five times as much."

Arjun nodded. "That's very enticing," he said, pocketing the check. "But there's a problem with me going all the way across the world: making a sale in the office isn't like making a sale on the road. I'm not really a software person. What if they have questions that I can't answer?"

"The bulk of the deal has been worked out already," Adam replied. "You're mostly there to hash out any final details. And, besides, you're not going alone."

"Are you coming with me?" Arjun asked.

Adam shook his head. "I'm sending one of your direct reports with you. A coder. It's—ah!" He pointed out the window into the bullpen. "There he is: Kevin McPherson. I believe you went to his bachelor party a few weeks back."

Arjun swiveled in the chair. Kevin McPherson was digging into a plate of chicken wings, his Birkenstock-clad feet slung up on his desk. A gob of ranch dressing had dripped onto his lurid Hawaiian shirt. The two men watched as Kevin swabbed it away with his index finger and licked it off. "It was a divorce party, actually," Arjun replied, turning back to his boss. "You can't be serious, right?"

"That was an unfortunate tableau, I'll admit," said Adam, shrugging. "But Kevin is the best coder on your team by far, and I need my A-team on a sale this big. What do you say?"

Arjun's mouth opened and closed—but no retort came. "I guess I'm going to India."

Adam smiled. "Attaboy. I'll have my assistant email you the details." Arjun rose, and just as he was about to exit his boss's office, Adam spoke up. "Oh, and one more thing: Mr. Evans asked to speak to you this morning."

"Who's Mr. Evans?" Arjun asked, turning around.

"The editor-in-chief of the *San Francisco Current*. It's probably nothing. Just going over some house rules while you're over there, I'd wager."

Arjun nodded, and Adam sent him off. He descended downstairs and crossed the lobby to the *Current*'s offices. "I'm looking for Mr. Evans," he said to the receptionist.

"He's downstairs," she told him. "In the old storage closet."

So that's what it is. "Spare office," my ass, Arjun thought bitterly, taking the stairs down another level, where the world grew smaller and danker. He squeezed through the crowded hallway and pushed open the door to his room, only to find two people waiting there for him. Only one was Mr. Evans, a tired-looking man in his late-fifties. Much to Arjun's surprise, the other person was the green-eyed woman who had first accosted him over scones and once more over this very "office." She sat on the desk, one leg thrown carelessly over the side, and she regarded Arjun coolly as he stepped inside.

"Ah, Mr. Chowdhury," said Mr. Evans. "It's good to see you. How are you liking the office so far?"

"It's fine," he replied tersely, crossing his arms. "Small. I'm sorry, but what is *she* doing here?"

"Right," said Mr. Evans, fiddling with his spectacles. "It's come to my attention that our newest employee was already working out of this space before we agreed to rent it to you. Obviously, the *Current* must prioritize our own employees, but we still want to be good neighbors to you folks up at PSI. With that said, I'm going to ask if you'd mind sharing the space."

Arjun was incredulous. *"Share?"* he repeated. "This place is a shoebox. We won't both fit in here." He glanced at the woman for confirmation; she remained as impassive as a sphinx.

Mr. Evans looked helplessly at Arjun, a sort of *my-hands-are-tied* gesture. "I'm sorry, Mr. Chowdhury," he said. "I can offer you a reduced rate on the office—but, for now, I'm afraid this is how things will have to be."

Mr. Evans gave Arjun one final apology, then sidestepped between him and the green-eyed woman. *Did that really just happen?* Arjun wondered, too stunned to speak.

It was the woman who broke the silence. "I don't like this any more than you do," she assured him. "I'd totally understand if you wanted to work from a coffee shop or something."

Arjun noticed a slight mocking smile that passed over her lips. She was right: he could go upstairs and beg Adam to put him somewhere else, *anywhere* else. But Arjun was nothing if not stubborn—and, besides, the office was rightfully his. *It's the scones all over again*, he thought. He wouldn't let this woman take something from him simply by complaining. *You won this battle*, he thought, staring at the self-satisfied expression on her perfectly symmetrical face. *But I'll win the war.*

He set his bag down on the table. "I think I'll be perfectly happy here," he said, carefully injecting just the right amount of smugness into his voice. "We haven't been formally introduced, by the way," he said, sticking out his hand. "My name is Arjun Chowdhury."

She rolled her eyes, as though exasperated that he'd taken up her challenge. "I'm Manisha Nandan," she told him. "But everyone calls me Nisha."

CHAPTER
Seven

India was hot.

No, thought Arjun, sitting on the tarmac of the Rajiv Gandhi International Airport, *"hot" is an insufficient word.* India was sweltering, baking, scorching. It was a heavy, suffocating heat, so dense with humidity that he could have stuck a straw into his mouth and sucked moisture right out of the air.

He dabbed at his forehead with a sodden handkerchief and stared out the window of his business-class seat. The plane had been taxiing for half an hour, but thirty minutes may as well have been a century. Arjun had stripped down to his undershirt—but, still, his face and body were sticky with sweat.

He glanced over to the seat beside him, wondering if Kevin McPherson was as miserable as he was. If so, he didn't show it: Kevin was fast asleep, his head flopped over one side of his neck pillow. "Figures," Arjun muttered under his breath. He leaned back into his seat and closed his eyes.

As his mind wandered, it found its way off that sweltering plane, off the subcontinent, across the ocean, and back to San Francisco. It meandered down Market Street, to the offices of

PSI, and it descended a flight of stairs and crossed through a cramped hallway. The journey happened quickly, subconsciously; this was, after all, a path that he'd taken dozens (if not hundreds) of times over the past two weeks. And, as he arrived at the battered red door, he knew who would be there waiting for him: the same person who'd been there every single time.

Yes—he was still thinking of Nisha Nandan.

The day she'd moved in had been a tense one. Adam had sent Arjun hundreds of pages of documents in preparation for the pitch at Peacock, and he spent the afternoon hunched over his laptop, trying not to notice the beautiful woman sitting six inches away from his face.

Of course, Nisha didn't make ignoring her easy. She typed furiously on her computer, each keystroke delivered like a champion boxer's punch. The pattering sound reverberated through the tiny office, a rainstorm of clicks. "Can you stop that?" Arjun finally asked, peering around the boxy desktop that separated him from Nisha. "It's really distracting."

She stopped typing just long enough to smile sweetly at him. "Thank you for telling me that."

She began to type even more loudly.

Arjun felt himself fuming. *Two can play at that game*, he thought. He began a new barrage on his own keyboard, the clacking of his keys growing louder than hers. *Had enough yet?* he wanted to ask.

But Nisha was not deterred in the slightest. She began hitting her keyboard even *harder*. This, of course, made Arjun do the same—and then, Nisha redoubled her assault on her laptop, the computer practically bouncing against ·the table with every thunderous keystroke. The tiny office began to sound just like a firing range.

The barrage continued for what seemed like hours. There

were no windows in the room, and it was difficult to get a sense of the passage of time. Besides, the incessant keyboard sounds made it hard to concentrate on anything. Finally, Nisha stopped typing. She leaned over the computer. "What are you still doing here?" she asked.

"What does it look like?" Arjun replied irritably. "I'm working."

"No shit," she said. "What I meant was: why haven't you left yet? It's Valentine's Day, you know. If you have a girl-friend, she's going to be *pissed*."

He shook his head and turned his attention back to his laptop. "Well, then, it's a good thing that I'm single."

She raised an eyebrow. "You're single?"

"Yes. Why? Is that hard to believe?"

She thought it over for a second. "Nope."

"What about you, hot stuff?" he shot back. "I might still be here without a valentine—but so are you."

Nisha scoffed, but Arjun saw a hint of real sadness behind her bright-green eyes. He felt a pang of regret. "I'm sorry," he said quickly. "That was uncalled for."

"Whatever," she said, rolling her eyes. "Just get back to work."

And so it went, the two of them working wordlessly. Thankfully, the war of keyboards had reached a détente, and the office was mercifully quiet. In the silence, Arjun occasion-ally caught himself sneaking glances at Nisha over his laptop screen. The first time they'd met, he'd noticed her green eyes, as bright and intense as emeralds. Now, he couldn't *stop* noticing them: the way they seemed to shine and shimmer even underneath the buzzing yellow lightbulb, their own luminescence making them impervious to the poor lighting.

Arjun wanted to dislike her, of course, and why shouldn't he? She'd had no right to accost him over those scones, to ambush him with her boss and strong-arm him into sharing an already too-small office. *But*, he thought, enthralled by the way Nisha's nose scrunched up in concentration, *it's hard to dislike someone so beautiful.*

He opened his mouth, ready to speak. *I think we got off on the wrong foot*, he wanted to say. Perhaps he'd suggest going back to Ron's coffee shop, where he could buy her a chocolate chip scone as a peace offering.

His eyes met her, and, for a moment, Arjun felt a spark of electricity. It was a spark that he'd felt a few times before, bringing him back to one moment in particular: the moment he'd first laid eyes on Vicky Chang in econ section freshman year. *Wouldn't that be something?* he wondered, his gaze lingering on the tiny gold ring sparkling inside the fold of Nisha's left nostril.

He felt himself start to smile—but Nisha only narrowed her eyes venomously. "Can you stop staring at me?" she spat, giving him a look of such utter contempt that he actually felt a chill pass through him. "It's *creepy.*"

And that was that. The two weeks after that exchange dragged by in silence, with Arjun completing his work as quickly as possible and refusing to acknowledge the presence of the woman sharing the former storage closet with him.

If Arjun had hoped that India would be a respite from his new office (and, most crucially, his new office mate), he had hoped wrong. The plane taxied for another half hour, by which point he was seriously contemplating pushing open the exit-row door and jumping down the emergency slide. *Sure, I might get shot by airport security*, he mused, staring long-ingly out the window, *but it would be worth it just to get off of this damn airplane.*

Finally, the intercom squawked overhead. "Sorry for the delay, everyone," came the captain's voice, which was made all the more grating by its pleasant Danish accent. "We'll disembark shortly. Thank you for flying British Airways, and welcome to Hyderabad."

After finally getting off the plane (and vowing never to fly British Airways again), Arjun walked to baggage claim with Kevin. They would only be in India for a week, so Arjun had packed light: all of his belongings fit into his carry-on bag. Kevin, on the other hand, had taken a more maximalist approach. He'd brought two large garishly red suitcases made of molded plastic that reminded Arjun of a grocery store toboggan. "You know we're only here for a few days, right?" he asked, helping Kevin lug the second suitcase off of the carousel.

Kevin only shrugged. "I like to be prepared."

There was a long line of taxis queued up outside the airport exit, and dozens of drivers jockeyed for fares. "Where you are going?" called one in English, jogging beside Arjun as he walked briskly by. "I will take you there most cheaply."

"Taj Krishna," Arjun replied, nonplussed.

"No problem at all, sir," the driver said, nodding vigorously. "Two thousand rupees, it is nothing."

That seemed reasonable to Arjun, but another driver interjected just before he could agree. "*Arre!*" the second driver exclaimed. "Two thousand rupees for a few kilometers! That man is a crook. I will take you for one thousand."

"*Sale*, even one thousand is robbery!" shouted a third driver, a cigarette wagging between his fingers. "Trying to take advantage of Americans. Come, I will take you for five hundred."

The sooner Arjun got out of the heat, the better. "Done," he said to the five-hundred-rupee man, who led them to a waiting cab and loaded their luggage into the trunk with surprising alacrity. Arjun slid into the backseat with Kevin. "Do you have AC?" he asked.

The driver gave him a quizzical look through the rearview

mirror, then shook his head. *Of course not*, Arjun thought miserably, turning the crank to lower the window.

As if the wait on the tarmac hadn't been enough, the ride to the hotel took almost an hour. The workday was just beginning, and the city hummed to life as the cab crawled toward its destination. There were people everywhere: kids in blue school uniforms, complete with black neckties; women in saris faded with dust; men lugging vegetable carts along the road. Horns blared almost the entire way, and Arjun saw tiny rickshaws scooting alongside rusty Marutis and even some cars of German and Japanese origin.

"I'm starving," Kevin said as the driver helped them unload their suitcases from the trunk. "You know, I could really go for a hamburger."

"You're probably in the wrong place, then," Arjun replied testily, tipping the driver. Adam D'Antonio might have forced Arjun to bring Kevin along—but he wasn't in the mood to play babysitter.

The hotel lobby was open and airy. Light poured in through large windows and bounced off the immaculate white marble floors, making the space appear much larger than it actually was. As Arjun stepped inside, he heard the low hum of the air conditioner, and he nearly burst into tears as he felt the slight breeze against his skin. Kevin walked off and reappeared with a carafe of ice water. Arjun could have kissed him. He drank one glass, then another. Kevin dipped a napkin into his glass and dabbed it all over his face and neck. "Good idea," Arjun said, doing the same (and not caring how ridiculous he must have looked to the hotel staff).

He and Kevin retrieved their room keys from the front desk. "I'm off to get some sleep," he said, rubbing his tired eyes with a knuckle. "We can meet up for dinner later, if you'd like."

"Works for me," Kevin replied. He glanced over Arjun's shoulder. "Hey, do you know that lady? She's waving at you."

Arjun whipped around. *Oh, no,* he thought. *Is that really her?*

It was. Dhanya Agarwal sat on one of the leather couches in the lobby, her bangles jingling as she waved him over. "Arjun!" she called, her voice carrying across the space. "Come, *beta!* I've been waiting for you!"

"Is that the person we're pitching to?" Kevin asked. "I thought it was supposed to be a guy."

"It is," Arjun said hastily. "She's, uh…well, she's my aunt. I forgot that I was supposed to meet her here. You go ahead, Kevin. I'll see you tonight."

Kevin shrugged and headed for the elevator bay, evidently satisfied by Arjun's answer. Arjun made his way across the lobby. "Hello, Dhanya Auntie," he said, allowing her to embrace him. "What a nice surprise."

She beamed. "The pleasure is all mine, *beta*. It was such a treat to meet you in San Francisco. When your mother told me you'd be in Hyderabad for work, I just *knew* I had to come see you!"

Of course, my mom is involved in this, thought Arjun. "You didn't have to come all this way," he said. "I feel terrible, making you fly all the way across the world just to meet me."

Dhanya shook her head. "It's no trouble—I was here anyway! I have many clients in India, so I spend two months here and two months in the US. Back and forth, like a grandfather clock!"

Dhanya must have been in her sixties; Arjun had to admire her vigor. "Well, it's lovely to see you, Auntie," he said, stifling a yawn. "I'm very jet-lagged, so I'll probably sleep now. But I'll see you in San Francisco soon enough, won't I?"

"Perhaps that won't be necessary," she said with an artful

smile. She reached for her large black purse and produced a manila envelope. She handed it to Arjun as discreetly as a government official slipping mission documents to a spy.

He peered inside the folder. "Are these…biodatas?"

"Good eye. I took the liberty of passing your information along to some of my clients. These are a few girls who have already agreed to meet with you. Now, the decision of whom to meet is up to you. Well, you and your mother, of course. You'll call her to review the girls' profiles, won't you?"

Arjun looked over the enclosed biodatas, complete with headshots the size of postage stamps. He'd completed his own biodata, of course—but this was the first time he was seeing them from the other side. *These are so brief,* he thought, scanning the pages. He knew it was impossible to capture a whole personality in such a basic format (in fact, this was the very reason that he tended to stay away from dating apps). *What if I miss out on someone great just because her biodata is lacking?* he wondered.

There was another thing that caught his notice, too. "Dhanya Auntie, all of these girls live here, in Hyderabad."

She nodded. "That's right. The girl you'll marry will most likely be from India, anyway, so it made perfect sense to conduct these meetings while you were here!"

That was news to Arjun. "Dhanya Auntie, I never said anything about marrying a girl from India."

"And you didn't have to! Trust me, *beta*—I've selected each of these girls myself. They are all of a sweet disposition, with good educations and respectable family backgrounds. I know you'll hit it off with at least one of them!"

Dhanya's phone pinged before Arjun could respond. "*Hai, Ram,*" she groaned. "I must run to another client's home. It was so lovely to see you, Arjun."

He sighed. "You, too, Dhanya Auntie," he said, stowing the biodatas back into the folder and tucking it under his arm. He hugged Dhanya again, and with that, the matchmaker swept across the lobby. There was a sleek black car waiting for her by the entrance, and it whisked her off in a cloud of yellow dust.

Hyderabad was almost eleven hours ahead of Des Moines, so Arjun waited around his hotel room until it became an acceptable time to FaceTime his mother. Luckily, she was already up when he called. "How was your flight?" she asked him, sounding incredibly chipper for six in the morning.

"It was fine, Mom," he said, deciding not to mention the wait on the tarmac (which would have led to a lecture about not flying on western airlines, he was sure).

"Good, good," she replied. "I'm assuming you're calling to go over the biodatas? Dhanya faxed me copies this morning."

So that's *why she's so happy*, Arjun thought. "Yes, I have them right here. I thought I'd wait for you to open them."

Sarita smiled. "That was smart of you. After all, it's my job to guide you in finding a suitable partner."

That sentence felt like a centipede crawling over Arjun's spine. "Whatever you say, Mom," he said, sliding the sheaf of papers out of the folder and onto the desk. "All right: first girl, Kavya Jayaram."

Sarita nodded. "Nice-looking girl. Good teeth."

Arjun couldn't help but laugh. "Really, Mom? 'Good teeth'?"

"What? I notice what I notice. So, what do you think of this Kavya?"

He scanned over the biodata. "She seems nice," he said finally. "And she's an accountant."

"Parents are good, as well," said Sarita. "Both doctors. Shall we go ahead and set up the meeting?"

Arjun sighed and pushed the paper aside. "I don't know," he said. "Doesn't this feel…I don't know, a bit *superficial* to you? I mean, we're literally evaluating women based on a photo and a few lines of text. This process really doesn't offend your feminist side?"

Sarita scoffed. "And the alternative is, what? Tinder? The *Bachelor*? People *are* superficial—and so is this process. But that doesn't mean that Kavya isn't a very nice girl who could make a very nice wife. So, I ask again: would you like to meet her?"

He shook his head. "No," he said. "Let's see if there's someone I like better in this pile."

It went on like that for the next several hours, with Arjun and Sarita discussing each woman's biodata and trying to cross-reference the names on Facebook and Google to learn more about them. This tactic did them no good: there were a billion people in India, after all, and there were always at least a dozen people with any given name.

Finally, Arjun had his name: Malini Arora, a twenty-six-year-old software engineer with large brown eyes and a slightly upturned nose. She seemed to satisfy Sarita, too. "You picked well," she said. "I can call Dhanya and tell her, if you'd like."

Arjun assented and hung up the phone. He flopped onto his mattress and glanced at the alarm clock on the bedside table. It was nearly ten, and he'd totally forgotten about dinner with Kevin. But, before he could feel bad about blowing Kevin off, he was asleep.

Kevin was waiting for Arjun in the lobby the following morning. At Arjun's insistence, he'd swapped out his Birkenstocks and Hawaiian shirt for a smart linen ensemble. Still, his style hadn't gone totally conventional: he had a swamp-green briefcase tucked under his arm, the leather stamped with a crocodile pattern. "What's in there?" Arjun asked.

"Snacks, mostly," Kevin replied.

Arjun couldn't help but chuckle. "Come on," he said. "Taxi's waiting."

This was not Arjun's first trip to Hyderabad. Growing up, he'd spent a few weeks in the city every summer, living with his father's parents in their tenth-floor apartment. He'd followed his grandmother on her daily peregrinations to the city's various temples, and he'd learned cooking from his grandfather. As a child, Arjun had loved India, so different from his home in Iowa: louder and brighter, simultaneously faster and slower paced. And this was to say nothing of the monkeys, which had fascinated him with their quick movements and curious, almost human expressions. More than anything, though, India was his grandparents—and, when they died, India became locked away, like ice freezing over a lake.

Arjun had last returned to Hyderabad in high school for his grandmother's funeral. Since then, the city had lived only in his mind, shrouded in the sepia haze of the past. Now, driving to the site of their meeting, the color was flooding back into his memories of the place. Shade trees lined the avenues, and fruit sellers and newsstands cropped up along the sides of the roadway. Bicyclists and scooters weaved through a line of yellow rickshaws—which had stopped for a white cow crossing just ahead, its hump bobbing from side to side as it went.

Despite all that had remained the same as Arjun remembered, what struck him the most was how much the city had changed since its last visit. Glass buildings towered proudly over the avenues and were emblazoned with the names of American technology companies: Microsoft and Dell, Google and Amazon. It was almost as though Silicon Valley had fashioned itself an Indian twin. Arjun found himself contemplating what his life would look like if his parents had never left India. *Would I be working in one of these skyscrapers?* he wondered, leaning against the car window.

The car stopped outside one of the buildings, which stood taller than the rest. There was a multicolored sign on the façade, ten stories above the street: PEACOCK INTERNATIONAL. They stepped out of the cab. "You ready?" Kevin asked, glancing over at Arjun.

He craned his neck up to stare at the huge peacock-shaped insignia. "As ready as I'll ever be."

The building's lobby was as enormous and resplendent as a palace. Live trees stood around the perimeter of the lobby, and there was a large circular koi pond in one corner, complete with a wooden bridge and mini waterfall. There were sitting areas and a coffee bar, and, in the center of the lobby, the peacock logo appeared once more in a floor mosaic twenty feet across. *An impressive lobby for an impressive company,* Arjun thought.

He'd conducted extensive research on Peacock in the weeks leading up to this trip. It was primarily a telecom company with operations in India and Southeast Asia. Peacock was also expanding its footprint in the personal banking space; that was why Arjun had come all the way to India, having drilled the sales pitch so many times that he could have recited it backwards (and in his sleep, too). Still, despite all of his preparation, Arjun could feel the sweat beading on his palms, and he wiped his hands on his trousers.

He and Kevin approached the young man sitting at the front desk. "We're from Pay Systems, Incorporated," he said. "We have a twelve o'clock appointment with Charan Murthi."

The receptionist squinted at his desktop. "Ah, yes. Arjun Chowdhury and Kevin McPherson. Unfortunately, Mr. Murthi was called away to Beijing this week. We have you up on the seventeenth floor with Mr. Wellstone."

Arjun frowned. Back in San Francisco, Adam had given him a dossier on Charan Murthi: his likes and dislikes, where he'd grown up, and where he'd gone to school. Not only did Arjun not know these things about this "Mr. Wellstone"—he'd never even heard of the man.

The receptionist noted Arjun's perplexed expression. "Is there a problem, sir?" he asked. Arjun glanced over at Kevin. He was looking at Arjun, too, awaiting a response.

"That should be fine," Arjun said, and the receptionist directed them to the elevator bank. *What am I walking into?* Arjun wondered as he stepped into the elevator, a golden-capped glass cylinder that reminded him of an expensive jar in which a rich woman might store cotton balls.

The lobby grew smaller beneath them. "Are you okay?" Kevin asked as the elevator whirred up to seventeen. "Your hands are balled up like you're about to hit something."

Arjun looked down; Kevin was right. He relaxed his hands, flexing his fingers. "I feel like there's something going on," he said. "They changed the person we're meeting with, without telling us in advance. And, where there's one surprise, there's always another."

The elevator doors slid open, and before them stood a verdant living wall planted with a variety of ferns and creeping vines. Rivulets of water ran from the ceiling, glistening on the dark-green leaves.

A man stood in front of the wall, waiting to greet them. *This must be Wellstone,* Arjun surmised. Despite the heat outside, the man was wearing an argyle sweater vest over his crisp white dress shirt. Round, wire-framed glasses rested upon the bridge of his aquiline nose.

"Hey, guys!" he called, beaming. His voice had a slight Boston accent. "I hope you had a great flight in."

He's American? thought Arjun, marveling at the irony of traveling halfway around the world for this meeting. "It wasn't too bad," he replied, shaking the other man's hand.

"Glad to hear it," the man said. "I'm Ed Wellstone, by the

way. I'm sorry about the mix-up earlier; I know I'm not who you were expecting. But I promise, I don't bite!"

"It's no trouble," Arjun replied. "I'm Arjun Chowdhury, Vice President at PSI. This is Kevin McPherson, one of our senior software engineers."

"Lovely to meet both of you," Wellstone replied, shaking Kevin's hand. "Let's head to my office, shall we?" He led them around the living wall, revealing a more conventional open office space.

Arjun and Kevin followed Wellstone down the main aisle, past cubicles and conference rooms, and finally, to an immense office on the other side of the floor. There was a sitting area in front of the desk, with chairs and a table. A projector sat on the table, casting blue light onto a screen.

Wellstone sat at the head of the table, and Arjun sat beside him as Kevin hooked up his laptop to the projector. "So, I have to ask—" Arjun began.

"How did I get here?" Wellstone replied, smiling. "I know, I must seem out of place here in Hyderabad."

"I'm sorry, I didn't mean to offend," Arjun said sheepishly.

"Not at all," Wellstone said. "I'm a native son of Boston: I grew up in Back Bay, and I went to Northeastern and then to Harvard Business School. The truth is, I met a woman in business school, and we fell in love. She wanted to return home, and after we got married, that's just what we did."

Arjun nodded. "She must be a remarkable person."

Wellstone smiled and toyed with his wedding ring. "She is." He glanced up at Kevin. "But, as much as I'd enjoy talking more about love, I do have another meeting scheduled after this one. Are you ready to present?"

Kevin nodded. "The floor is yours, Arjun."

"Right," he said. He stood and walked over to the screen. "Well, first off, we want to thank you again for your time today. We're here to present our—PSI's—proposal to Peacock International."

Arjun looked to Wellstone for some sort of confirmation. The other man smiled warmly.

He forged on. "Peacock is the leader in most of the markets in which it operates. But there is one area where it's falling behind: banking. Now, Peacock offers banking services to many geographical areas that larger banks don't occupy. In the past, that has allowed your firm to have a monopoly over all of these different locations. However, your monopoly is under threat as companies like Virgo and TriStar move into those traditionally underserved markets. That means that Peacock now finds itself in the position of having to provide new incentives to customers so that they'll continue to use Peacock for all of their banking needs.

"That's where we come in," Arjun continued. "PSI offers unparalleled software infrastructure to support banking activities. We'll augment your physical locations with digital services so customers can open accounts, deposit and withdraw money, and even invest in the stock market—all from their mobile phones."

Arjun moved through the rest of the presentation, describing PSI's offerings in detail. It was a comprehensive pitch, polished by hours of preparatory work. Still, as he flicked through the slides, Arjun began to feel nervous.

It was Wellstone. As the presentation progressed, a chill had settled over the other man's demeanor. Where initially Wellstone had appeared warm and encouraging, now he seemed aloof and disinterested. He even pulled out his phone and answered a text message at one point. *Am I blowing this?* Arjun wondered, trying to keep his thoughts from racing as he spoke.

No, he told himself. *He's just playing hard to get.* That was a common tactic, something every first-year learned in business school: in a negotiation, the winner is the person who appears most likely to walk away. *But,* Arjun thought, *most of the groundwork for this deal has already been laid. We've been in negotiations for months; I'm only here to close. So why do I feel like this guy is messing with me?*

Finally, Arjun reached his last slide. "As you know, my colleagues have already sent you documents containing all of the deal parameters we've discussed today," he said, attempting to ease his disquieting thoughts. "I'd like to answer any questions you might still have."

Wellstone was silent, and for a moment, Arjun thought he would continue his silence indefinitely. Finally, he frowned. He said only one word:

"No."

A grenade went off inside Arjun's skull, filling it with an angry buzzing sound. "No?" he repeated, his voice dulled with confusion. "What do you mean?"

"I mean that this deal is no longer acceptable to our firm," Wellstone replied, leaning back in his chair.

Arjun shook his head. "I'm sorry, but I was under the impression that this had been basically worked out."

Wellstone frowned. "Nothing is ever really 'worked out' until the paperwork is actually signed. Our priorities have changed since we last spoke to your team. At this time, we feel that the resources devoted to this project are…inordinate."

Wellstone's blue eyes gleamed with amusement. He'd relished that last word, drawing out each syllable: *in-or-di-nate.*

He's toying with me, Arjun realized. *He's trying to lower the price of the deal.*

Arjun didn't know if he was authorized to offer a reduced price. Of course, he could call Adam D'Antonio and ask, but he knew the negotiation would be over if he left the room. *Besides,* he thought, *if I really* could *offer a lower price, Adam would have mentioned something back in San Francisco.*

Arjun realized that he hadn't said anything in what felt like several minutes. He was still standing beside the table, the projector remote in his hand. He'd never felt more stupid, like a knight on a battlefield with a pool noodle for a sword. *Think,* he told himself. He'd always been good at solving problems of all kinds—*And what is this, if not another problem to be solved?* he thought.

The beginnings of an answer were forming in his mind. He met Wellstone's stare, trying to appear as confident as possible. "I understand your hesitation," he said slowly, like a deer venturing out of the safety of the forest. "The amount of money we're asking for is very large. And you might think that the approach we've just presented to you isn't unique enough. Too cookie-cutter. After all, if we give you the same stuff as we give everyone, what's to stop your competitors from hiring us to do this for them?"

Arjun thought he saw the subtlest of nods from the other man. *It's working,* he realized. *He's on the hook—now, reel him in.*

"We can offer you a suite of custom features," he continued. "A set of software tools that will be unique to Peacock International. We'll help you stand leagues apart from the competition."

Wellstone straightened slightly. "And what sorts of features are you referring to?" he asked, his voice even. Still, Arjun could sense his interest, hiding behind his words like the face behind a mask.

Arjun shifted nervously. He hadn't thought this far ahead. *Work the problem,* he thought. *What does he want more than anything?*

"Data," he began. "Most of your customers use mobile phones as their primary, or only, internet-capable device. Wi-fi is scarce in many areas, which pushes customers to use cellular data instead. Online banking, therefore, is an enormous expense for these users—if they even have reception in the first place."

Arjun looked over to Kevin, who'd been observing silently for the entire presentation, scarcely moving in his low-slung chair. "What if there was a way to drastically lower the amount of data used in online banking?" he asked. "What if there was a way to make Peacock services much, much cheaper than the competition?"

Wellstone shook his head, chuckling slightly. "It's a nice idea," he said patronizingly. "But it's impossible. Online banking is necessarily data-intensive. There's no way to get around it."

For the first time, Kevin spoke up. "That's incorrect," he said, oblivious to his lack of diplomacy. "Maybe there's no way for *your* software engineers to get around the data issue —but I'm a much better coder than they are. Are you familiar with network effects?"

Wellstone shook his head. *Where's he going with this?* Arjun wondered, looking over at Kevin.

"Essentially," Kevin continued, "users could 'piggyback' on other users' phones, provided those other users also have the app. If you opened the app, the computational load would be spread to other phones. It'd be a minuscule amount, barely noticeable. In turn, when those other users use the app, *their* data load would be distributed onto your phone, as well. This would dramatically lower data usage for every user overall."

Kevin had struck gold. Sparks lit up in Wellstone's eyes. "This isn't just theoretical, is it?" he asked, his tone growing suddenly animated. "You can actually do this?"

"I've done it before," Kevin said casually. "If you have a whiteboard, I could explain how it works."

Wellstone relayed Kevin's request to his secretary, who brought a rolling whiteboard into the room. In a flurry of movement, Kevin sketched out his ideas in red marker.

Arjun watched as Kevin explained, occasionally cutting in to ask Kevin to provide more details when Wellstone looked confused. Eventually, Kevin's drawings grew so dense that Wellstone had another whiteboard brought in. Arjun continually looked at the other man, and he felt nervous anticipation fluttering in his chest. *Is he taking this well?* he wondered.

Finally, Kevin finished. He stood between the two whiteboards and capped the marker. He glanced at Arjun, and that was his cue to bring it home.

He stood and cleared his throat. "So, there you have it," he said. "Now, do we have a deal?"

Eight

"Holy shit," Arjun said, walking briskly out of the building with Kevin. "Did we really just do that?"

Kevin grinned back at him. "Yes, we did."

Arjun clapped him on the back. "This calls for some champagne at the hotel. It's on me."

"We don't have to wait that long," said Kevin. He kneeled on the sidewalk and opened his briefcase. There was a small champagne bottle inside, nestled between candy bars and bags of chips. He pulled out the bottle and handed it to Arjun. "Like I said, I like to be prepared. Here's to you, Arjun."

He laughed in delight. "Here's to *us*," he said. He uncorked the bottle, and champagne spurted all over the sidewalk.

The celebrations did not end there. Arjun felt invincible, as though all of his blood had been replaced by divine ichor. He basked in the glow of his victory on the long cab ride back to the hotel, and he did his best to appear humble when Adam D'Antonio called him and promised him a commission check "so big it'll make your eyes bleed" (he hoped that last part was figurative).

They stepped into the lobby of the Taj Krishna, greeted by

the cool breeze from the AC. "Do you want to get dinner here tonight?" Arjun asked. "The food is supposed to be the best in Hyderabad."

"Actually," Kevin replied, "I had something else in mind. Have you ever heard of Gokul Rathore?"

Arjun shook his head, unsure whether that was a person, place, or something else entirely.

"He's a chef," Kevin explained. "He runs a restaurant here in Hyderabad. It's nothing as fancy as the Taj Krishna, but it's the essence of South Indian cooking. I've watched videos about Gokul, and the way he uses ingredients—the creativity, the economy—it's not like anything I've seen before."

Arjun smiled. "Kevin, I didn't know you were such a foodie!" he replied, pleasantly surprised.

Kevin shrugged. "I've always loved food. If I weren't a software engineer, I'd probably be a cook. Anyway, do you want to check out the restaurant?"

"I'd love to," Arjun said.

Gokul Rathore's restaurant was not really a restaurant at all. It was in an outdoor food hall, a rambling assembly of small stalls with corrugated tin roofs supported by thin wooden poles and bolts of cloth separating each stall. Arjun followed Kevin through the maze, weaving through people and ducking beneath the colorful cotton fabric hung overhead to block out the sun. The smells wafted through the narrow alleyway, each one of them torturously delicious: here, the hiss of *vadas* being deep-fried, the sizzle of a *dosa* on the griddle; just beside the honey-sweet smell of *gulab jamun*, the burble of richly spiced *rasam*.

Homesickness tugged at Arjun, like a pinch behind the navel—not for a place, but for a time. The smells brought Arjun back to his childhood, to those Sunday mornings when the snow fell thick and white outside and the windows grew translucent with frost. Arjun's mother would wake him up with a hot bowl of *pongal* and *sambar,* and they would eat together in the kitchen. *Back when there were three of us,* Arjun thought wistfully, thinking of how his father always wolfed down his first bowl and waited for Sarita's approval to get seconds.

Gokul's stall was in the back corner, beneath a span of teal fabric emblazoned with a golden lotus. There was a folding table, beyond which Arjun could see huge pots of bubbling oil and a *tawa* that looked to be four feet across. It was blazing hot inside the kitchen, and Arjun could already feel sweat trickling down his forehead. A man—thin, twenties, with a scimitar nose—was elbow-deep in a *tandoor.* "Gokul!" Kevin called, sliding past the table. Arjun followed.

"Kevin McPherson, yes?" Gokul replied, extricating his arm from the oven and not even bothering to look in their direction.

"That's right," said Kevin. "This is my colleague, Arjun." Arjun folded his hands, and Gokul gave him a cursory once-over. "I want to thank you for getting back to me."

"You were very persistent. How many emails did you send to me? Twenty?"

"Something like that."

"Well, you made it all the way here," Gokul said. "And you didn't come just to be fed, I take it?"

Kevin shook his head. "I was hoping you could teach me how to make your *dum aloo?*"

"Ah," said Gokul. "Of course. You saw the video on YouTube, did you? And now, you want to learn how to cook my most famous dish."

Kevin nodded.

"Very well," sighed Gokul. "You can start by dicing some onions." Gokul turned to Arjun. "And what about you? Can you be of use in a kitchen?"

"Um…I'd like to think so," Arjun said.

"We'll see," Gokul replied. He gestured to a sack of potatoes resting against the leg of the folding table. "Peel them and cut them into quarters."

Arjun nodded. Gokul handed him a small knife, and Arjun got to work. He'd only ever used a vegetable peeler to remove potato skins, and it was slow going with a knife. Once he'd peeled three potatoes, Gokul had evidently seen enough. He snatched the knife from Arjun and made quick work of the rest of the potatoes, removing each skin with one fluid twist of the blade.

Kevin had finished with the onions, and Gokul dumped the quartered potatoes into a pot of boiling water. "We can prepare the gravy in the meantime," he said. There was a large metal tin nearby, and when he opened it, Arjun could see that it was full of colorful spices. Gokul selected bay leaves, cardamom, ginger root, and a head of garlic. He handed the ginger and garlic to Kevin, with instructions to peel both. "There are tomatoes there," he told Arjun. Arjun handed them over, and Gokul dumped them into a huge mortar resting on the ground, along with a handful of cashews and the chopped onions. "Crush them," he told Arjun, giving him a meter-long wooden dowel to use as a pestle. In the meantime, Gokul went off to fry the spices on the *tawa*.

Arjun mashed the tomatoes until his arms ached, and all that was left in the mortar was a thick, gray-white paste. Gokul came over to inspect his work. "Good," he said, adding the paste to the *tawa*. "Make sure this doesn't burn," he told Kevin. The potatoes had finished boiling, and Arjun helped Gokul drain them before placing them on the *tawa* to fry lightly. Gokul went back to the spice tin and returned with a painter's palette of spices: yellow turmeric, bright-red chili powder, green coriander powder, and a half dozen others. He mixed the spices in with the paste, and Arjun watched the whole mixture turn a vibrant, sunset-colored orange.

Gokul tasted the gravy with a spoon, then frowned. He added salt, then some more *garam masala*. He tasted it again, then added a squeeze of lemon. Another taste, and he nodded, pleased. He mixed the potatoes with the gravy. "It's done," he said, scooping up a potato with the spoon; covered in sauce, the morsel glistened like a jewel. "Try this," he said, giving the spoon to Arjun.

The potato was the best that Arjun had ever eaten. *Or was that even a potato?* Arjun thought—because, surely, this couldn't be the same humble root vegetable he'd eaten thousands of times. He'd never tasted anything like it: so richly flavored, the flavors cascading over one another like notes in a symphony. "This is amazing," he said to Gokul as the chef fed Kevin. "Is it this good every time?"

Gokul smiled. "Every time."

"Can you give me the recipe?" Arjun ventured.

Gokul shook his head. "There's no recipe," he said, as though that were the silliest question in the world.

"What do you mean?" asked Arjun. "Surely, you've written something down *somewhere*. How else would you know what to add and when?"

Gokul chuckled. "Cooking is not like computer science, my friend. There's no algorithm that you can follow. The best food is made from the *heart*—and knowing something is good comes from tasting it along the way. Ask yourself: how does it make you feel as you make it?"

Arjun nodded. What Gokul said actually made sense. "Fine, no recipe," Arjun said. "Can I have another potato?"

Arjun spent the cab ride back to the hotel half-asleep, in the clutches of a wicked food coma. He'd inhaled a whole tureen of *dum aloo*, several *laccha parathas*, and a heaping plate of *hakka* noodles. Beside him in the backseat, Kevin McPherson appeared to have been similarly affected. "Thanks for taking me today," Arjun told Kevin. "I really enjoyed meeting Gokul."

Kevin shrugged. "Don't mention it. He's a genius, isn't he? His food was the best I've ever had."

Arjun laughed. "No arguments here. And, again, you were *amazing* today. Really amazing. You practically had Wellstone eating out of your hand."

"Thanks," Kevin replied. "You know, it's almost surprising to hear this from you. I don't know; I guess I always got the sense that you didn't like me."

"I like you," said Arjun. Kevin gave him a dubious look. "Well, okay," he admitted. "It was hard to look past the Birkenstocks. And the Hawaiian shirts! Why do you own so many of them?"

Kevin shrugged. "They're comfortable and stylish. Am I wrong?"

"Yes, but…well, that's not the point. What I'm trying to say is that I misjudged you, Kevin. I'm sorry."

Kevin smiled. "I appreciate that."

Arjun leaned back and sighed. "You know, as good as making that sale felt, cooking with Gokul felt *better*. My dad used to tell me that feeding people was the closest we could come to godliness. I've never been particularly religious, but I felt *something* today."

"Maybe feeding people is something you should pursue more seriously," Kevin said. "I'm sure you could figure it out, if that's what you really want."

"I've actually been thinking about opening a restaurant of my own," Arjun replied. "But that's always been my problem: *thinking*. Too much thinking and not enough doing."

"Maybe that's because it's just been *your* dream," Kevin said. "You're more okay letting yourself down than you are letting other people down. Have you ever thought about bringing on a partner?"

An idea popped into Arjun's head. "What about you?" he

asked. "You clearly know your way around a kitchen. I'm developing a menu. Is that something you'd be interested in helping me with?"

Kevin grinned. "When can I start?" he asked.

Arjun woke the next day to a loud knocking on his door. When he glanced at the alarm clock beside the bed, he saw it was past noon. He opened the door to find a valet carrying a bottle of Johnnie Walker Blue Label. The whiskey was courtesy of Ed Wellstone, who'd also enclosed a note: *I'm hosting a small get-together in the office tonight. I'd love it if you could attend. Details are provided below.*

Arjun set the note on his dresser and went to go shower. It would have been nice to linger on the events of the previous day—the pitch with Wellstone, the meal with Gokul Rathore —but, for the moment, he had more pressing things on his mind.

Today, he was meeting his first prospective match.

Malini Arora was twenty-six years old, slim, and fair-skinned, with long hair that fell past her waist. She'd attended Osmania University and worked as a software engineer at Microsoft. Under the biodata section titled "Expectations for Marriage," she'd written: "I am looking for a true partner, to be supportive in all things: family, career, and life."

Arjun had given up on his own "Expectations" section, and he'd written something similarly banal. Still, Malini was the perfect match—at least, on paper. Like Arjun, she wanted two children. She was close with her parents, loved reading old novels, and played tennis. She was a concert pianist, and she spent her weekends at a local food bank.

Arjun had texted Dhanya around ten o'clock the previous night. To his surprise, she'd responded immediately, and gave him a time and place to meet Malini for lunch.

. . .

Arjun changed into a tailored suit and caught a cab downstairs, giving the address to the driver as he ducked into the backseat. "Jubilee Hills. Fancy place," the driver said in Hindi as the car bumped along the roads.

It occurred to Arjun that he should not arrive empty-handed. He had the driver stop by a roadside stand. *Does Malini prefer roses?* he wondered, staring at the bouquets set in buckets full of water. *Or would lilies be better?* Arjun settled for a large bunch of red roses, paid the man running the stand, and got back into the car.

Arjun was unfamiliar with Hyderabad's various neighborhoods, and he'd thought the address would lead him to a restaurant. Instead, the car turned into a clearly opulent neighborhood. Large houses presided over the street, many constructed in the modern style that would not have been out of place in Westwood or Seattle. Sidewalks crisscrossed lush parks, and people walked golden retrievers and German shepherds. In the distance, Arjun could see the downtown, the gleaming skyscrapers shrouded in haze.

The car stopped in front of a heavy black gate framed by shrubbery. The driver reached out the window and pressed the intercom button. He glanced back at Arjun, clearly meaning for him to speak. "Arjun Chowdhury, here to see Malini," he said, his voice creaky with nervous anticipation.

The gate swung open.

Arjun exited the car in front of the house and knocked on the driver's window. He rolled it down, and Arjun leaned over. "Wait here," he said quietly, handing the driver several hundred-rupee notes. He was in an unfamiliar place, and he didn't know how this meeting would go. He would rather not be stuck on the family's lawn, waiting for a cab if it went badly.

He turned and walked up the front steps. *This is it,* he

thought, smoothing the creases on his jacket. *In thirty seconds, you could be meeting your wife.*

He rang the doorbell.

A lock turned, and a man stood in the doorway. He was short and thin, with a graying mustache; Arjun surmised that this was Malini's father. *What's the etiquette here?* he wondered, beginning to panic. *Should I bow?* he thought, before dismissing the idea. *He's not a king.*

"*Namaste*, Arora *sahib*," Arjun decided, folding his hands in front of his chest and inclining his head slightly. *You look like a complete ass*, he thought, picturing one of those bobble-heads that sat on a dashboard, their expressions vacant as their heads wiggled idiotically.

The man smirked. "I'm Shomu, the servant," he replied in Hindi. "Arora *sahib* is in the living room, with the rest of the family."

I forgot that they have servants here, thought Arjun, slightly relieved that he hadn't made a fool of himself in front of his prospective father-in-law. *But I don't know what he's being so smug about.*

He followed Shomu through the foyer, which was hung with ornate tapestries and paintings depicting Hindu myths: blue-skinned Krishna, recumbent, lay surrounded by attendants and wives; the goddess of death, Kali, planted a foot atop a vanquished enemy, her tongue lolling from her mouth.

A group of people sat on the set of posh black leather couches in the living room. The entire family had assembled: Malini's parents and grandparents, her brothers and sisters, and at least two babies (though, hopefully, not Malini's—what a thing to leave off a biodata!).

Arjun felt his stomach tighten as his gaze fell upon Malini herself. She looked a bit different than she had in her photograph—but, of course, her photo had just been a headshot a few inches wide. Malini had wide eyes fringed by heavy lashes, with a small purple *bindi* on her forehead. Her hair was pleated, intertwined with jasmine buds whose scent wafted across the living room. She wore a green *sari*, and her golden bangles jingled like wind chimes when she stood.

Arjun's mouth went dry. *How do I introduce myself?* he wondered again, knowing that he would be addressing the whole family. Would a simple "Hello" suffice? Surely, he couldn't say the truth: "My name is Arjun, and I'm here because, in a few months, I'd like to marry your daughter and whisk her off to America."

He cleared his throat. *"Namaste,"* he said instead, awkwardly balancing the flowers in the crook of his arm as he folded his hands.

A large man rose from the group, huffing with effort as he stood. He wore thick glasses and a gold chain that would've put most American rappers to shame. *"Namaste,"* he replied, his small eyes looking Arjun up and down. Arjun knew what he was thinking: *So, this is the man who's come to marry my daughter.*

Arjun introduced himself to the rest of the family members, kneeling to touch the feet of the elders, as was customary. Finally, he arrived at Malini herself. "These are for you," he said, handing her the flowers.

"Thank you," she replied, accepting the bouquet. She spoke softly and kept her eyes low. Arjun saw Malini's grandmothers whispering and glancing towards the kitchen. He looked, too, and saw a vase brimming with dozens of perfect, plump roses. *Damn it*, he thought.

Arjun took the place offered to him, a round ottoman so low that his knees came halfway up his shoulders when he sat. "So, Malini—" he began.

Her father cut in instead. "You are a long way from home," he said in thickly accented English. "You came all this way just to meet Malini?"

Arjun tried to steady his nerves. "Of course," he said, smiling as broadly as he dared.

Malini's father laughed, a big booming guffaw that seemed to shake the room. "Good boy," he said. "So, how much do you make?"

Arjun raised an eyebrow. He'd answered this question on the biodata—but to have it be asked so bluntly, not two minutes after meeting this man, was like a splash of cold water to the face. "Three hundred thousand dollars," he said hesitantly. "That's not counting bonuses. And I have stock options that just vested, too. Those are worth a lot more."

Malini's father nodded, clearly impressed. "So much money for such a young man."

"Not young," corrected Malini's mother, a heavyset woman in dark eyeliner. "You're thirty, aren't you, Arjun? Most boys your age are already married."

That was not a question. *Shake it off*, he told himself. "I wanted to establish myself before marriage," he said, trying to project confidence. "It was important to me to make sure I could support myself and my wife when the time came."

Malini's mother nodded. Arjun sensed that she was warming quickly to him—but he sensed wrong. "Is that the only thing, then?" she said, her tone suddenly mocking. "Money?"

He frowned. "I'm sorry, I'm not following." He glanced at Malini, hoping she would finally speak up and say something. Instead, she stared down at her hands folded in her lap.

"There are other things that go into one's readiness for marriage besides money," Malini's mother continued. "Why do you feel that you're ready to be married?"

Arjun knew the answer immediately, this time. "My own father was married around this age," he said. "I think he would have wanted me to be, too."

The hour that followed was among the most agonizing of Arjun's life. He felt like a criminal defendant in front of a panel of lawyers, taking questions on everything from his career goals to his ideal family size to whether or not he snored (or if he minded that Malini did). All the while, his eyes made silent entreaties to Malini, begging her to speak up and stop the interrogation. It didn't work; she remained as mute as a figure in one of the tapestries hanging above.

Finally, Malini's father rose. "Thank you for coming," he said to Arjun, clapping him a bit too hard on the shoulder. "We'll let you know if we'd like another meeting."

That was all that Arjun needed to hear. He practically shot to his feet. "It was nice to meet you, Malini," he said—though, in truth, he didn't feel like he'd met her at all.

"You, as well," she replied. Arjun realized that this was the longest sentence she'd uttered all afternoon.

He bade a hurried farewell to Malini's family, and he walked as quickly as he dared to the door. There was a strange queasy feeling in his stomach that only amplified when he shut the car door behind him. *That was awful*, he thought with a huge exhale as he threw his head back against the headrest. The whole thing had felt oddly like a job interview—but was that normal? After all, it had started with a biodata, which was basically a glorified resume.

And I barely talked to Malini, he thought. Was she just shy? Or did the women usually let their families take the lead in these initial meetings?

Oh, and there was also that thing that Malini's father had said: "...*if* we'd like another meeting."

Arjun wondered if he'd made a bad impression. *The roses were stupid*, he decided. Sitting with all these thoughts buzzing around his head, the journey back to the Taj Krishna felt interminable.

When he arrived at the hotel again, he realized that the solution to all of his problems was staring him in the face. *It's so simple*, he thought, walking towards the bar. A few glasses of whiskey, and this would all be just a bad memory. But, to his surprise, he found Kevin waiting in the lobby, dressed in a blazer and khaki pants. "You look sharp," Arjun said, pleasantly surprised. "What's the occasion?"

Kevin raised an eyebrow. "You got a bottle from Wellstone, too, right? Did you see the note about the mixer?"

Arjun groaned. *Damn it*, he thought. He glanced at his watch, wondering if there was time to head upstairs for a shower. *You're already wearing a suit*, he mused. "All right," he said to Kevin. "I'm ready if you're ready."

Arjun's first thought upon arriving was that Wellstone had dramatically undersold his "small get-together." The Peacock building was lit up like a Christmas tree, with colored lights dancing on the sleek glass façade. A row of cars lined up at the entrance: Porsches and Mercedes, Audis and Maseratis, and even a Lamborghini or two. The people exiting the cars were dressed in glittering dresses and fashionable tuxedos. "What's going on here?" Kevin asked, leaning over to Arjun as they stepped out into the humid night.

"That," he replied, pointing. Someone had placed a large sign just before the sliding doors: a constellation of red and yellow mums was pinned to a large foam display board, forming the words HYDERABAD EDUCATION GALA. "I guess it's a charity event."

Kevin laughed. "Well, it looks like the two of us are a little underdressed. I hope you brought your wallet."

Arjun smiled. He and Kevin went inside together.

The giant lobby had been transformed into a reception hall, with tables dotting the floor and a stage at the far end opposite the koi pond. A band was playing Michael Jackson covers interspersed with Bollywood hits from standards like *Main Hoon Na* and *Kabhi Khushi Kabhie Gham*. After signing in and receiving nametags, Arjun and Kevin watched the band play for a little while. "They're pretty good!" Kevin said, clapping as the band wrapped up a rendition of "Billie Jean" (sung partially in Hindi).

"We should find Wellstone," Arjun replied.

"Go ahead," Kevin said, shouting over the music as another song began. "I'm going to hang out here for a bit. Maybe try to get closer to the band."

Walking away from the crowd assembled near the stage, Arjun left Kevin to listen to a mashup of "Man in the Mirror" and "Maahi Ve". He milled around the lobby for a while, nodding at the people who passed him but not making conversation. After that afternoon's meeting with Malini, he was in no mood to socialize. He wanted to find Wellstone, say hello, and sneak out into the night.

Wellstone, evidently, had other plans. Arjun circled the entire lobby twice, but the bespectacled Bostonian was nowhere to be found. *Maybe the bartender has seen him*, he thought. *And it'd be a good excuse to finally get that drink.*

He walked over to the bar, which had been set up by the elevator bank. He asked the bartender if he'd seen Wellstone. "Tall guy?" Arjun asked. "*White* guy," he elaborated, hoping that would clear things up.

The bartender only shook his head. Arjun sighed and ordered a whiskey, rocks. "He never comes to these things," said a man standing nearby.

"Of course, he doesn't," Arjun muttered.

He felt his phone buzz in his pocket; it was a call from Dhanya. Arjun set his drink down and made for the men's room, where he could speak to her privately. Thankfully, the bathroom was empty, and he picked up the phone. "Hi, Dhanya Auntie," he said, his voice echoing off the white tile walls. "What can I do for you?"

Dhanya laughed. "You're just like my other American clients," she said. "Straight to business. I wanted to congratulate you, *beta*. Malini's family really liked you. They're wondering if you'd like to meet her again before you leave."

That was news to Arjun. "They would?"

"You sound surprised."

"Well, I didn't really get to know Malini very well," he replied. "That's an understatement, actually. I spent the entire meeting talking to her parents while she just sat there, mute. Is that normal?"

Arjun heard Dhanya make an approving noise at the other end of the line. "What is it you say in the States? 'Different strokes for different folks.' Sometimes, the parents lead the discussion; other times, it's up to the children. What did you think of Malini?"

Arjun was surprised at how quickly he came up with an answer. "Please thank her family for their hospitality…but I don't think I'll see her again."

Dhanya was silent for a moment. "That's perfectly fine," she replied. "Would you tell me why not? It will help me to find a better match for you next time."

"She was too timid," Arjun decided after a moment. "I want my wife to be confident enough to take the lead in an intimidating situation. To say what she really thinks. And, even though I only met her once, I don't think Malini is that kind of woman."

"Very well," Dhanya said. "I'll look over my database, then. Hopefully, I can find another meeting for you while you're still in India. I'll talk to you soon, Arjun."

Arjun said goodbye and hung up.

He leaned against the wall and gave a long sigh, like the air being let out of a football. He hadn't said this to Dhanya, but he dreaded the prospect of another meeting. This afternoon was so painfully awkward that he wondered whether he could subject himself to the same thing again. "Maybe you should let it go, Arjun," he told himself, staring at his reflection in the mirror. "Maybe an arranged marriage just isn't for you."

He heard a toilet flush. A latch clicked, and one of the stall doors swung open. An elegant woman in a red dress walked out, smiling faintly. She washed her hands, casting a sideways smirk at Arjun. "This is the men's room," Arjun stammered, pointing to the urinal.

"The women's line is always too long," she replied, chuckling softly. She reached into her purse and drew out a small silver box. She opened it and pulled out a cigarette. "Who'd have thought I'd find juicier gossip in the men's room, though?" She set the cigarette between her lips and sucked in, then exhaled the smoke in a thin, continuous stream.

"That was my friend," said Arjun, stumbling over the lie. "He's having a rough day."

"His name is Arjun, too?" She pointed to his nametag with the tip of her glowing cigarette, and Arjun felt himself turn as red as her dress. "It's all right," she said, chuckling. "Is this the first meeting you've had?"

There was no point in continuing the charade now. "That was the first," he replied. "But I'm thinking that it might be the last."

"Because of her parents?"

"That was part of it. I don't think our personalities were a match, though. I want someone more…"

"Domineering?" she supplied.

He shook his head. "Someone more outgoing."

"Well, that doesn't mean the whole process is a bust. Maybe the next girl you meet will have the personality you're looking for."

"It's not that," Arjun said. "I'm getting an arranged marriage because I've been told that compatibility from the outset is the most important foundation for a lasting relationship. And compatibility isn't just what you do for a living or whether you sleep with the fan on. Chemistry is just as important—and, if I can't guarantee that, what's the point of going through the whole song and dance?"

The woman took another drag; smoke spiraled from the

tip of her cigarette. "Let me ask you a question. What do you think is more romantic: an arranged marriage or a love marriage?"

Arjun knew the answer immediately, but he felt guilty saying it. "A love marriage."

She tutted. "Let me ask again, a different way. Which idea is more beautiful: that one is destined to find enduring love with only one person? Or that he can build a lasting love with anyone?"

Arjun had to think about that. "I don't know," he said, genuinely unsure. "Neither idea is more beautiful than the other. They're just…different."

"Ah," she replied, waggling the cigarette between her fingers. "Now you see. All your life, you've been used to thinking of love one way. Now, you must think in the other way. Not better, not worse—but, as you say, different. It takes some getting used to."

It occurred to Arjun that he was having the biggest philosophical debate of his life in a men's room. "So, what do I do now? I don't want another meeting like the one I just had."

The woman shrugged. "Set yourself up for success," she said. "You know, geography isn't as trivial as we'd like to think it is. Maybe you'll hit it off better with an ABCD, like you. You know: American-born confused—"

"*Desi*," Arjun finished, chuckling. "I know what it means."

The woman smiled, dropped the cigarette into the sink, and let out a jet of water to extinguish it. "Best of luck, Arjun," she said, opening the bathroom door. "I hope you find what you're looking for."

CHAPTER

Nine

I t took Arjun twenty-seven hours to get back to San Francisco, and by the time he rolled his bags into his apartment and flopped onto the couch, the sun had long since set. He was fatigued from traveling, but he wasn't sleepy. A week in India had reversed his circadian rhythm, and despite the late hour, he was wide awake.

Luckily, Dan and Erica were awake, too. When Arjun texted to ask what they were up to, Dan told him they were getting burritos from the taqueria below their apartment and asked if he wanted to join. Arjun had eaten nothing but airplane food all day, and the mere thought of a Mission-style burrito was enough to make him salivate like a dog. He called an Uber to their apartment and entered the taqueria on the ground floor.

Dan and Erica were in their usual spot, a booth tucked into the back corner, surrounded by metal shelving units laden with tortillas. "The conquering hero returns," Dan said, rising to embrace Arjun.

"We figured you'd be hungry, so we got you food," said Erica, handing Arjun a plate of tacos *al pastor* and a mandarin Jarritos.

"You are my favorite person in the world right now," Arjun said gratefully, sliding into the booth next to Dan. He bit into one of the tacos, and the succulent orange meat was the best thing he'd ever tasted: hot and richly spiced, its steam perfuming his mouth. Since his encounter with Gokul Rathore, food and cooking were never far from his mind; now, he was wondering if there was some way to make Indian tacos. *"Chicken tikka tacos" has a nice ring to it,* he mused. That was probably a question for Kevin McPherson; on the plane ride back, Kevin had promised to whip up some new recipes for Arjun, should he ever need them for his restaurant.

"How was India?" asked Erica, dipping a cheesy *birria* taco into a bowl full of consommé. "Besides the sale, I mean."

Arjun almost blurted out something about his meeting with Malini—then, he remembered that Dan and Erica still didn't know that he was looking for an arranged marriage (or that he'd decided to pursue Indian American women exclusively from now on). He suddenly realized how odd it was to hide such a big secret from his best friends. *Should I tell them?* he wondered. Can *I tell them?*

"India was good," he said instead, through a mouthful of meat. "Hot."

"Did you get us anything?" asked Dan, glancing meaningfully at the tote bag Arjun had brought with him. Arjun produced a small wooden elephant for Dan and a dazzling red *sari* for Erica. She insisted on trying on the garment there and then, and she suggested that they ascend to the apartment. The three of them gathered up their food and headed upstairs.

"So, it was a huge sale, right?" Erica asked as they climbed. "Did your boss give you some kind of reward for pulling it off?"

Arjun nodded. "It was really interesting, actually. When Adam called me, he told me what this could mean for my career. I'm a VP now—but I could be Senior Vice President very soon, then Division Head. Adam said I could even be sitting in *his* chair in a few years. Imagine me, the CFO."

"That's great," Dan said. "But there was still a commission check, right?"

Arjun laughed. "A big one."

"What are you going to do with all of that money?"

He shrugged. "I was thinking of buying my condo."

Erica frowned. "That place? It's a bachelor pad, Arjun. Why not put a down payment on a family home?"

"Yeah, maybe. Or maybe I'll find myself a new office."

"What's wrong with your old office?" asked Dan.

"A pipe burst in the ceiling," Arjun explained. "I got moved to this dingy little spot in the basement of the *San Francisco Current*." He frowned. "And don't even get me started on my new office mate."

"You're sharing an office?" Erica asked.

He nodded. Then, without thinking, he rattled off his list of ever-growing grievances concerning Nisha Nandan: her incessant phone calls, her loud laugh, the way she always oh-so-subtly pushed her mountain of books onto *his* side of the desk.

Dan laughed. "She sounds like the worst person ever," he said. "Does she have an awful name, too? I'm picturing a 'Prudence.' Or maybe a 'Bertha.'"

"That's sexist," Erica put in. "What if *I* was named Prudence?"

Dan shrugged. "Then I'd be writing you letters asking what to do about my terribly named fiancée."

Erica gave him a playful shove. "Her name isn't so bad," Arjun admitted. "It's Nisha Nandan."

Dan raised an eyebrow. "Nisha Nandan?" he repeated. They had arrived outside the apartment, and Erica turned the lock and let them inside. "Where have I heard that name before?"

"She's a journalist," offered Arjun, walking over to the kitchen table and taking a seat with his food. "Maybe you've seen her byline somewhere."

Dan shook his head. "That's not it." He stood and walked to the rickety wooden bookshelf set beneath the window. He squatted down and scanned his finger across the rows of spines. His finger stopped on one book, a paperback with a bright-fuchsia cover. He pulled it off the shelf and brought it to the table. "Take a look," he said, handing the book to Arjun.

Arjun examined the cover. It was one of those classic romance novel covers: two impossibly good-looking models locked in an embrace. Only the woman's face was visible, and contorted with longing. Above the figures, in big, loopy letters, was the title: *The Kiss of Eternity*. "Right there," Dan said, pointing to the bottom of the cover. "Nisha Nandan. She's a writer."

Arjun sipped on his soda. "Come on, Dan—there must be hundreds of Nisha Nandans in the world. Trust me: the Nisha I know is most definitely not a romance novelist."

Dan opened the book and flipped to the back cover. "Is this her?" he asked, pointing to the author's photo.

Arjun nearly spit out his drink. The woman's hair was straighter than Nisha's, and she was wearing glasses—but she had the same sharp nose and dazzling green eyes. "Oh my God," he said. "That's her."

Erica emerged from the bedroom, draped in her new *sari*. The garment fit her perfectly, and the sequins stitched into the silk glittered like diamonds. She leaned over Arjun's shoulder and looked at the picture. "She's pretty," she said. "You should ask her out."

"As if," he scoffed.

"It's just as well," said Dan, reading the blurb. "It looks like she's married."

"No, she's not," said Arjun. "She doesn't wear a wedding ring."

"Lots of married people don't wear wedding rings," said Dan. He read aloud: "'Nisha Nandan graduated from Northwestern University with a degree in English literature. She lives in Denver with her cat, Susan, and her husband, Parth.'"

Dan lent *The Kiss of Eternity* to Arjun, who fully expected an enjoyable hate-read. It would be fun to go through Nisha's writing and tear it apart, then sit opposite her with the smug satisfaction that he'd read her book (and knew about her secret life peddling garbage to the masses).

The novel's plot centered around a pair of childhood friends, the bullheaded Raymond and the bookish Adeline, who lived in neighboring country estates in 1900s England. At first, Raymond loathed Adeline, and she returned the feeling: Raymond thought her too meek, and she thought him too brash. Gradually, though, Adeline introduced Raymond to her favorite books, and Raymond helped her to stand up to her domineering father. They grew inseparable, and they shared their first kiss beneath an apple tree.

When they reached their teenage years, however, everything fell apart. Adeline's father moved their family to Germany to start a textile factory, and she and Raymond fell out of touch. Ten years passed, and World War One began; after Raymond's older brother was killed in the fighting, he decided to enlist, too. Raymond was blinded in battle and marched to a prison camp in Germany.

Unbeknownst to Raymond, one of the nurses at his camp was Adeline, though neither of them recognized the other. As Adeline tended to Raymond's injuries, their love for one another rekindled. Eventually, she smuggled him out of the camp and hid him from the German army until the war ended. At the end of the novel, Raymond and Adeline each figured out who the other was, and they married and moved back to England.

Despite his generally low opinion of romance novels (not to mention his generally low opinion of Nisha Nandan), Arjun spent the weekend devouring the book. Much to his chagrin, she was a fantastic writer, deftly weaving scenes together and meticulously crafting the English countryside, the battlefield trenches, and Adeline's small factory town with sparkling prose. Arjun found himself tearing through the last few chapters, hoping for the moment the two lovers recognized one another. When the reunion finally came, he felt his eyes grow misty. *Damn it*, he thought, setting the book down. There were many adjectives he'd wished he could apply to this book—but why was *amazing* the only one he could think of?

When Arjun arrived at work on Monday, he didn't even stop upstairs to see if his office had been fixed, as he'd done every day since the pipe had burst. Instead, he made a beeline for the small office in the basement. The door was closed, and he pushed it open to find Nisha Nandan typing away at her computer.

She narrowed her eyes when she saw him. "Oh. I was beginning to hope that I'd just imagined you."

"No such luck, I'm afraid," he said, setting down his things. His eyes drifted to Nisha's left hand. *No, I'm not crazy*, he told himself. *She's not wearing a ring.*

He wanted desperately to ask her if she was married, as her blurb had indicated. *The Kiss of Eternity* had come out five years ago, though—perhaps she'd gotten a divorce? Of course, Arjun didn't even know *why* this mattered. He was getting an arranged marriage, and whether or not Nisha had a husband was really none of his business, anyway (not that he would ever be remotely interested in her in that way, he reminded himself).

He sat down opposite her. He had a long list of tasks to

complete for PSI that day, and he opened his laptop. Still, he could not concentrate. His mind was far away in the English countryside, with Adeline and Raymond. *The Kiss of Eternity* was such a romantic, life-affirming story. How could this beautiful, cynical woman have written such a thing? And why had she never written another novel? Arjun searched Nisha's green eyes. *Is she still in there?* he wondered. *Some other Nisha Nandan?*

"*Ahem.*" Nisha cleared her throat and looked expectantly at him.

"What is it?" asked Arjun, snapping out of his thoughts.

"I was about to ask you the same thing," she replied. "I thought I told you to stop staring at me."

"Oh," Arjun said. "Sorry."

"Just...keep your eyes on your own paper, okay?"

He nodded, and Nisha resumed typing. "Wait," he said. "I have something to tell you."

She sighed with exasperation. "Arjun, unless you're telling me that you're finally letting me have this office all to myself—"

"I read your book," he said.

Her posture grew instantly defensive. She crossed her arms and seemed to lean as far away from him as was possible in the cramped space. "I don't know what you're talking about," she said, averting her eyes.

"Maybe this will help," Arjun said, reaching into his backpack. He drew out Dan's copy of *The Kiss of Eternity* and set it on the desk between them. He opened it to the last page, where the author's bio was stamped onto the back cover. "That's you," he said, pointing to the photo. "You wrote this book, Nisha."

She shook her head. "So, what—you're stalking me now?"

"No. I was telling someone about you, and he had read it, so...it doesn't matter. Your book was really good, Nisha. Maybe one of the best I've ever read."

She scoffed. Then, suddenly, she snatched the *The Kiss of Eternity* up from the table. With a single, fluid movement, she pitched it against the wall. The sound echoed through the office, as loud as a thunderclap.

Arjun stared at the book, which lay face-down on the floor like a dead bird. His mouth gaped open. "Nisha, what the hell?" he asked, looking back at her with wide eyes.

But Nisha Nandan didn't reply. She buried her face in her hands, and her shoulders shook with soft little sobs.

For a moment, Arjun didn't move. Then, without speaking, he went around the table and crouched beside her. He put his hand on her shoulder and gave it a gentle squeeze.

He was almost surprised when she embraced him, held him tightly, and cried softly into his jacket. And he was even more surprised when he wrapped his arms around her, too.

CHAPTER
Ten

"I'm sorry," Nisha said, sniffling. "I hate being seen like this. Especially by *you*."

"Says the woman who's using my jacket as her own personal Kleenex," Arjun replied.

She laughed weakly. "I'm sorry," she said again. She swabbed her red-tipped nose with Arjun's collar.

"It's all right." Without thinking, he wiped the tears from her cheeks with his thumb. "We don't have to talk about it, if you don't want to."

"It's fine," she said. "I can tell you." His arm was still wrapped around her. She looked around the office. "Can it not be here, though?"

He nodded and stood, then helped her to her feet. "Come on," he said. "I know just the place."

"Are you sure you didn't bring me here to murder me?" Nisha asked, panting as she hiked up the steep hill behind Arjun.

"Why would I want to murder you?" he laughed.

"I don't know. Finally get that office to yourself?"

He smiled. "I'll take it under advisement."

They arrived at a large wooden sign that said, in bright-white letters, BUENA VISTA PARK. Nisha groaned, staring up at the incline ahead of them. "Another hill?"

"Come on," said Arjun, extending a hand behind him. She took it and followed him up.

Stairs roughly hewn from wood ascended to the top of a massive hill. Eucalyptus and oak trees towered over the hillside; cypress bushes crept along the meandering, sand-swept paths. The air here smelled sacred, prehistoric, as though this place had been here forever and would continue to be long after the city below fell away. "I can't believe I've never heard of this place before," said Nisha, craning her neck to look up at the trees. "It's like a forest in the middle of the city."

"And we're not even at the best part yet," said Arjun. "Come on, we're almost there."

They continued forward through a tunnel made of dark-green foliage. Finally, the dense canopy parted, and the steel-colored sky became visible through the trees. They had reached the summit, an expansive meadow laced with dirt trails. There was an old wooden bench in the shadow of a tall cypress tree, and Arjun and Nisha sat.

San Francisco unfurled before them, the vista framed by branches. Arjun could see almost the entire city: skyscrapers huddling in the distance, rows of houses washed in pastels—muted purples and warm yellows, baby blues and terra-cotta reds. The Golden Gate stood tall against the sky, the rusty red bridge winding a curve around the distant green hills. Sunlight glinted off the dark waters of the bay. Nisha shook her head in wonder. "Wow."

"This is my favorite place in the city," Arjun told her, leaning back and draping his arm over the back of the bench. "When things get overwhelming, I come to this park and just sit for a while." He looked at her. "I can sit here with you, if you want. Or I can let you be alone."

Nisha shook her head. "Stay." Arjun's right hand was resting on his thigh, and she laid her hand on his and gave it a squeeze.

Birds chittered in the trees. Across the park, Arjun heard a little girl shrieking in delight, being chased by her brother. Wildflowers dotted the hillside, purple and yellow and orange, and Arjun saw a jewel-green hummingbird darting between the petals.

He took a deep breath. Her hand was still resting on top of his. He glanced over at her and saw that her eyes were closed. It looked almost as though she was meditating.

He had nearly forgotten what Nisha looked like in the daylight. She was beautiful, the sharp line of her nose limned in sunlight. Arjun heard a new sound now: his own heartbeat, a metronome keeping time against the whispering breeze.

Finally, she broke her silence. "I miss it," she said. "Being a writer, I mean. I grew up devouring romance novels: Jane Austen, the Brontë sisters, basically anything from Harlequin. My favorite, though, was Edith Wharton. Have you ever read *The Age of Innocence?*"

Arjun shook his head. "I can't say that I have."

"Anyway…she had a way of creating characters that felt so *real*, you know? Like they could walk off the page and exist in our world, just like you and me. All my life, I wanted to write books like that."

"You did," Arjun told her. "Nisha, I've never read anything like *The Kiss of Eternity.*"

She smiled softly. "It only took me three months to write," she said, her voice swelling with pride. "It just poured out of me, Arjun. Like it wasn't *me* writing it; it was like a ghost was driving my fingers over the keyboard."

She paused, and when she stared out into the distant hills, it was like she was staring not across space but across *time*—viewing the past version of herself as through a fogged window. "Do you know what I do now?"

He shook his head.

"I sit at my computer—and I just *wait*. Sometimes, I stare at the document for hours, just watching the cursor blink. Like a candle sputtering until, finally, it goes out." Arjun saw a tear glittering in the corner of Nisha's eye. "I don't have it anymore, Arjun," she said. Her voice sounded far away, like it was coming from across the bay.

"The married me, *she* was the writer," Nisha continued. "*She* was the one who could draft up a manuscript in a few weeks, the one whose head was swimming with ideas. You can't conjure emotions out of thin air; they have to come from *somewhere*. When I was with my ex-husband, I had a love story that was all mine. It was a deep well of emotions to draw on, and I channeled it all into *The Kiss of Eternity*. When I got a divorce, that well dried up. And seeing that book now reminds me of everything I lost."

She sighed. "After the split, I wanted to get as far away from Denver as possible, so I took the first out-of-state job I could find. Part of me thought San Francisco would be a reset for me. A way to get back to where I was. But I still feel irretrievably broken."

Arjun shook his head. "You don't really believe that, do you?"

Nisha shrugged. "I'm never getting married again," she told him, her voice full of steely determination. "I mean, if you really believe in true love, it means you don't believe in second chances, either. And, if you don't believe in love at all anymore—then what's the point?"

"The past is the past," said Arjun, wishing that he could take his own advice. "And, it's just a feeling I have, but maybe San Francisco is the place to find what you're looking for. Being here could help remove whatever blockage is stopping you from writing."

Nisha smiled wanly. "That's a nice thought, Arjun. But San Francisco is just a city."

He shook his head. "You're wrong, Nisha," he told her. He pointed off into the distance. "They call this place 'The Golden City,'" he said. "Maybe it's because, for a long while, there really was gold in these hills. Or maybe it's because of the bridge, or the way the sunlight seems to gild the streets in the early evening. But do you know what the real treasure is here?"

Nisha's green eyes sparkled like distant stars. "What is it?"

"*Opportunity*," he said. "Because San Francisco, more than anywhere else in the world, is a place where people come to make their own destiny. From the gold rush to gay rights, to the startup boom: whatever the future holds for you, *this* is the best place to grab life by the ears and take it where you want to go."

Arjun looked into Nisha's eyes, as green as life itself. "There really is magic here. You just have to look for it."

Her breath made a small white cloud in the air. Arjun was suddenly aware of how close they were. He could feel the warmth of her body, could smell the citrus scent of her hair. Was it just him, or was she leaning closer? He felt his pulse quicken, felt his breath catch in his chest.

"I'm getting an arranged marriage," he blurted. "I haven't told anyone. But it's happening."

Nisha nodded. "Okay," she said.

She turned towards the city, and she rested her head on his shoulder. For a long while, she and Arjun just sat there on that bench, admiring the view.

CHAPTER
Eleven

Okay, so maybe Arjun didn't hate Nisha Nandan after all.

They'd sat on the bench until San Francisco's midday cold settled over the park. "I think I'm going to head home," Nisha said. "I don't know about going back to the office today."

Arjun nodded. "Okay. Can I walk you back?"

She shook her head. "I'll be fine."

Arjun stood. "I'll see you tomorrow, Nisha," he said, squeezing her shoulder. He started his descent.

"Wait!" she called, her voice carrying over the wind.

He turned around to see her striding towards him. "What is it?"

"I just want to say…thanks for…just thanks." Nisha stepped tentatively towards him, her arms slightly outstretched. Arjun embraced her and felt the softness of her hair against his cheek.

They pulled apart.

. . .

Back at home that evening, Arjun found that Nisha still lingered in his thoughts. When he closed his eyes, he saw her face: her eyes, her nose, the curve of her lips. He bought a copy of *The Age of Innocence* at the bookstore near his house, and as he read, it was Nisha's voice in his head.

Arjun stayed up late reading. When he woke up, there was a new feeling in his chest: was he really looking forward to seeing Nisha again?

Apparently, the feeling was mutual. He arrived at the basement office to find a chocolate chip scone on the desk. "It's a peace offering," Nisha explained.

Arjun took a bite of the scone, still warm and crumbly. "Offering accepted," he said, his mouth full of chocolate.

They had lunch together that day, and every day after. On Wednesday, they ate at a Thai food truck parked outside Salesforce Tower, and they took the long way back to the office, down Mission Street. "Have you been here before?" Arjun asked, gesturing to one of the glass storefronts as they passed.

"Anthony's Book Company?" asked Nisha, peering inside. "I have, actually. This was one of the places that hosted me for a reading during my book tour."

Arjun smiled. "Well, we have to go inside, then." He bounded over to the door and held it open for Nisha. "Let's see if we can find your book."

The store contained three stories, with a bright-blue staircase near the back. Bookshelves lined the walls, with free-standing displays interspersed in between. Arjun had always loved bookstores; walking into one always made him feel a bit awestruck, the weight of millions of words bearing down on him.

"Where do you think you are?" Arjun asked, bending at the waist to browse one of the bookshelves. "With the other N's? Or in the romance section?"

"I'm not sure," Nisha said. "Every place does it differently, you know."

"Well, *The Kiss of Eternity* would be hard to miss. It is bright pink, after all."

She laughed. "Let's split up, then. You can search through the letters. I'll head upstairs for the romance section."

Arjun scanned the N section three times, but he couldn't find Nisha's book. He approached the register. "Hi," he said. "I'm wondering if you have *The Kiss of Eternity?* The author's name is Nisha Nandan."

The clerk, a thin and gray-haired man, nodded. "Let me check," he said, typing the title on his computer. "It looks like we do have one copy in stock," he said, sliding past the desk. Arjun followed him across the store to a small section near the back. He saw the sign hanging above the section—and his heart sank. "Here it is," the clerk said, plucking the sole remaining copy of *The Kiss of Eternity* from a milk crate and handing it to Arjun.

There was a bright-red sticker taped to the front cover: 50% OFF. Arjun glanced up at the sign again. LAST CHANCE, it said.

He heard footsteps descending the staircase, and he saw Nisha coming downstairs again. Quickly, he hooked his thumbnail under the edge of the sticker; in one swift motion, he peeled it off. He crumpled the sticker into a tight little ball and hid it in his pocket. "Here it is," Arjun said, showing the book to Nisha.

"Wow," she said, a grin stretching across her face. "I've crossed over to the 'General Fiction' section. I have to say: it feels pretty good."

Arjun laughed. He led Nisha back to the N section and slid *The Kiss of Eternity* back onto the shelf where it belonged. "We should probably get back to work," he said, and she nodded.

Stepping back outside, Arjun was glad Nisha hadn't

witnessed his deception. Yes, lying was bad—but he hated to think of her finding her novel in the clearance section, along with outdated calendars, old cookbooks, and other castoffs. Still, he'd failed to realize one thing: the clearance section was visible from the top of the staircase, and Nisha Nandan had seen it all.

When, on Friday, Arjun told Nisha that he was fulfilling his inebriated promise to Dan and Erica and getting a dog, she insisted on coming with him. She showed up at his apartment on Saturday at nine o'clock on the dot, holding two steaming carryout cups of coffee. "This place is huge," she said, stepping inside and handing him his drink. "Although I find it concerning that the only artwork you have here is a *Tintin* poster."

Arjun glanced back at the poster. "You know what that is?"

"Please," she replied. "Did you know that, in that particular issue, Hergé suggested that there was water under the moon's surface? We didn't discover that there actually *was* water on the moon until the seventies—more than twenty years after publication."

He smiled. "I didn't know that."

"So," said Nisha, "today's the day, huh? Are you excited?"

He shrugged, pulling on his jacket. "I'm more worried than excited," he said. "I've never had a dog before."

"Really? Not even as a kid?"

He shook his head. "My family always talked about it, but we were too busy to ever actually get one. It's probably for the best, though. We eventually found out that my dad was allergic to dogs. Like, really allergic."

Nisha grinned. "How does he feel about you getting one now, then?"

Arjun rubbed the back of his neck. "He died when I was a sophomore in college."

A shadow passed over her face. "I'm so sorry," she said. "I shouldn't have pried."

"Don't worry about it," he said, trying his best to smile reassuringly. "It happened a long time ago."

The San Francisco SPCA was in the Mission, two miles away from Arjun's condo. It was a swanky-looking building that would have fit in on the Stanford campus or as the home of one of the venture capital firms on Sandhill Road. There was a wide plaza shaded by swaying palms, and Arjun and Nisha crossed and went inside.

The inside of the building was pristine and white, like a hospital wing built exclusively for wealthy patients. Clinicians shuttled through the hallways in multicolored scrubs; owners queued with their pets in front of the veterinary wing. Arjun threw away his empty coffee cup and approached the front desk. "Hi," he said. "I'm looking for the pound."

The volunteer, a young woman in a red SPCA t-shirt, narrowed her eyes. "The 'pound'?" she repeated venomously. "We don't *have* a 'pound' here, sir."

Arjun heard Nisha walk up beside him. "He meant the *adoption center*," she said, shaking her head at him. The volunteer pointed the way, and Arjun followed Nisha down the hall. "Come on, man," she chided, batting his arm.

They turned a corner and arrived at a set of double doors. Arjun could hear the sounds of dogs just behind: pawing and scraping, barking and whining. He stopped. "I don't know about this," he said. "I mean, am I even capable of taking care of a dog?"

Nisha shook her head. "You're overthinking it."

"You've met me, right?" he replied. "Overthinking things is kind of what I do."

She laughed. "You want to be married, right? So, I assume you want kids someday?" He nodded. "Well, then," she said, "think of this as practice. Adorable, furry practice." She looked expectantly at Arjun. "You ready?"

He took a breath. "Yes."

Nisha pushed open the doors and led Arjun into the kennel.

There were rows of wire doors along either side of the hallway, so they could see all of the dogs inside as they passed. Arjun felt his heart begin to thaw as he saw each dog: a German shepherd who raised his huge head from his paws as he walked by; a black Labrador who began to bark excitedly; a Shih Tzu that stood up on her rear legs, scratching furiously at the door as though she might break through.

"Do you have an appointment?" asked the volunteer manning the kennel, a middle-aged woman dressed in violet scrubs. Arjun gave her the details, and she confirmed his information on her clipboard. "Perfect," she said. "Arjun Chowdhury, with the two-bedroom on Folsom Street. First-time owner, requesting something non-shedding." She smiled at Nisha, then back at him. "I'm sorry, Arjun—you didn't mention you had a partner."

"We're just friends," said Nisha, beating him to it. Arjun felt a weird flutter in his stomach, the same sensation he'd felt when he saw Nisha for the first time. Despite himself, he'd almost *liked* it when the volunteer assumed that he and Nisha were a couple.

The woman looked at her clipboard. "Well, it's your lucky day. We just had someone surrender a dog that I think would be perfect for you. You can take her home today, if you'd like."

Nisha grabbed his arm excitedly. "Can we see her?" Arjun asked. The volunteer led them down the hallway. She opened one of the doors and kneeled, beckoning to the dog inside with a small treat.

The dog stepped out slowly, sniffing the air. She had bright, clear eyes and curly golden fur that reminded Arjun of a teddy bear he'd owned as a child. "This is Daisy," said the volunteer, clipping a leash onto the dog's collar as she fed her the treat. "She's a mix between a cocker spaniel and a poodle. Hypoallergenic, just like you requested."

"Why did the previous owner surrender her?" he asked, kneeling and letting Daisy lick his hand.

"No behavior issues," said the volunteer. "He had to move out of the country unexpectedly. As you can see, she's a very sweet dog. And she's already housebroken, which is one fewer thing to worry about."

"You should get her," Nisha whispered, nuzzling Daisy's head. The dog's tail began to wag rapidly, as though she understood Nisha and was in total agreement. "I mean, can you resist this face?"

Arjun grinned, and Daisy leaped up and put her paws on his shoulders. She nuzzled his ear with her nose, and he laughed and scooped her up under his arm. "I'll take her," he said.

It turned out not to be so simple. The volunteer brought them into a back room, where she made Arjun fill out at least twenty different forms, scanned his driver's license, and promised/threatened to send someone to conduct a house visit if he didn't check in with the shelter in a week. After they finished, Arjun let Nisha pick out a collar and a leash for his new dog, along with a bag of treats and a fluffy pink tennis ball. They thanked the shelter staff and stepped out into the sunshine, with Daisy tugging eagerly at her leash. There was a park nearby, and Arjun unclipped Daisy from her leash and rolled the tennis ball across the grass for her to retrieve.

"So, obviously, we can't call her 'Daisy' anymore," Nisha said as Arjun took the ball from his new dog's mouth and tossed it again.

He laughed. "What do you mean, 'obviously'?"

"Does she look like a 'Daisy' to you?" asked Nisha, as though that were an obvious statement to be making. "And, besides," she said, "'Daisy' is such a cookie-cutter name. I know three other dogs named Daisy."

"You know more than three dogs?"

"Well, I know them from Facebook," she admitted. "So, what do you think?"

Daisy was walking back with the ball, tail wagging. "Can you even rename a dog?" Arjun asked.

"Sure, you can." Nisha kneeled and offered a treat to Daisy, who gobbled it up and began licking her face. "What does she look like to you?" She stared into Daisy's eyes. "Are you a Scout? Rocket? How about…Morticia?"

"I was always more of a Brady Bunch guy," Arjun said bemusedly.

"Well, you could always help me out, you know."

"What about Sally?"

A quizzical expression came over Nisha's face. "Why Sally?"

"Her fur," Arjun said. "Blonde and curly. It reminds me of Meg Ryan's hair in *When Harry Met Sally*. So, you know, Sally."

Nisha nodded slowly.

"You hate it," he said.

She smiled. "No, it's great. Sally it is."

Arjun clipped the leash onto his newly christened dog, and they continued down the street. "You know, I've never actually seen that movie?" said Nisha.

"Which? *When Harry Met Sally*?"

She nodded. "That's the one."

Arjun stopped in his tracks. "You can't be serious. You—a bestselling romance author—have never seen *When Harry Met Sally*? The greatest romantic comedy of all time?"

"That's right," she replied. "I mean, I've *tried* to watch it.

But I could never make it past the opening scene. You know, with the old people talking on the couch? They were *terrible* actors."

"That's the point!" Arjun countered. "It's candid!"

"It's *tacky*," Nisha corrected.

He shook his head. "Nisha, that is my favorite movie. If we're going to be friends, you need to see it."

The corner of Nisha's mouth hitched up in a sly smile. "If you say so. You know, I think it's on Netflix. Do you want to come over later and watch?"

Arjun checked his watch. "I wish I could," he said. "But I have another meeting today."

"Another meeting? Working on the weekend, are we?"

He smiled awkwardly. "It's not for work."

Nisha clocked his meaning, and her expression fell for just an instant. "Anyway," he asked, rubbing the back of his neck, "can I get a rain check?"

"Yeah, of course," Nisha replied, sounding as cool as ever. "I'll see you at work on Monday."

Arjun didn't have much time to enjoy his new dog by himself. He walked Sally back to his place, loaded her into his car, and headed to the San Francisco International Airport, where his mother's flight had just landed. "That's not yours, is it?" Sarita asked as Arjun loaded her suitcase into the trunk. She pointed at Sally, who had curled up in the passenger seat.

"I just got her," said Arjun, sliding behind the wheel. "Sally, meet my emotional baggage. Emotional baggage, meet Sally."

Sarita scoffed. "I can't believe you could be so irresponsible."

Arjun scooped up his dog and put her in his mother's arms. "You'll grow to love her," he said. On cue, Sally snuggled into Sarita's arms. Arjun wondered if Sally did, indeed, understand English.

His mother looked down at the dog, then sighed. "She *is* quite cute," she admitted, stroking Sally's velvety ear.

Much to Arjun's chagrin, Sally spent the night in Sarita's room. When he woke his mother with coffee and the Sunday edition of the *San Francisco Current*, he found Sally cuddled up in bed beside her. Sarita insisted on walking Sally up and down the block while Arjun made breakfast, and he watched them skip over the sidewalk with mounting jealousy.

He glanced anxiously at the clock as he and Sarita ate. "Are you nervous?" she asked, sipping her coffee. Arjun nodded. "Remember, this isn't your first meeting."

"And I was nervous then, too," he replied, sawing away at his omelet with a butter knife. "This feels more *real* to me, somehow. Last time, I was a guest. This time—well, everyone is coming *here*."

After his meeting with Malini, Arjun told Dhanya Agrawal that he preferred to meet an American girl, and she'd been very obliging. In fact, she'd sent over a potential match the day after he'd asked: an anesthesiologist named Simran. He'd agreed to the meeting, and Dhanya had set it up and asked if her family could visit him in San Francisco.

"It will be fine, Arjun," said Sarita, waving her hand. "Don't stress."

"How could I *not* stress?" he countered. "This isn't like a normal date, Mom. If I go out to coffee with a girl and it goes well, I can see her again or not. If this meeting goes well...I could *marry* this girl."

Sarita raised an eyebrow. "That's the point, *beta*."

Arjun sighed. "Right," he said, standing. "If you need me, I'm going to go stress-clean my room."

"While you're at it, could you run a vacuum through mine, too?" Sarita asked, sneaking Sally a piece of her omelet beneath the table. "Oh, and if you have the time, my clothes need ironing."

The doorbell rang at eleven o'clock sharp. "I'll get it," said Sarita, rising from the couch and walking towards the door. "Take a breath, Arjun," she said, her hand on the doorknob. "You're white as a ghost."

He wiped his sweaty hands on his trousers. *This is it*, he thought. *In the next two minutes, I could be meeting the person I'm going to spend the rest of my life with.* He stared up at his *Tintin* poster, and a small part of him wished that he could be transported to the moon, far away from all of this pressure.

He heard the front door swing open. "Come in!" Sarita said, and Arjun heard shuffling feet and the general chatter of people. *How many are there?* he wondered, standing to try and get a better view.

Sarita moved to the side, and Arjun saw the crowd on his front step. There were at least a dozen people there, and Arjun stood and greeted each one as they made their way toward the living area. He hadn't expected this many guests, and he made trips to the bedroom and the guest room for more seating: his desk chair, the bench at the foot of his bed, and the small stool in the bathroom. Simran had arrived with generations of family support, from squirming infants to stooped elders. Yet, there was no sign of Simran herself.

A few people were closer to Arjun's age, including three similar-looking women who must have been sisters. *Which one looks most like the biodata?* he wondered, embracing Dhanya the matchmaker, who had come in last.

Dhanya began her introductions. "Sarita, Arjun: it's my pleasure to announce the Khatri family of Cedar Rapids, Iowa. Here we have the parents, Shivam and Rupal—" Dhanya indicated the two middle-aged people in Indian dress —"Shivam's parents, Ishan and Ishana; and Rupal's parents,

Gaurav and Sahana." Arjun folded his hands in greeting as Dhanya rattled off the names of the assembled siblings and cousins, though he might as well have been listening to her read from the Yellow Pages. It was like the ocean was roaring in his ears, drowning out all the noise. *I don't care about any of them*, he thought, his heart in his throat. *Where is Simran?*

Dhanya answered his question. "Finally, the woman of the hour: Dr. Simran Khatri."

Arjun held his breath. He looked expectantly at the three women, doing his best to appear as nonchalant as possible.

None of them moved. A hush fell over the room, like a crowd waiting for fireworks. *Which one is she?* wondered Arjun, examining the women—but they didn't give any indication.

From the entryway, he heard the tinkling of anklets.

Arjun's first thought was that this woman made him feel severely underdressed. She was wearing a beautiful pink *sari* snared with delicate green vines. Her eyes were shadowed with dusky makeup, a sharp accent against her honey-colored skin. Henna tattoos adorned her palms, the patterns as intricate as lace. She bowed her head demurely and touched Sarita's feet. "*Namaste*, Auntie," she said. "My name is Simran."

The woman rose, and her eyes met Arjun's. There was a veiled expectation in those eyes, and Arjun did not know what she wanted him to say—only that, clearly, he was meant to say *something*. "I'm Arjun," he decided. "It's very nice to meet you, Simran. Or should I call you Dr. Khatri?"

She laughed. *That's a good sign*, thought Arjun, his chest rising with hope. "Simran is fine," she said.

Dhanya beamed. "Excellent! Shall we all sit?"

"Of course," said Sarita. "My apologies—if I'd known so many of you were coming, I might have suggested a different venue. You know, my house is in Iowa, as well."

"It's no trouble," said Simran's father—whose name Arjun was struggling to remember. "We're all going skiing in Tahoe in a few days, so this was on the way. Thank you for welcoming us into your home, Arjun."

It struck him how odd this entire enterprise was. Here were two families: strangers, all tiptoeing around one another. In a few months, though, they could all be one family centered around him and Simran. His mouth began to dry up at the very thought of it.

Dhanya seemed to anticipate the awkwardness, and she kicked off the conversation. "I've given each of you the other's biodata," she said. "Do you have anything you'd like to discuss?"

"Yes," said Arjun, remembering the conversation topics he'd drilled with Sarita the night before. "Simran, I understand that you're an anesthesiologist. How do you like that job?"

"I enjoy it," she replied from the couch. The coffee table was like a chasm separating the two of them. Simran's relatives watched her eagerly, like spectators at a prize fight. Arjun became aware of how ridiculous he must look, perched on the kitchen stool like a gargoyle. "My hours are quite demanding," Simran said. "But the opportunity to practice medicine is amazing."

"Simran was at the top of her class at ISU Medical School," Simran's mother said proudly.

"That's very impressive," Arjun replied. He searched for the next thing to say. Usually, a first date was an opportunity to learn more about the other person: their family and their interests, where they went to school, their favorite foods. Having studied the biodata the previous night, Arjun already knew all of that—and, of course, there was the added complication that his date did not usually bring her whole family along.

Simran's father cleared his throat. "Obviously, Simran has had a lot of time to evaluate her priorities. What makes you think you're ready for marriage?"

Arjun had known a question like that was coming. "I'm in the right place for it," he replied. "I have a great home, a great job—a great life. The missing piece for me is someone to share it with."

"I have already completed an assessment of Arjun," Dhanya put in. "I assure you, his intentions are good."

Arjun could have kissed her. Simran's father nodded, though he seemed a bit annoyed that his opportunity to grill his prospective son-in-law had been snatched away.

The rest of the conversation was relatively tame, with each family member asking Arjun a few questions and him answering while trying to appear as marriageable as possible. Arjun made sure to include Simran in the conversation, though he and Sarita were vastly outnumbered, and his questions to her rarely deviated from Sarita's meticulous script.

Finally, Dhanya suggested that the family meeting end. "This is about the kids, after all," she said. "Why don't you two go off and get to know one another better? Arjun, do you have anything planned?"

He nodded, stood, and bade farewell to Simran's family; Sarita would entertain them for a while before they left.

Simran followed him to the entryway. She did not say anything—only cast sidelong glances, perhaps hoping that he would initiate conversation. "That was something, wasn't it?" Arjun asked in a hushed voice as he slipped on his shoes.

She smiled. "I'm sorry about the third degree. My parents —my father especially—are very protective."

They stepped outside. "So, where are you taking me?" she asked.

"Where do you usually go?" said Arjun.

"A coffee shop," she said with a laugh. She had a nice laugh, the kind that Arjun knew he'd enjoy hearing for the rest of his life. "One guy took me to the library once."

He chuckled. "We're not going to the library," he said. "Do you have a change of clothes?"

Arjun had rented a new car just for this occasion, a sparkling Porsche Boxster in storm gray. He drove into the San Francisco Zoo parking lot, sliding into a spot marked "compact."

Simran stepped out of the car. They'd stopped off at her hotel just before, and she'd changed into jeans, a pair of Converse high-tops, and a navy-blue Columbia puffer coat with a bright-orange zipper. "This is new," she said, smiling. "I've never had a guy bring me to the zoo before."

"You're not one of those people who hates zoos, are you?" asked Arjun. He had traded his stiff *kurta* for a dark-gray Patagonia fleece.

"People hate zoos?"

"You'd be surprised," he replied. They continued through the parking lot and toward the zoo entrance. Arjun had purchased the tickets on his phone, and the clerk scanned the passes.

They passed through the lobby and back outside again, where a large sign displayed the various exhibits. The sky was a steely gray, and Arjun hoped it wouldn't rain. "Where to first?" he asked.

Simran didn't hesitate. "Africa," she said, pointing to the sign. "I want to see the giraffes."

"Africa it is."

They walked down the wide path toward the African exhibit, which was the closest to the entrance. Other people meandered by, mostly families with young children in tow. Arjun had a passing thought that he would like to bring his own children here one day. Then, he realized that those children could belong to him and the woman walking just a few steps away. He felt suddenly lightheaded, as though all the blood in his body had rushed toward his feet.

"So, you said you'd met other suitors," he said, sticking his hands in his pockets and admiring a flock of ostriches doing laps in their exhibit. "What did you think of them?"

Simran smiled coyly. "That's private, isn't it? What happens when the next guy asks what I thought of you?"

"Maybe there won't be a next guy."

She laughed. "You're quick."

A herd of gemsbok grazed on a pile of hay. They were beautiful animals with smooth silver coats and slender, spiraling horns. Simran leaned against the guardrail and gazed out at the herd. The air smelled like popcorn, and Arjun turned to see a food cart a few yards away. "Do you want a lemonade?" he asked, gesturing to the cart.

She shook her head. "I'm good for now. To tell you the truth, I hate sweets."

Arjun raised an eyebrow. "You hate sweets? That wasn't on the biodata," he said jokingly.

"Is that a dealbreaker?"

"I think I can make it work."

"So, if it's not our mutual love of junk food," she asked, "why *do* you think Dhanya matched us?"

"That's a good question," he said, leaning on the rail beside her. "Something in the biodatas, I guess."

"Yes, but what specifically? There had to have been a reason."

"I don't know," he replied. "Maybe it'll become more apparent when we spend more time together. I think you being a doctor had a lot to do with it, though."

Simran seemed surprised by that. "Really? A lot of guys are scared off when they find out that I have an MD."

"Why would that matter?"

She shrugged. "Most American-born guys who go for an arranged marriage tend to be pretty traditional. You know, the husband works, and the wife stays home and takes care of the kids. Or if she does work, it's something totally menial.

My job, on the other hand…I practically live at the hospital. You really wouldn't have a problem with that?"

Arjun shrugged. "My mom is a doctor, you know."

Simran grinned. "So, what you're saying is: Freud was right?"

Arjun rolled his eyes. He couldn't help but laugh.

They continued down the trail. There was a bench near the gorilla preserve, and Arjun suggested they sit and watch them for a while. "So—how am I doing so far?" he asked as a silverback strutted up to the glass and examined his reflection.

Simran looked thoughtful for a moment. "Pretty solid, I'd say. The zoo was a strong move." They were sitting close together, their shoulders almost touching. Arjun cast a glance at her. She was beautiful, there was no doubt about it. The light reflecting off of the glass spiderwebbed across her face, and a lock of black hair hung over her forehead. For a moment he was tempted to move it aside. *Would that be too intimate?* he wondered. After all, he had only known Simran for a few hours—certainly, it would be very familiar.

But, then again—that was the game, wasn't it? This wasn't just another first date. *We could literally be married within the year*, he thought.

They stood and continued through the zoo, conversing more as they observed the animals. Simran told Arjun about her three sisters while they looked at brilliantly colored poison frogs. Arjun told Simran about his disastrous meeting with Malini while toucans leaped on a net strung above their heads. In truth, he was more inclined to listen than to talk. He wondered if Simran's voice—light and pleasant, with a tendency to rush to the end of sentences—could be the voice he'd listen to for the rest of his life.

Despite his latent misgivings about the arranged marriage process, Arjun was struck by how *normal* this date seemed— and then was struck that he hadn't considered this meeting to be "normal" in the first place. He liked Simran, and she seemed to like him. *Why should this experience be inferior just because we didn't meet at a bookstore or in line for coffee?* he asked himself. He remembered the words of the woman in the Peacock bathroom: *Not better. Not worse. Just different.*

"So, what happens next?" he asked as they walked toward the capybara exhibit. "Assuming that anything does happen."

Simran smiled. "I want to see you again," she said. "Are you planning on making a trip to Iowa anytime soon?"

"Maybe," he replied. "I've been traveling for work recently, so I might be back there soon. And I try to get out to visit my mom every few months. When are you thinking of returning to SF?"

"I don't know. Like I said, I work pretty insane hours, so it'll probably be tough for me to get out here again."

Arjun nodded. "This might be jumping the gun a little bit, but do you have an idea of where you'd want to work if you came to live here?"

Simran knit her brows. "What do you mean?"

"Like, a clinic in San Francisco," he said. "Or maybe even in South Bay, if you don't mind the commute."

She shook her head. "I'm not moving to California. Arjun, one of the reasons I wanted to meet you was because you're from Iowa, too. I thought you'd want to move back."

He frowned. "What gave you that idea?"

"Well, your biodata said you'd be open to relocating." A concerned expression darkened her face like an ink stain.

"I meant, like…to the *Peninsula*," he said. "I wouldn't leave the Bay Area."

"You wouldn't want to return to Iowa to start a family?" she asked. "Don't you want your kids to have the same experiences you did growing up? To have the same sense of home?"

Arjun shook his head. "Simran, Iowa hasn't been home for me for ten years now. I've spent basically my entire adulthood here in SF, and I really love it. If anything, *this* is the place that I want to share with my kids." He watched the capybara munch on a pile of hay. "You really wouldn't move here? I mean, it's *San Francisco*. What do they have in Iowa that we don't have here?"

"My parents," said Simran with a wistful expression. "They're getting older, and I want to be close to them. I thought that...well, I thought that you might want to be near your mom, too."

Arjun nodded. "I lost my dad when I was twenty," he said. "It was the most painful thing I've ever experienced. I know that I *should* realize that my mom is getting older, but some part of me just...well, it's tough to acknowledge. She's all I have. And, if she starts to lose speed, I know I can give her a better life here than in the Midwest. The winters are certainly more forgiving."

"You're not wrong there," Simran said, staring up at the sky. "Are you sure, Arjun? Like, *really* sure?"

"I'm sorry," he said. "It's not in the cards for me."

Arjun braced for a protest, an argument—but none came. Simran only gave a sad smile. "I guess it's not meant to be," she said. "Want to go look at the kangaroos?"

"Aw, I liked her," said Nisha, sitting cross-legged on the floor of Arjun's kitchen. "You're really not going to see her again?"

Arjun, simmering a sauce on the stovetop, shook his head.

"I'm sorry," she said. She was playing tug-of-war with Sally, who was pulling away at a Gumby toy that Nisha had bought for her. "That really sucks."

"That's the thing," responded Arjun, dipping a spoon into the sauce to taste it. "It was great."

Nisha laughed. "Did you hit your head or something?" she asked, letting Sally wrest the toy away from her. "You didn't get the girl. That's a *bad* thing, isn't it?"

"That's not the point, though," he replied. "The relocation issue was a major deal-breaker for both of us. Normally, it would have taken months—or years—of dating for it to surface. Instead, because we came into our first meeting from the perspective that marriage was on the table, we found out about it immediately, before either of us was all that invested. Imagine all the heartache we both avoided."

"It's efficient, I'll give you that." Nisha scratched Sally behind the ear, and the dog rolled over for a belly rub.

Arjun had been trying—and failing—to recreate Gokul Rathore's *dum aloo* recipe for nearly a week. He brought over the spoon and crouched in front of Nisha. "Blow," he said, and Nisha did. "What do you think?"

"It's getting there," she said, her mouth wide open to vent the heat, her words thick with steam. "So, do you have any more of these meetings set up?"

"Not at the moment," Arjun said, swabbing a dribble of sauce from the corner of Nisha's mouth with his thumb before returning to the stove. "The matchmaker sent me a few more biodatas last night, and I still need to go through them. Who knows, though—the next woman I meet might be absolutely perfect."

Nisha laughed.

"What's so funny?" he asked.

"It's nothing," she said. "It's just…do you really think that 'perfect' is achievable where love is concerned?"

He shrugged. "Why not? Perfection exists, you know. I can look at a Matisse painting or listen to a Mozart sonata and think, 'That's perfect.' Why should love be any different?"

Nisha shrugged. "I don't know, isn't perfection sort of antithetical to the idea of love itself? Like, yeah, you have this internal checklist—in your case, a *literal* checklist—of everything you're looking for. But doesn't that seem a little too…sanitized?"

He frowned. "Sanitized?"

She nodded. "Like, would your Matisse be as beautiful if it were drawn by a computer? The beautiful thing about love, I think, is how *human* it is. And humans are messy, Arjun. Despite how much you might want to—you can't control everything all the time."

He considered what she'd just said. It sounded remarkably similar to his conversation with Vinay a few months ago. But his mind flashed back to the telephone message he'd received a few weeks back. Of course, Nisha didn't know about Vicky Chang, but Arjun knew there must have been hairline cracks in that relationship before everything blew up. *Things don't just fall apart for no reason,* he thought. An arranged marriage was an opportunity—and, if he *could* pick, why shouldn't he? Yes, Arjun was set on making sure the foundation of his marriage was as solid as possible...but wasn't that the best course of action when *building* something?

"Well, I'm not the only perfectionist here," he said. "You are, too, Nisha—just in a different way."

"What do you mean?"

"Your writer's block. Staring at the blank page, not writing anything at all. It's not because you don't have the ideas anymore. It's because you're afraid your ideas aren't perfect. You and I are much more similar than you think."

"You seem to know a lot about writing, suddenly," she said, smiling sarcastically.

He shook his head. "I know that it's a lot easier to fix something that's imperfect than to build something from scratch. God knows that's why I've made fifteen terrible versions of this dish."

Nisha nodded. "And what about the arranged marriage? Is that what you're doing there, too?"

He shrugged. "I guess so," he said. He tasted the sauce one last time. "Food's ready, by the way."

Arjun and Nisha returned to the office after having lunch at his apartment. He had a few meetings at the PSI complex, but he returned to the basement office around five.

"Hey, random question: did you find it hard to make friends here?" Nisha asked him, standing as she gathered her things.

"At first," he admitted. "Why do you ask?"

"Well, it's been six months since I moved to SF. And, so

far, the only real friend I have is you. And I hated you at first. Like, *really* hated you."

Arjun laughed. "At least you have Sally." His dog was resting her in the corner of the room, and she perked up at the mention of her name. "Do you have plans tonight?"

Nisha shook her head. Arjun pulled out his phone and shot off a few text messages. "Come on," he said. "I'm taking you to Kiki's."

Nisha raised an eyebrow. "What's Kiki's?"

Kiki's was ostensibly a Hawaiian-themed bar, but other than a single drink called the "Tiki-la Sunrise," there was no indication of the tropical theme. The bar was dark and low ceilinged, and the walls were covered in chipped green paint washed golden by the strings of fairy lights hung from the ceiling. There were pool tables in the center of the bar, and black vinyl booths ringed around them, hugging the walls.

"This is my favorite watering hole in the city," Arjun explained, leading Nisha into the bar; after work, he'd dropped Sally off at his place and met Nisha outside Kiki's at seven. "Mostly because they have the cheapest drinks in San Francisco."

"Oh? Are they any good?" Nisha had changed into a floral-patterned dress underneath a slim-waisted black leather jacket.

"The absolute worst," he replied, grinning. He and Nisha made their way to the back of the room, where Dan and Erica sat in one of the booths. "Hey guys," said Arjun. "This is Nisha Nandan. Nisha, these are my best friends, Dan and Erica."

"Aww," said Dan. "I'm your best friend?"

"For now," Arjun said, sliding into the booth behind Nisha.

The waitress came by with a steaming plate of appetizers and four beers. "We got here early," Dan said, popping a few tater tots into his mouth. "Please, dig in." Arjun removed the lime wedge from the edge of the glass and squeezed it into his beer; he noticed that Nisha did the same.

"So, Arjun says that you two share an office," said Erica, sipping her drink. "How's that going?"

"It's going well!" said Nisha. "It's very cozy, but we make do. Arjun brings his dog to the office most days now, which is a great perk when you're at your laptop writing all day."

"I'm so jealous," Erica said. "We haven't even gotten the chance to meet her yet."

"Well, you guys are the busy ones," Arjun said. "They're getting married soon, and the wedding preparations have been keeping them stuck in their apartment most days," he explained to Nisha.

"Congratulations," she said. "Let us know if you ever need any help. I'm an expert at stuffing envelopes."

Erica smiled. "Careful, we might just take you up on that."

"So, Nisha, what kind of writing do you do at the *Current*?" asked Dan.

"I'm in the *Reviews* section," she replied. "I find cool books —or, more often, my editor finds books *he* thinks are cool— and I write about them. I do it all: fiction, nonfiction, cookbooks, and photography books. But I draw the line at picture books."

"That's amazing," said Dan. "Have you heard of *Madame Midnight's*? It's an erotic bookstore. But don't worry—everything is done very tastefully."

"This will be a while," Erica said quietly to Arjun as Dan explained the store's offerings to Nisha. "I might trade this IPA for something a little more...palatable. Want to come with?"

"Sure," said Arjun, sliding out of the booth. He and Erica approached the bar and ordered a pitcher of Anchor lager.

"I like her," Erica said, leaning against the bar. "And, I have to say, you make a very cute couple."

Arjun pursed his lips. "A couple? No, we're just friends."

She seemed surprised. "Oh. I'm sorry, I just thought… never mind."

Arjun felt suddenly defensive. "What makes you think we're together?" he asked.

She shook her head. "Forget it. It's nothing."

"It's not nothing. What is it?"

"Fine," said Erica. "I've known you for a long time now, Arjun. And, let me tell you, the look on your face right now… well, you have the same look you did the first time you introduced me to Vicky Chang."

Arjun felt his face redden. "It's strictly platonic," he sputtered. The bartender set the pitcher down on the bar, and the amber beer sloshed around inside and spilled down the sides.

"Whatever you say," said Erica, grabbing the pitcher by the handle. "Come on, I'm sure they're waiting for us."

They returned to the booth. Dan was deep in conversation with Nisha. "You're still talking about *Madame Midnight's*?" asked Arjun incredulously, taking his place beside Nisha again. "Honestly, Dan, no one will ever love that place like you do."

"We were having a different conversation, thank you very much," said Dan.

"About what?" Erica asked.

"About Arjun," Dan replied. "Nisha was just telling me that he *cooked* for her today."

Erica raised an eyebrow and prodded Arjun with her elbow. "You cooked for her?" She turned toward Nisha. "He's only cooked for us a handful of times."

"And it was delicious," Dan said. "Did he tell you about his restaurant yet?"

Nisha looked at Arjun. "Restaurant?" she asked. "You never told me about a restaurant."

Arjun smiled, slightly embarrassed. "Yeah. It's an idea that I've been kicking around for a few years. Just something to occupy my free time."

"It's a *great* idea," said Dan. "Arjun was always feeding people in college. And he's obsessed with creating new recipes. He once made me these kimchi donuts. I thought they'd be terrible—but they were the best donuts I've ever had."

"Well," said Nisha, patting Arjun on the arm, "I'll be your taste tester anytime you need me."

Arjun chuckled. "You promise?"

She smiled. "Promise."

Dan and Erica decided to call it a night after a few more drinks, but Arjun felt strangely energized. "Do you want to walk around?" he asked Nisha as Dan and Erica piled into the backseat of their Uber.

"Where to?" The evening cold kissed her cheeks, turning them rose red.

"How about Hayes Valley?" he suggested. "We're just a short walk away."

"Sure," said Nisha. She drew her jacket closer to her body, and Arjun felt the sudden impulse to wrap his arm around her. *Strictly platonic*, he reminded himself.

They walked on, down an empty stretch of Market Street. The night swirled inky blue around them, and the silvery moonlight glow suffused through the darkness like a watercolor. A tram whooshed past, ghostly green in the darkness. "Hey," said Nisha, stopping suddenly. The yellow of a street-lamp shone in her hair, giving her a temporary halo.

"What is it?" asked Arjun.

She shuffled her feet. "I just wanted to say…thanks."

"Thanks?" he asked. "What for?"

Nisha shrugged. "When I moved to SF, I was lonely for a long time. Now, though…I'm not so lonely anymore. I know I joke about it, but I'm really happy I met you."

For a moment, he didn't know what to say. "I'm happy I

met you, too," he told her, finally. "I don't find it easy to open up to people, but with you…well, I'm glad I can."

The streets narrowed. Hayes Valley was usually a bustling neighborhood, but at this hour, all of the shops along the avenues were shuttered and darkened.

Arjun stopped in front of one of the buildings. "This is it," he said.

"What am I looking at?" Nisha asked. She was shivering slightly, and suddenly, she grabbed Arjun's arm and held it tightly against her body.

"This storefront has been empty for a few months now," said Arjun. "It's the place I'd put my restaurant, if I ever worked up the nerve to put in an offer."

"So why not do it?" she asked.

"What if I start my restaurant and it fails? Ideas are safe, you know. But reality…reality is hard."

She laughed. "You know, I got a good piece of advice this morning: 'Just focus on making *something*—and worry about making it perfect later.'"

Arjun chuckled softly.

"Sometimes," said Nisha, "you just have to go for it."

Her eyes locked with his. The green of her irises drank in the light of the full moon, and a wisp of hair drifted across her face. Arjun could feel himself turning toward her; subtly, her body moved, too. Her hand pressed against his chest, the steady beat of his heart pounding against her fingers.

And then she was drifting toward him, and he toward her. He caressed her chin with his fingers, drawing her close.

Their lips pulsed together like ocean waves.

There was a firework exploding in Arjun's chest: a ball of heat enveloping him and Nisha, consuming their bodies, the entire street, the entire world.

They pulled apart. Nisha was looking at him, an expectant look in her eyes. Arjun swallowed hard, and the clarity overtook him. *Oh, no,* he thought.

Thirteen

Arjun's childhood home was smaller than he remembered. *Smaller*, he thought...*and emptier*.

He stood in the foyer, having just arrived in Iowa after the four-hour flight from San Francisco. His legs were still sore from sitting for so long, and he slipped off his shoes and left his rollaway bag near the door. "Can I fix you something to eat?" asked Sarita, who'd picked him up from the airport in her sleek silver Mercedes. "I made *chana masala*."

"Sounds perfect," said Arjun. He followed his mother into the kitchen, their footsteps echoing through the house. He traced his hand along the walls, feeling the familiar irregularities in the paint he'd discovered as a child, his fingers like radar waves probing marine depths.

The kitchen smelled faintly of masalas and other spices. It was an airy space, with a big set of windows looking out over the snow-covered backyard. Though it was April now, it was still nearly freezing in Iowa. The *chana masala* burbled and popped on the stove, and Sarita scooped a spoonful of chickpeas out onto a plate along with a heap of basmati rice. "Eat up," she said.

The doorbell rang, and Sarita went to answer it. It was

Dan and Erica. They shed their winter coats and draped them over the back of the couch. "That smells delicious," Dan said, and Sarita fixed him and Erica their own plates.

"I'm so glad you two made it back out to Iowa," Sarita said as they sat at the dining table. "It's always such a treat to see you."

"The pleasure is ours," Dan said, his mouth full of food. "Where else are we going to get this kind of food?"

Sarita chuckled. "Careful, Dan. Your mother might get jealous if she hears you talking this way."

They ate for a while, reminiscing about school dances, old teachers, the big storm that toppled a tree right through Dan's living room. Being with his friends in San Francisco was one thing—but being here, where the memories had actually happened, made Arjun almost feel as though he were sixteen years old again, wrapped in the tight, comforting embrace of the past.

Erica checked her phone. "It looks like my parents just pulled up outside. Dan, do you want to head out?"

Dan shoveled the rest of his food into his mouth and nodded. He and Erica thanked Sarita for her hospitality, and Arjun followed them outside to chat briefly with Erica's parents.

The kitchen was spotless when Arjun returned, red-cheeked, inside. Sarita was waiting for him with a full trash bag. "I'm going to take a shower," said Arjun, taking the trash outside before heading upstairs. He stripped out of his plane clothes and turned on the hot water. He closed his eyes, and he was right back outside that empty storefront on Hayes Street.

Arjun hadn't thought much about what Nisha's lips would taste like...but now he knew. They tasted like vanilla and moonlight, like petrichor and red wine.

He looked aside as they pulled apart. "I'm sorry."

"Don't be," she replied, the stars gleaming in her eyes.

"That shouldn't have happened. You're a really good friend, Nisha. But—"

"It's okay," she said. "It was only a kiss. I was just…confused."

"You mean it?" he asked. To his surprise, he felt a little hurt. "Because I do like you, Nisha. It's just…I really do want to get married. Soon. And you… it's like you said, you never want to get married again."

"Honestly, Arjun, it's fine. Let's just forget this ever happened, okay?"

He nodded. "Thanks."

But, of course, he hadn't forgotten. Despite his best efforts, that kiss had stirred something in him, as though a pile of kindling had been stacked inside his body, and Nisha was the spark. They'd parted soon after, and it had been three days since they'd seen one another (Dan and Erica having held him to his word and conscripted him into packaging wedding invitations). Still, not a moment had passed without Arjun recalling the sensation of Nisha's lips on his—not when he was stuffing envelopes, and not even here in Iowa.

Arjun heard Sarita calling him, and he turned off the shower. Dressed in his bathrobe, he ventured back downstairs. "Mom?"

"Right here," she said. She was in the living room, standing in front of a large, framed photograph. "Can you help me hang this?" she asked, gesturing to the white floral garland in her hand. "It keeps slipping off."

"Of course," he said.

The man in the photograph had Arjun's eyes: deep-set and so brown they seemed almost black. There was a twinkle in those eyes, a spark of light captured by the camera flash, and the man was smiling as though he was looking at something amusing just beyond the frame. He had a sparse head of hair, just beginning to gray around the temples. A silver Omega Speedmaster gleamed on his wrist.

Arjun took the garland from his mother and carefully hung it on the frame. He stepped back. Sarita came up next to him and hugged his arm like a life raft. "I can't believe it's been ten years," she said.

"Neither can I," he replied. He glanced down at his watch, the very same Speedmaster that his father had worn.

She sighed. "We had such plans, you know. Traveling the world, growing old together. Now…" She trailed off. "I get lonely, Arjun. As I grow older, I feel it more."

Arjun nodded slowly. "You don't have to be alone," he said cautiously. "I'm sure Dad would have wanted you to be happy."

Sarita sighed. "We talked about it. You know, one of those 'what-if' conversations. He always said I should remarry if he died first. It's been such a long time…but I don't think I'll ever find that kind of love again."

Arjun hugged his mother tighter. "I'm here for you, Mom."

"I know," she replied. "Helping you to find a wife has been good for me, actually. It reminds me of my courtship with Ravi."

"What was he like?" asked Arjun. "Back then, I mean."

His mother smiled wistfully. "He was very sweet," she said. "Arranged marriages were different back then. There was only the initial meeting between our families. It lasted all of fifteen minutes, and afterward, we went our separate ways. I didn't see him again until the wedding, but he made sure I knew he was thinking of me. He wrote me letters, you know. Love letters."

Arjun raised an eyebrow. "Dad wrote love letters?" he asked, delighted. His father had been an engineer; Arjun had never known him to be the sappy type.

Sarita laughed. "Oh, yes," she said. "He wrote beautifully,

almost like poetry. And he never stopped, either. Whenever we were apart, even for a day, he would send me a letter."

"Do you still have them?"

"Somewhere. I tried to read them again when he died, but it was too much for me to bear. Even now, I can't bring myself to do it." She sniffled. "I want that for you. That sort of love. And if I'm pushing you toward marriage—it's only because it was the source of my happiness for so many years."

Arjun was in his bedroom watching television when the doorbell rang a few hours later. Sarita burst into his bedroom, a panicked expression on her face. "They're not supposed to be here for another hour!" she exclaimed. She noted Arjun's *kurta* and frowned. "And you should wear the red one, instead. It will make you look much more virile, don't you think?"

"Gross, Mom," replied Arjun—but he went to his closet and picked out the red *kurta*, anyway. He pulled it over his head, and Sarita came by to adjust the collar. She rubbed her hands through his hair, trying to tame any unruly strands. *"Mom,"* protested Arjun as she brought out a bottle of coconut oil. "I don't want to smell like an Almond Joy."

"Fine," Sarita said, relenting. "It's just your future wife. What do I care?"

He followed her downstairs. He could see people outside the front door, their figures hazy through the frosted glass windows. "Are you ready?" Sarita asked. Arjun nodded, and she opened the door.

Arjun's match, Devi, was twenty-nine years old, with short, wavy hair and a small lotus tattoo in the crook of her elbow. Neither of the two women standing outside the door was twenty-nine, and there were no tattoos in sight. "Revathi," said Sarita, sounding a bit confused. "Oh, and Manjula is here, too."

"Hello, *bhabi*," said Revathi, the older of the two women. She was tall and fair-skinned, with a streak of gray running through her coarse black hair.

Manjula, short and round and draped in a peacock-green *sari*, sashayed past Sarita and into the house. "It is *so cold* in this state," she said. "Honestly, *bhabi,* I don't know how you can stand to live here."

"Neither can I," said Revathi, closing the door behind her. "My invitation is always open, if you want to come stay with me in Milwaukee."

Manjula shook her head. "That place is no warmer than it is here!" she proclaimed. "Now, *Florida,* on the other hand…"

"I am perfectly happy exactly where I am," Sarita interjected. "My question is: what are the both of *you* doing here?"

"Arjun is getting married," said Revathi. "And these things are a family affair, aren't they?"

Sarita looked momentarily lost for words. "Yes," she said. "*Our* family. Me and Arjun."

"You're forgetting someone, no?" said Manjula. "And, since Ravi can't be here, who better than his sisters to stand in his place? Arjun, *beta,* what do you think?"

Truthfully, the last thing Arjun wanted was for his aunts to barge in on his meeting—but he was powerless against decorum. "It's a very nice surprise," he said, putting the emphasis on *surprise.* "Are you hungry?"

"I could eat," said Manjula.

"As long as it's not the *matar paneer* we had last time," added Revathi. "Do you remember those peas, Manju? Hard as rocks!"

Manjula snickered. Arjun glanced at his mother, who had a pained expression on her face, as though she would like nothing more than to find an *actual* rock and smash in her sister-in-law's face. Instead, Sarita said, "You're in luck. I have some leftover *chana masala* that I'm sure will live up to your standards."

Arjun led his aunts to the couches in the living room while his mother went off to prepare the food. The two women sat beside one another, their proximity highlighting their differences: Revathi lean and severe as a jungle cat, Manjula plump and bubbly as a domestic tabby. Still, they were more alike than not: the same deep-set eyes, the same thin lips—even the hands, with spindly and delicate fingers like one might find on a concert pianist. Arjun's father had possessed these traits, too, and seeing them so clearly in his sisters made his absence seem even more pronounced.

"I must say, Arjun, I was so happy when I heard that you were getting an arranged marriage," said Manjula.

"And how *did* you hear, exactly?" he asked. He'd sworn Sarita to secrecy. Of course, the truth would have come out eventually—but he would have preferred that "eventually" arrive when the save-the-dates were sent.

"Dhanya Agarwal is a dear friend of mine," Manjula explained. "And besides, she posts all of her clients' biodatas on Facebook."

Arjun made a mental note to tell Dhanya that she was under no circumstances to discuss him with any prying relatives—or put anything about him on the internet. *There's doctor-patient confidentiality,* he mused. *Surely, matchmaker-suitor confidentiality must exist, too.*

Sarita arrived with the food. "Please, eat quickly," she said, handing each woman a steaming plate and some fresh *roti*. "We're expecting them any minute now."

Revathi scooped up some chickpeas with her *roti* and took a bite. She made no comment, which meant that the curry was excellent. "We were just discussing Arjun's decision to marry," she said, covering her mouth daintily with one hand. "At least, to marry traditionally."

"Yes," said Sarita, sitting on the couch next to Arjun. "It was a weighty decision, but the right one."

"The right one, indeed!" said Revathi. "It is so good to see a nice boy like you staying true to his culture. We were worried about you for a long while, you know."

Arjun frowned. "Worried? Why?"

"Well, you were running around with that Chinese girl for so long," Revathi said. "And *cohabitating* with her, even." She huffed. "Only our brother could be so permissive," she muttered just loudly enough for Arjun to hear.

Arjun could feel anger boiling underneath his skin. His mother seemed to sense it, too, and she put a hand on his knee before he could explode at his aunt. "Vicky was a nice girl," Sarita said diplomatically. "She helped Arjun a lot after Ravi's passing."

"If you say so," said Revathi. "But, at the end of the day, that relationship did not start properly."

Arjun frowned. "And what is that supposed to mean?" he asked, his voice rigid with indignation.

Manjula cut in. "Your *bhua* did not mean to offend you, Arjun," she said. "I can speak from firsthand experience. My Divya married for love: her husband, Tom. At first, I was hesitant because, ever since my daughter was born, I imagined her with a handsome Indian groom—a groom that I had helped her to choose. But, I thought: *He makes her happy. Who am I to stand in the way?*"

Manjula shook her head sorrowfully. "Neither of you know this yet, but Tom and Divya are getting a divorce."

Arjun felt a pang of sadness. He'd always liked his cousin Divya, though they only spoke at family gatherings once or twice a year. And Tom was nice enough, if a bit awkward. "I'm very sorry to hear that," he said.

"It was about culture and values, at the end of the day," Manjula said. "Now, of course, it's possible for people from different backgrounds to be happy together. But it's much easier if they start with a common foundation."

Revathi was nodding. "You don't want to ruin your future, Arjun," she said. "Divya is a nice girl—but it'll be more difficult for her to remarry now, even if she chooses to get an arranged marriage this time. After all, what mother would let her son be with a divorcée?"

Arjun's cheeks were growing warm. *What is this, the eighteenth century?* he wanted to shout. *How could you talk like this about your niece—your daughter?*

Before he could verbalize his thoughts, cooler heads prevailed. Chewing out his aunts would do him no good. "Mom, I'd like to try some of your *chana*," he said through gritted teeth.

"Of course," replied Sarita, and together, they walked to the kitchen to commiserate over their uninvited guests.

Devi's family arrived soon after. Arjun went to answer the door this time. He gave himself a once-over in the foyer mirror, re-doing a button on his *kurta* that had slipped from its hold. Then, he opened the door.

Devi stood on the stoop. While Simran had brought what seemed like her entire extended family, Devi was accompanied only by her parents. She was dressed in a simple blue *sari* blouse, which she wore over white denim pants.

Arjun folded his hands in a *namaste* greeting and ushered the family inside. He gamely made small talk, asking them how their flight from Pennsylvania had been and thanking them for traveling such a long way to meet him. Devi's father, a thin man with a pencil mustache, was certainly less intimidating than Malini's or Simran's fathers had been, and he smiled and nodded at Arjun as they spoke.

They arrived at the living room, and Arjun introduced the family to his aunts and bade them sit on one of the couches. Sarita emerged from the kitchen with a tray of biscuits and a steaming kettle of *chai*. Devi's father took a Parle G biscuit from the tray, nibbling away at the corner like a mouse.

The standard questions followed: how much Arjun made,

what he did for fun, whether he had ever committed any serious crimes ("I got a speeding ticket in high school, but that's about it," Arjun had replied; his aunts exchanged a disapproving glance).

Arjun made it a priority to speak more to Devi than to her parents, and mercifully, her mother and father were happy to oblige. He asked her about her job as an actuary and her time at Penn State (to his surprise, Devi had played Division I hockey).

"That's all very impressive," Revathi said. "But, tell me: do you cook?"

Devi frowned.

"I can hold my own in the kitchen," Arjun interjected. "I don't expect my partner to make my meals for me."

Devi's parents nodded in approval. Devi seemed impressed by the answer, her frown shifting into a slight smile.

Finally, Arjun asked whether Devi would be open to moving to San Francisco. She smiled. "Of course."

Arjun had planned dinner at Il Casaro, an Italian restaurant he'd frequented as a child. It had been the site of most of his birthdays and a celebration place after special occasions like his high school graduation or his victory in the local spelling bee.

He'd reserved a table beside the window, which overlooked the darkened street. The table was set with a white tablecloth, and a flickering candle cast a dramatic light over Devi's delicate features. Arjun tried his best to be open and charming, though all of his questions were suffused with the knowledge that he might be sitting across the table from his future wife. *Can I see it with her?* he wondered, sipping a glass of rich red wine and realizing that Devi was likely conducting a similar calculus on him. Devi was dark-eyed and beautiful, and she seemed intelligent, but something about her gave

Arjun pause. *What is it?* he asked himself, parsing her every word and expression.

He pulled out his phone, wanting to find something new to talk about. "This is my dog," he said, showing Devi a photo of Sally. "I got her a few months ago."

Devi nodded, munching on a piece of garlic bread. "She's very pretty," she said. "Why'd you name her 'Sally'?"

"After a character from a movie," he replied. "Do you like dogs?"

She nodded. "I love dogs."

He smiled. *Finally, something we have in common.* "I'm really glad to hear that. All dog lovers, I think, are good people."

"Well," said Devi, "Hitler loved dogs."

Arjun didn't know how to respond to that.

The appetizer course ended, and the waiter brought out the entrees. "So, what does the rest of your life look like?" Arjun asked, twirling fettuccine around his fork.

Devi speared a piece of ravioli. "The rest of my life?" she repeated. "Like, after I go back home to Pennsylvania?"

"Sure," said Arjun. "But I was thinking more long-term. Where do you see yourself in thirty years?"

She raised an eyebrow. "That's a long time from now. Does anybody know what their life will look like in thirty years? I mean, is that something that you think about?"

He nodded. "Yes, it is," he said. "I have a house in San Francisco: an old Victorian, right in the middle of the city. I have two or three kids, and they're just starting families of their own. My wife and I spend our time traveling the world, and, at night, we sit in our bed, reading books side-by-side until we fall asleep."

Devi didn't say anything for a moment. "That's...a lot," she replied at last, shrinking back in her chair as though intimidated by his grand plan. "You're only thirty, you know. Isn't it a little weird to plan things in that amount of detail?"

"Maybe," he admitted. "But that's what I do. You really never think about these kinds of things?"

She shook her head. "I've been trying to live in the present. You know, take things as they come. I think we spend too much time worrying about what the future will bring."

"So, why did you decide to pursue an arranged marriage?" Arjun asked. "Isn't that a pretty forward-thinking pursuit?"

She shrugged. "Getting married is just what people do at this age, I guess."

"Yeah, but why an arranged marriage?"

"I don't know. The path of least resistance, maybe? If I'm being honest, I'm still not totally sure I'll go through with it in the end."

He frowned. "What do you mean?"

"I'm still young," she said. "Like, yeah, there's society's expectations of me. And, of course, my parents' expectations, too. But I still have plenty of time. Tell me: if something totally wonderful and serendipitous happened—you met your soulmate on the street, say—you really wouldn't drop this whole thing?"

The waiter came by to refill their glasses. Arjun stared out at the darkened street, considering what Devi had just said. Just a few months ago, the idea of pursuing an arranged marriage had been unfathomable to him.

*And yet…*here he was.

"I think you and I are really similar," he said. "We're in this process—but we're not really *in* it. I think some small part of us is still hoping that someone will come and bail us out. But it's time for us to commit, Devi. At least, it's time for *me* to commit. To the process, I mean," he added.

Devi smiled at him, the kind of smile that was half pity and half *Oh my God, I'm sitting across from a crazy person.* "This has been…interesting," she said. "I think you're really nice, Arjun, but I don't think we're a match."

Before he could reply, there was a sudden, insistent knock on the window. Arjun and Devi jumped in their seats. He turned to see two people, a man and a woman, standing in coats and hats just outside. The man grinned widely, but the woman wore a confused expression that Arjun knew well.

Arjun felt the color drain from his face. *What the hell are they doing here?* he wondered.

"Do you know them?" Devi asked, still looking a bit perturbed. She gave a slight wave to the people outside.

"Yeah," said Arjun, burying his face in his napkin. "They're my best friends."

After dropping Devi off at her hotel (and exchanging the world's most awkward hug), Arjun checked his phone to see a flurry of text messages from Dan. He sighed. *Let's go on a drive,* he replied, feeling a pit yawn open in his stomach.

Dan's house was on the other side of town, and he drove there straight from the hotel. He rang the doorbell, and Dan and Erica emerged. "Hey, guys," Arjun said sheepishly. "We can talk about it, just…later, okay?"

They exchanged a look. "Okay," they said in unison.

The three of them got into the car. Erica sat in the passenger seat beside Arjun, and Dan sat in the middle seat just behind. Arjun backed out of the driveway and onto the road. "Where are we going?" asked Dan.

"Same place as always," Arjun replied, glancing into the rearview mirror.

It was a short drive to SuperAmerica. The gas station shone like a beacon in the darkness, the fluorescent red, white, and blue sign as bright as the midday sun. Arjun pulled his car up beside one of the pumps and got out, opening the door for Dan. He heard the passenger door close. "Oh, man," said Erica, staring up at the sign. "How long has it been?"

Arjun squinted in the light. "Ten years, give or take?"

She smiled. "Too long."

Dan shook his head. "Guys, we were here last Christmas."

Arjun laughed. "Right."

They went into the mini-mart, which was open 24/7. They made a beeline to the back of the store. Thankfully, it was still there: an ancient Icee machine, groaning and wheezing like an old man as it churned up tubs of vibrant cherry and blue raspberry slushies.

Arjun pulled on the handle and poured himself a cup of blue raspberry. Dan picked the same flavor, and Erica got a cherry Icee for herself. They paid and walked back to the car. Arjun drove out of the parking lot and parked beneath a streetlamp a few blocks away.

"That hits the spot," he said contentedly, sucking the Icee through the extra-wide straw. "Do you remember cutting class to get these? Oh, and those little snack cakes Erica liked —what were they called, again?"

"Ho-Hos," said Erica, looking vampiric with her lips stained bloodred by syrup. She sighed. "Look, Arjun, this is nice—but you didn't bring us out here just to get slushies, did you?"

For a moment, he contemplated lying. After all, he'd made it this far without telling Dan and Erica about his decision. *No more hiding*, he decided. *It's time to commit.*

"No," he said. "That's not the only reason."

"The girl we saw you with," Dan guessed. "Don't tell us: you have a long-lost sister? Or are you secretly a spy, and she's your handler?"

Arjun laughed. "Dan, I love you—but you are the world's worst guesser."

Dan rolled his eyes. "Well, if it's not that, what is it?"

Arjun sighed. He felt like a steam engine, the pressure building up inside him. It was just a few words, wasn't it? Then why were they so hard to say?

He cleared his throat. "I'm getting an arranged marriage," he said, the words streaming out of his mouth as though he'd just flicked a release valve. "That woman you saw—Devi—she was one of my matches."

From the rearview mirror, Arjun saw Dan's mouth gape open. "You mean…" He faltered for words. "You're going to *marry* her?"

"No," said Arjun. "Not Devi. But, the point is, I'm going to marry *someone*. I'm going to be married by the end of the year."

Silence followed. Then, Erica spoke. "But why?" she asked. "As long as we've known you, you've always wanted to pursue your own great love story. Why would you throw all of that away for an arranged marriage with someone you barely know?"

Arjun shook his head. "Guys, you know that I want to be married more than anything. But it hasn't worked out. And the one time that I thought I'd found my soulmate, with Vicky…well, you know how that ended. I'm just done with it. I'm sick of searching for love and failing. And arranged marriages have worked for millions of people. Billions, maybe. Why not me?"

Dan and Erica said nothing. "It's really not a big deal, you guys," said Arjun, his face growing hot despite his cold drink. "I've made my peace with this decision. I need you to be okay with this, too."

His friends exchanged a glance through the mirror. "Okay," Erica said finally, squeezing his forearm. "We support you."

Their flight to San Francisco left the following afternoon. Arjun sat at the gate while Dan and Erica went off to buy snacks at one of the nearby newsstands. His phone buzzed; it was a text from Nisha. *How'd it go?* the message said.

I'll tell you all about it when I get back, he replied.

That bad?

No. Just wasn't what I was looking for. Can I pick up Sally tomorrow morning?

Of course. By the way, I have something to show you.

What is it?

Arjun's phone buzzed again. Nisha had sent him a picture this time. It was a selfie: her in a white t-shirt, clutching a notebook to her chest. *I wrote something today. The first thing I've written in months.*

He smiled. *Can I read it?*

A few dots appeared on his screen; Nisha was clearly typing and re-typing her answer. *It's private…for now.*

More dots. Arjun waited for the next text—and, when it came, he felt his heart start to race.

When are you back in SF? I miss you.

Arjun sat back in the chair and let out a long exhale. He thought about the last three words of Nisha's text. Had she meant what he thought she'd meant? What he secretly *hoped* she'd meant? He wondered if she'd typed the letters out and deleted them once, twice, three times. If she'd paced around the room, trying to come up with the perfect thing to send him. If she'd agonized over the text the way he'd agonized over her since they'd kissed outside the abandoned storefront. Part of him hoped she had.

Why bother wondering, though? he asked himself. *It's like she said, it didn't matter.*

But perhaps it did matter. For, at that very moment, Nisha Nandan was sitting on the edge of her mattress, her phone gripped tightly between her fingers, waiting for his response.

More matches followed…and more disappointments.

There was Harshita, a pug-nosed lawyer whom Sarita deemed "unacceptable" because of her honking, goose-like laugh.

There was Anu, slight and soft-spoken, who seemed to enjoy the company of her seven cats more than she had Arjun's.

There was Aditi, who, when they were alone, had asked Arjun whether he was open to wearing a wolf costume in the bedroom (he was not).

There were Priya, Neha, Daksha, Arya, Meena, Sandhya, and Trisha, all of whom were perfectly nice (and some of whom even warranted a second or even third meeting) but ultimately were not a fit because of personality differences, a lack of chemistry—or, in Meena's case, a mother just as intractable as Sarita.

And then there was Nisha Nandan.

Three months passed quickly between work and match-making. Arjun was away from San Francisco on most weekends—a sales pitch in Tulsa, a client presentation in Kansas City, meetings with matches all over the country—and he barely saw Dan or Erica (who were occupied with wedding planning more often than not). The one constant in his life was Nisha, whom he still saw every day at the office.

Not that they spent much time in there these days. "Let's go out somewhere," Arjun had said to her the day after he returned from his trip to Iowa. He'd barely done any work; instead, he'd spent his time surreptitiously examining Nisha's expression for the slightest hint of what she'd meant when she told him that she missed him.

"Where did you have in mind?" she asked, folding down her laptop screen.

He shrugged. "It's San Francisco. I'm sure we'll figure something out."

"Arjun, I have a lot of work to get through today."

"You have work to get through every day. Come on, play hooky with me. You're writing again, right? Surely, a jaunt around the Golden City will inspire you more than sitting in this depressing little office."

Nisha laughed. "I can't argue with that."

And that was where it all began.

They toured the Presidio on a slow Monday and hiked up to Coit Tower when the Wednesday workload had sapped them of energy. They meandered down Jackson Street, and Arjun tried not to be annoyed as Nisha sampled every variety of hand cream at an expensive boutique. "Come on, live a little," Nisha said, squirting lotion into his palm. "Smell it— it's called 'Exploding Sunrise.'"

Arjun rubbed in the lotion and smelled his hands. "What's an exploding sunrise supposed to smell like? Tires on fire?" Nisha laughed and stroked his arm, and Arjun felt a jolt of electricity race up to his heart.

"What have you been working on lately?" he asked her on a perfect April Sunday, as they sat on their bench at Buena Vista Park. Though they'd toured dozens of spots in the city, this was the one that they kept returning to. The sun was setting, and the Golden Gate Bridge cast a dark, matchstick outline against the brilliant sky.

Nisha nodded. "I've been writing every day," she said. "You know that, though."

"Yeah, but anything you'll actually let me see? Come on—how do I know you're not just faking me out?"

She laughed. "Fine," she said, reaching into her backpack. She drew out a composition notebook and cracked it open for Arjun to see. There were entire pages filled with her neat script, done in green pen; she flipped through the notebook and opened it to a dog-eared page. "You can read this one," she said.

She didn't need to ask twice.

It was a short story, only a few pages long, and Arjun read aloud: "'The roses were in full bloom the day Jesse died. It was a memory he carried with him as he passed into the afterlife, struggling to pull it through the veil separating the living from the dead. Evelyn had always loved roses. He watched her as she kneeled beside the rosebush, tears glittering like diamonds on her cheeks. But try as he might to comfort her, Jesse could not. He felt like a fly, tap-tapping on a glass window.'"

It didn't take long for Arjun to finish the story, and he closed the notebook when he was done. He looked up at Nisha. "It's a ghost story," she explained.

He shook his head. "It's a love story," he said.

She smiled. "I guess."

"It's really good, Nisha. Does this mean you're seeing someone new?"

"Nope," she replied. "What about you? Any more meetings on the horizon?"

He nodded. "Dhanya sent over some more biodatas yesterday. I'm aiming to have another meeting or two next weekend."

Nisha was silent for a moment. She took a deep breath,

inhaling the sweet scent of the magnolia trees just coming into bloom. "Hey, can I ask you a personal question?"

He sat up straighter. "Okay."

"Does it ever frustrate you? That you haven't matched with the right person yet? I mean, you've been at this process for months."

He shrugged. "I know this journey is supposed to be expedient, but I'm still looking for a real connection. That just takes longer, I guess. Especially since no one is marching anyone down the aisle anymore. Which is a good thing," he added hastily, noticing Nisha's bemused expression. "Who knows—maybe I'm still too picky."

Nisha grinned. "Oh, you're definitely too picky." She turned her body towards him, leaning one elbow on the back of the bench. "You never told me why, you know."

"Why what?"

"Why you're getting an arranged marriage in the first place."

"Oh," said Arjun. "Why does there have to be a reason? You know, in lots of places, an arranged marriage is actually the default."

Nisha smiled. "Come on, Arjun. I like to think I know you pretty well by now. There's a reason behind everything you do."

He sighed. Nisha knew so much about him—but she didn't know this. *Can I tell her?* he wondered. Even now, the memory was painful, an old wound that had never scarred over.

"I met Vicky Chang when I was nineteen," he told her. "I wish we had some adorable meet-cute, but it was nothing like that. We were assigned to the same econ section, and the other kids were stoned or absent most of the time. Vicky and I hit it off, and eventually, I worked up the courage to ask her out on a real date.

"We'd only been together for six months when my dad

died. I told my mom that I'd take the rest of the year off from Yale or even transfer to the University of Iowa so I could be closer to her. But it was *Vicky* who called her and told her that I had to come back to school, that *she'd* be my support system in Connecticut."

Arjun felt his throat tighten. "That was Vicky. And she really *was* there for me. Sure, I had Dan and Erica, but Vicky was the one I'd go to when things got too overwhelming, when I had a funny story to tell my dad before realizing he wasn't here anymore.

"After college, the two of us got accepted to Stanford GSB together, and I thought, *This is it. Kismet.* A sign from the universe that this girl and I were meant to be together forever. We stayed strong through business school, and when we graduated, the two of us found jobs in SF: me at Intellia, which eventually became a part of PSI, and her at a private equity firm in FiDi. We shared a tiny one-bedroom in SoMa, and we were so busy that we barely saw each other. But we were happy. At least, I thought we were happy.

"Dan tried to talk me out of proposing. I don't know, maybe he saw something I didn't, but he told me: *You're too young for this, Arjun. Give it a few years.* Still, I loved Vicky. I wanted her to be my wife. And so, I bought a ring, took Vicky to Baker Beach, and got down on one knee.

"I knew something was wrong when she didn't say 'yes' immediately. I don't know how long that silence lasted, but it felt like a century. When she finally spoke, she said something that I will remember forever: 'I love you, but I don't want to marry you.'"

Arjun clenched his teeth and felt his jaw muscle pulse under his cheek. His throat was locking up, but Nisha was looking at him, and he needed to finish his story.

"She told me that she'd been having doubts for a while," he continued. "'People say falling in love is like being struck by lightning,' she said. She didn't know if people actually felt like that or just sang about it—but, on the off chance that that feeling existed, she owed it to herself to find it. And she said that she'd never found that with me."

The breeze picked up around them, stirring the leaves above. It was a low, soft sound, barely perceptible, but Arjun felt as though the very earth was quaking underneath him. "How could I not have seen it?" he asked Nisha. "We were together for five years. I thought she loved me. I certainly loved her. But it wasn't enough. And, ever since Vicky, it's never been enough."

Nisha nodded slowly. She looked at him with those dazzling eyes, green as springtime. "That sounds really painful," she said. "But can I be honest? Like, brutally honest?"

He nodded.

"Vicky was only twenty-five, Arjun. You can't even rent a car when you're twenty-five. Are you really going to let *her* get in the way of your happiness?"

"And what does that even look like? My happiness?"

Nisha leaned closer. Arjun could feel the intensity of her gaze, could almost taste the way the light filtered through the trees and dappled her lips. "I don't know," she said. Her voice was soft as velvet.

Arjun knew what he wanted to do then. He and Nisha had never talked about their kiss—but, in that moment, he wanted nothing more than to kiss her again.

But that was his heart talking. And where had that ever gotten him?

He leaned in and kissed Nisha on the cheek. He felt his lips linger. "I should go," he whispered, his lips a millimeter from her perfect ear.

He stood and walked down the hill alone.

CHAPTER
Fifteen

Arjun sat alone on a bench at Fisherman's Wharf, the sea breeze whipping off the ocean and filling his nose with its sweet salt smell. His almost-kiss with Nisha, not yet two days ago, still played on a loop in his head. Some part of him wished he could go back and tell her how he really felt, but he knew where that would lead. One heartbreak had been enough—and, as much as he liked Nisha, he couldn't take that risk again. *Like you told Devi*, he thought, *it's time to commit.*

At noon, Arjun had received another biodata from Dhanya. A new woman, Sophia, wanted to meet him today at six o'clock. Due to the short notice, Sarita couldn't make it from Iowa, and Dhanya told Arjun that Sophia's parents wouldn't be there, either. Arjun thought it was funny: this was almost like a normal first date…except that both his and Sophia's parents had already approved it.

From the corner of his eye, he saw a woman approaching. She was slim and fair-skinned, with hair that had been dyed blonde at the ends. She wore dark jeans, a purple blouse, and a fashionable pair of eyeglasses. "Are you Arjun?" she asked him.

He stood. "Hey," he said, trying to put Nisha out of his mind. "You're Sophia?"

"That's me," she said. "I never know how to introduce myself at these meetings. Would a hug be too informal?"

He smiled. "No, a hug would be perfect." They embraced, and Arjun could smell her chocolate-scented perfume.

"Thanks for indulging me, by the way," said Sophia as they pulled apart. "I know Fisherman's Wharf is a tourist trap...but I'm a tourist, right? I mean, I grew up in Los Angeles—well, Pasadena—but it's not like it's convenient to get up to SF, is it?" She sighed. "Sorry. Am I talking a lot? I'm talking a lot, aren't I?"

He laughed. "No, you're fine. Dhanya mentioned that you were here for work. Anything special?"

"I just had my final interview at Stanford," she explained. "I finished my postdoc at Caltech in January, and I'm trying to be a professor. I really want to be either at Stanford or at Berkeley. Well, Stanford mostly. Berkeley is kind of my safety school, I guess. Not to perpetuate any stereotypes or anything. Wait, you didn't go to Berkeley, did you?"

Arjun shook his head. "I did my MBA at Stanford, so, in fact, Berkeley is fair game," he said with a grin. "So, Fisherman's Wharf. What do you want to see first?"

Sophia smiled, turning to face the boardwalk. "What does every tourist come to Fisherman's Wharf for?"

They wended their way through the plaza. It was a pleasant day, with the late April sun dispelling most of the low-hanging clouds. Sophia led the way, confidently weaving through the crowds of people who milled between the restaurants and shops on the boardwalk.

Pier 39 was in the rear of the Wharf, across a wooden dock lipped by a chain-link fence. The waters were gray-green and tranquil, except for the occasional ferry that passed through the bay. Today, the viewing gallery was uncharacteristically deserted.

"Where are they?" asked Sophia, her eyes narrowing behind her glasses. She leaned up against the fence. A gentle breeze blew toward her, and her blouse hugged her stomach.

Arjun looked out at the square docks bobbing in the marina. Usually, there were dozens of sea lions lazing at Pier 39: huge, loud animals with slick brown fur and a distinctive wild animal scent. Now, though, the docks were empty, without a single sea lion in sight. A seagull swooped over-head and splashed into the water. "Well, this was a bust," Sophia said disappointedly, turning away from the water.

Arjun shook his head. "Come on," he said, leading her away from the pier. They returned to the boardwalk.

He stopped at a small booth. "Two, please," he said, reaching into his wallet. The cashier handed him a pair of tickets. "This way." Without thinking, he reached his hand toward Sophia's. She took it. "It's right here," he said, pointing.

They had arrived at a giant carousel in the middle of the boardwalk. Animals of all kinds pranced around a huge circular platform, topped by a blue-and-white striped dome. Arjun handed his tickets to the attendant and stepped onto the platform. "What are you looking for?" asked Sophia as he went from animal to animal.

"This," he said, stopping. He patted one of the figures on the rump. It was a sea lion, its mouth open in mid-bark. "I know it's not quite the real thing…but it's pretty close, right?"

For a moment, Sophia looked at him like he was crazy. Then, she laughed. "I think you're right."

The platform began to rotate. Sophia swung onto the sea lion, and Arjun got onto a tiger beside. Circus music began to play from the speakers above, and the animals began to move up and down on their poles. "What do you think?" asked Arjun.

"Who needs real sea lions?" called Sophia, her voice rising over the music.

Watching her bob up and down, something strange transpired within Arjun—something that he didn't even notice until after the date had concluded. In an instant, he forgot the stakes involved in their date. He was no longer obsessively wondering if this woman could be his wife. It felt easy, natural...

And almost serendipitous, he would think later.

The music slowed, and so did the platform. Finally, it came to a stop, and Arjun and Sophia dismounted. He felt a bit dizzy, as though the ground were still spinning underneath him. Sophia took a few steps and careened into him, and he caught her in his arms. "So, what next?" she asked.

He shrugged. "How about some ice cream?"

They spent the next few hours at the boardwalk. They ate ice cream and browsed around the novelty shops frequented by tourists: magic stores, board game boutiques, a candy emporium, and an Alcatraz gift shop. They visited a booth that sold oysters customers could break open. After cracking three of them, Arjun found a tiny pearl winking inside the fourth. "Here," he said, handing the jewel to Sophia.

She held it up to her ear. "Big enough for an earring?" she asked.

He smiled. "Maybe a nose piercing," he said, indicating the fold beside his nostril.

"We do those here, you know," said the man working the booth, craggy and tanned, with a thick brown mustache that reminded Arjun of a caterpillar. "Oh, and belly buttons. You interested?"

Arjun and Sophia exchanged a look. Then, they burst out laughing.

They got dinner at an Italian restaurant a few blocks from the pier. The sky erupted into a brilliant show of purple and orange, the clouds running like egg yolks. Arjun sat outside with Sophia, watching the waves darken as the sun set. Sophia shivered. "Are you cold?" Arjun asked.

"A little bit," she admitted, rubbing her arms. "I'll be fine, though."

He nodded. "One sec," he said, rising from the table. He ran to a store just across the street and returned with a red plastic bag. He dug inside and handed a white hoodie to Sophia. "What do you think?"

She looked at the front and smiled, then turned the sweatshirt towards him. "'I HEART SF,'" she said, laughing and pulling it over her head. "I love it," she said, picking a piece of fluff off of her cheek. "But what about you?"

"I'll be warm in a second," he replied. He drew a matching hoodie out of the bag and slipped it over his head. "There," he said. "We make a good pair, I think."

Dinner arrived a few moments later: fresh pasta in a light summer sauce for Arjun and shrimp scampi for Sophia. They had wine, too—an expensive Napa red. "What are we toasting to?" she asked, raising the glass.

"To your new job," replied Arjun.

"I haven't gotten it, you know," said Sophia.

He smiled. "I've got a good feeling."

They tapped their glasses together, and the sound hung in the air like a chord strummed on an acoustic guitar.

Their conversation grew livelier as they ate. Arjun was surprised by how much he had in common with Sophia. She liked the same music, the same books and movies. She told Arjun about her first concert, a Pixies show at the Rose Bowl that she'd begged her parents to let her attend. Like Arjun, she'd gone to college on the East Coast. "Harvard, huh?" Arjun asked. "I'm a Yale grad—but I won't hold it against you."

Of course, they dived into the weightier stuff, too. Like Arjun, Sophia dreamed of raising a family in the Bay Area. She told him about her plans for the future: a house in Palo Alto with a big yard for kids and a dog or two. She wanted to stay in academia, write books about her economics research, and hold monthly salons at the house for her favorite students.

Arjun tried to picture himself in that life: walking around the house with Sally skipping behind him, or chasing his children around the backyard. It wasn't a clear picture, like the kind he got when he tried to visualize his own future—but it was an outline, like a painter's blocking strokes. He gazed at Sophia, wondering if this could really be it. *I mean, could it be this simple?* he asked himself. Sophia was smiling at him, and the sight of her set something stirring deep in his chest.

The waiter came by once they'd finished. "Dessert?" he asked, clasping his hands in front of his apron. Arjun glanced at Sophia, then shook his head.

"Just the check, please." The waiter left and returned with a black billfold.

"Can I ask you something?" Sophia said as Arjun slid his credit card inside.

"Shoot."

"How do you feel about all of this?"

"What do you mean?"

"I know arranged marriages are the norm in India. But, obviously, you grew up in America. You didn't have any reservations?"

Arjun sighed. He thought back to his conversation with Devi a few months ago. This time, he was less flustered.

"Honestly, I wrestled with it for a while," he said. "At first, I felt like a loser. Like I couldn't find anyone on my own, and I was in this situation as a last resort. But I think that this experience is what you make of it. It's not better or worse. It's just...if it works out, who cares how it happened?"

Sophia nodded. "I feel exactly the same way."

They left the restaurant and walked back to where they'd first met. The pier was as lively as ever. Music played faintly from the loudspeakers, and people walked about, conversing in a hundred different languages. The crescent moon cut a sliver into the velvet-black sky. "What time do you have to be back?" asked Arjun, sticking his hands into his pockets.

Sophia checked her phone. "I just called an Uber," she said. "I have some grading that I promised myself I'd start at nine." The night breeze ruffled her thick, dark hair like an affectionate hand. "I'd like to see you again."

"Me, too," Arjun replied instantly, and she smiled. She took his hand in hers, then leaned in and pecked him on the cheek.

A car pulled up to the curb. "Good night, Arjun," Sophia said, climbing inside.

As the car sped off into the night, Arjun could not help but feel as though the hands of fate, or time, or Dhanya the matchmaker, had carried him off and were bearing him along toward his true destiny: a destiny with the beautiful girl he'd met only a few hours ago.

CHAPTER
Sixteen

Nisha was back in the office the following day. Arjun heard the sharp clacking of her keyboard from the cramped basement hallway, standing between the towers of boxes. He paused in front of the open door for a moment, just out of view of the desk. *Should I go in?* he wondered, thinking of his almost-kiss with Nisha, just a few days past. Part of him toyed with the idea of returning to PSI and begging Adam D'Antonio for a workspace there—even if it was just the break room table.

He took a breath. *It's fine,* he told himself. *What is this, middle school? It was just one moment. She's probably forgotten about it by now.* And who knew? Maybe she really *had* forgotten; she hadn't so much as texted Arjun since Sunday. But he remembered just how much tension had permeated their moment on the park bench, how much *want* had lingered between them—unspoken, but as persistent as gravity.

He steeled himself and swung the door open.

Nisha was wearing pearl earrings and a green cable-knit sweater that brought out her eyes. She shut her laptop when she saw Arjun in the doorway. "Hey," she said, sounding much less tormented than he was.

"Hey," Arjun replied, rocking back and forth on his heels and trying his best not to sound uncomfortable. He considered several different options of things to say, but none of them seemed remotely sufficient. He decided to change the subject. "I had another meeting last night," he said.

Nisha raised an eyebrow. "Oh? How'd it go?"

"We're going to meet again," Arjun said. "I think she could be…well, this was the best meeting I've had so far."

She nodded. "I'm very happy for you."

Arjun rubbed the back of his neck. "Listen, Nisha, about what happened on Sunday…or about what almost happened—"

She held up a hand to stop him. "Let's not," she said, not unkindly. "I think it'd probably be easier for both of us if we didn't. Just…promise not to make things awkward, huh?"

He nodded. "I'll try my best. You know me, though: it's bound to happen sometime."

Nisha laughed. She leaned back in her chair and gestured to the empty spot across the desk. "So, do you want to sit? You can tell me all about that meeting of yours."

Arjun shook his head. "I can't stay," he said. "I've got a meeting upstairs in fifteen minutes. The work kind. I'm actually pretty excited for this one."

"Who are you meeting?"

"Emily Richter," he replied. He waited for a response, but Nisha didn't seem to clock what he'd just said. "Emily *Richter*," he repeated as though that would clarify anything. "You know, the most influential restaurateur in the Bay Area? She has three Michelin-star restaurants in San Francisco alone."

"That's very impressive," Nisha acknowledged—though, in Arjun's opinion, "impressive" hardly began to cover it.

"Anyway," he said, "she's looking to finance a new location. I guess PSI's loan rates have gotten pretty competitive, so she's coming up to meet with us. Well, to meet with me."

Nisha smiled.

"What is it?" Arjun asked.

"Nothing," she said. "It's just, this could be an opportunity for you as well."

He leaned against the doorframe. "What do you mean?"

"Well, she owns restaurants," said Nisha. "And you want to open a restaurant. You should talk to her about your idea."

"I can't do that," Arjun replied. "It's a clear conflict of interest."

She shrugged. "Maybe. But you want to open your own restaurant eventually, don't you? Who knows: Emily Richter might be just the person to help you make it happen."

He checked his watch. "I have to go," he said, and walked back down the hallway and up the stairs.

Emily Richter was already in one of the conference rooms on the second floor. She sat at the end of the table like some large raptorial bird, hunched over and ready to strike at any moment. Her mass of red curls was unruly as ever, and she wore the same simple outfit that Arjun had seen her don on the covers of dozens of magazines: black flare pants and a white blouse dotted with shiny black buttons.

She stood when she saw him enter. Arjun was nearly six feet tall, but Emily Richter was a few inches taller still. "Hello," he said, checking to make sure his palm wasn't sweating. "I'm Arjun Chowdhury."

She shook his hand and smiled. It was a quick shark smile that contained no warmth, and it came with a once-over that, while brief, gave Arjun the impression that Emily had just analyzed him on a molecular level. "Charmed," she said, exposing a pair of shiny canines.

"Before we begin," Arjun said, sitting, "I have to tell you that I'm a big fan. I've eaten at all of your restaurants, and I have all of your cookbooks."

She chuckled. "That's very nice of you to say. And which recipe would you say is your favorite?"

"That's a hard one," he replied. "The winter spanakopita was excellent. And I did love your peach clafoutis. But I'd have to say that my favorite recipe was the *mollejas de pollo*."

Emily raised an eyebrow. "You actually tried the chicken sweetbreads? I'm impressed. Most people are scared off by organ meats, even when I've served them at my restaurants. Tell me: are you a particularly adventurous eater?"

"I don't think so," he replied. "Just an aspiring restaurateur like yourself. But enough about me. We're here to discuss your new restaurant."

She waved her hand. "There will be plenty of time for business later. Tell me more about this restaurant of yours. Is it opening anytime soon?"

He shook his head. "I've been procrastinating for the last few years. But I've got a name and a location picked out. And I've been working on a menu."

She steepled her fingers in front of her and leaned her chin on them. Her eyes were like lighthouses, luminescent and irresistible. "Tell me more."

Arjun could scarcely believe this was happening. Emily Richter—*the* Emily Richter—was interested in *his* restaurant idea?

"It's called Raja's," he said. "I named it after my grandfather, who was the person who taught me how to really appreciate cooking. The menu is all Indian food. And, as far as location goes, there's this storefront on Hayes Street that's been empty for months now." He pulled out his phone and opened Google Maps to show her.

"And you think that this would be a good location for an Indian restaurant?" Emily replied, handing his phone back to him.

He nodded. "Foot traffic on Hayes Street is among the highest in the city. There are at least a dozen restaurants within a five-minute walk—but no Indian food. We all know that there's a huge appetite for Indian cuisine in San Francisco, especially given the demographic makeup of the city. So why wouldn't there be an Indian restaurant in one of its most trafficked areas?"

Emily smiled. "That makes sense, Arjun," she said. "I'll tell you what: I'd love to help you achieve this dream of yours. If you'd like, I can refer you to some great chefs. And, if you send me your recipes, I can help you to refine them and optimize them for a restaurant setting."

He felt his jaw drop. "Are...are you serious?" he stammered.

She laughed. "Of course," she said, giving him that same smile that just a moment ago had made him uneasy. "So, what do you say?"

Arjun was at a loss for words. He only nodded, dumbstruck by how inconceivably, magnificently well that had just gone. He felt like an amateur bicyclist who had stumbled into the Tour de France—and won.

The presentation that followed regarding the financing of Emily's new restaurant was a blur. Arjun didn't remember anything about the meeting: not what he said or what she said. He only remembered how it ended, with him shaking hands with Emily again and walking her back down to the lobby. Not five minutes after she'd departed in her sleek black Range Rover, Arjun received an email from her assistant, complete with an invitation to meet with Emily at her restaurant, Portofino.

Arjun decided that a celebratory pastry was in order. He crossed the street to the coffee shop, ordered a cappuccino and a muffin, and sat at one of the tables. Every sip of coffee tasted as sweet as nectar.

He saw a familiar figure striding across the street. It was Adam D'Antonio. Adam somehow looked even more massive than before, like he'd just begun a new workout routine or had started suiting up for the Cardinal again. "Arjun!" he said, smiling broadly as he entered the shop. "Fancy seeing you out and about. How are the muffins today?"

"Excellent, as always," Arjun replied, covering his mouth with one hand. "I would highly recommend the chocolate chip. I'd never tried it before—but it's excellent."

Adam shook his head. "I'm on a new diet!" he proclaimed, slapping his stomach. It made a sound like a hollow drum. "Maybe I'll come back on my cheat day." He made toward the counter before turning suddenly. "Hey, you had that pitch today! With that chef, Emily-something. How did it go?"

"Emily Richter," Arjun replied. "She said she'd think about it."

Adam frowned. "That's surprising," he said. "She didn't seem like the type to drag her feet." He shrugged. "It is what it is, I guess. You know, I have some news that might brighten your mood."

"What is it?"

"The plumber came last night," Adam said, flashing his million-watt smile. "Your office is finally fixed!"

Arjun felt an odd clenching sensation in his stomach, as though he'd just been dropped from an airplane. "Really?"

"Well, it might smell a little musty, but it's basically good as new. You can move back in this afternoon, if you'd like. I know you must be itching to get out of that dank little base-ment office, eh?"

"Would it be possible to stay?" blurted Arjun.

His boss furrowed his eyebrows. "Stay? In the basement?"

"Yes," Arjun replied. "In the basement."

Adam rubbed his chin. "Well, there's no reason you can't," he said thoughtfully. "And I have to say, your work has been even better ever since you moved in there. Are you sure about this?"

Arjun nodded. "I'm sure."

"All right," Adam said. "The basement it is. Now, if you'll excuse me, that egg white sandwich right there is calling my name." He went off to order, leaving Arjun alone at his table once more.

Arjun sighed and took another bite of his muffin. He couldn't recall the last time he'd felt this happy, the last time he'd taken a swing this big and had it pay off. *And,* he realized, *it was all thanks to Nisha.*

CHAPTER

Seventeen

The sun was setting, and purple dusk fell like a veil over the city. Arjun sat on a blanket in the middle of Alamo Square Park, feeling the coolness of evening settle over him. Someone had set up a large projector screen twenty feet across at the other end of the park and was projecting *Casablanca* for the few hundred people who had gathered to watch.

He heard footsteps in the grass behind him, and he scooted over to make room on the picnic blanket. "Get anything good?" he whispered.

Sophia shook her head. "They're out of popcorn," she replied, sitting next to him. "Luckily, I thought ahead." She reached into her purse and pulled out a bottle of wine and a pack of Twizzlers. "We can use them like straws," she said, pulling out one of the lurid red candy ropes, which flopped over her hand.

Arjun laughed. "That's a great idea," he said as Sophia settled onto the blanket beside him. "But how are we going to get the wine open?"

"I can take care of that," came a voice. Arjun winced, as though bracing himself for a blow. *This is it,* he thought.

. . .

Arjun had seen Sophia twice more since their first meeting on Monday. On Tuesday, the same day he'd met Emily Richter, he'd taken Sophia to the Museum of Modern Art. They walked around the huge building, examining abstract paintings and the huge, alien sculptures assembled by Alexander Calder. Like Erica, Sophia was well-read when it came to art, and Arjun was amused to find that she often knew more about various pieces than the museum's own docents. "What do you see when you look at this?" she'd asked him, tilting her head in front of a large abstract painting.

Arjun squinted. The painting was a series of multicolored, vertical lines overlaid one over the other: red and brown, gray and yellow. Each line had been painstakingly laid, as though the artist had used a ruler. "It's discordant," he said. "The lines are parallel, which would otherwise be pleasing. But do you see the line there, in the center?" He pointed. "The blue one. It's slightly angled. It's not much—probably only a few degrees—but it's enough to make you feel like..." He struggled to find the words.

"Like something is a little off?" Sophia said.

He nodded. "Yeah, that's right."

She laughed. "Come on. Let's go check out the Dutch masters."

On Thursday, Arjun and Sophia went to a Giants game. Kevin McPherson was a fan, and he had a pair of season tickets that he lent Arjun. The seats were fantastic: just a few rows behind the dugout. "I love baseball," Arjun told Sophia as "Charge" blared over the stadium speakers. "Nothing makes me feel more American."

"Can I be honest?" she asked, wearing the black-and-orange baseball cap that Arjun had purchased for her. "I don't get the point. It's just...men standing around in tights."

He smiled. "That isn't part of the appeal?"

Someone was up to bat, and there was a sharp crack as the baseball soared up to the top of the stands. The jumbotron showed the scrum of people fighting over the ball—only for a young boy to emerge with it in his mitt, laughing joyfully. "Come on," said Arjun, pointing. "That doesn't warm your heart?"

"That's not fair," she replied. "Everyone loves kids."

Walking out of the stadium in the gathering dark, Arjun realized something. "You know, there's nothing wrong with you," he said to Sophia.

She hitched up an eyebrow. "Do you say that to all the girls?"

He shook his head. "That came out wrong. What I meant to say is that throughout this whole process, we've been scoping each other out. Trying to figure out if we're really as compatible in real life as we are on paper. And the thing that I've realized is…I still don't have a reason to say 'no.'"

She smiled. "Me, neither," she said, and she threaded her arm through his.

Whatever comfort that Arjun had felt in that moment had now completely faded. His heart was in his throat as he turned to see the two people who had come to join them in the park. "These are my friends, Dan and Erica," he said to Sophia. "And this is Sophia. She's my…"

He was momentarily at a loss. What *was* Sophia to him, exactly? His new friend? His excursion companion? His "person-I-met-five-days-ago-and-might-soon-marry"?

"We're seeing one another," Sophia said helpfully, extending a hand. "Arjun has told me so much about you both. And I'm sure you'll have lots to tell me, too."

Dan laughed. "We might need to crack into that bottle first," he said, spreading his own blanket out over the grass.

Sophia leaned against Arjun as the movie played, and he

wondered if he could put his arm around her. In the other relationships he'd had, three dates in was generally when things began to get physical—but, of course, this relationship was not like his others. Cicadas sounded in the grass, drowning out Humphrey Bogart. Dan poured the wine, and Arjun attempted to drink it through a Twizzler (it didn't work).

The movie ended soon after, and Arjun rose to fold up his blanket. "What did you think?" Sophia asked, helping him to fold it lengthwise.

"I liked it," said Arjun—though, truthfully, he despised black-and-white movies.

Thankfully, Sophia didn't seem to notice. "You'd better," she said. "Honestly, I should have put that on the biodata: 'Must love *Casablanca*.'"

Dan stood and stretched his arms. "It's still early," he said. "Kiki's?"

"What's Kiki's?" asked Sophia.

Arjun and Dan exchanged a look. "You'll see," Arjun said, grinning.

The bar was a short Uber ride away, and it was more crowded than Arjun had ever seen; evidently, everyone else at the screening had the same idea. Dan went to get drinks while Sophia excused herself outside to take a call. Erica and Arjun stood against the wall, all of the booths having been occupied. She leaned over to him. "You and Sophia make a nice couple."

"Thanks," he replied. "I think so, too."

"Do you think you'll marry her?"

"I don't know," he admitted, thinking back to their conversation outside the ballpark. "I like her. We have a lot in common."

"And is that enough?"

He shrugged. "What else is there?"

A pool table opened up, and Arjun and Erica claimed it for the group. Dan returned as Arjun was chalking up his cue. "Where's Sophia?" he asked.

"Still outside," Arjun replied. "She said she had a phone call to take."

Dan grabbed the triangle from underneath the table and started racking up the balls. "She's a good one," he said, leaning over the table. "But, to be honest—and, please, don't take this the wrong way—I liked you with Nisha better."

Arjun frowned. "What do you mean?"

"I just think you two have good chemistry together," Dan said. "Like, you really get each other. Remind me again why you're not dating *her*?"

Arjun shook his head. "We're just friends," he said, perhaps a bit too forcefully. "And, besides, chemistry can be misleading. Not that I have that kind of chemistry with Nisha. We're just friends," he repeated for emphasis.

Dan shot a look at Erica, but he didn't press the point further. "All right," he said, rolling the cue ball across the table to Arjun. "You break."

Sophia returned after Erica had finished wiping the floor with Dan and Arjun. She looked flushed, as though she'd just gone running. "You were gone for a long time," Arjun said as Dan re-racked the balls. "Is everything alright?"

She nodded. "Everything is great," she said. She leaned over to Arjun and whispered: "I have something to tell you."

"What is it?" he asked.

She inclined her head towards the door. "Not here. Outside."

Arjun thought that was a bit strange, but he followed Sophia outside. A streetlamp buzzed overhead, and the music from the bar drifted faintly out onto the street. "Are you sure you're okay?" Arjun asked as Sophia paced the sidewalk in front of him.

She stopped. Then, she leaped towards him and grabbed his forearms. "I got the job!" she exclaimed. "I'm going to be a professor at *Stanford!*" Her eyes were wide, as though she herself didn't believe it.

Arjun let out a huge, booming laugh. "Are you serious? Sophia, that's amazing! I'm so happy for you!" He stepped forward, and Sophia allowed him to embrace her.

"Yeah," she said as they pulled apart, still sounding a bit breathless. "I'm not starting until August...but, God, there's so much I have to do. Find a car, a new place: maybe in Palo Alto, but maybe in SF? And I'll probably need a roommate, because this entire city is *criminally* expensive, but I'm also almost thirty—"

"Stay with me," Arjun replied immediately.

She cocked her head. "Like, move in with you?"

"Why not?" he said. "I have a big place right in the middle of the city. And I have a spare bedroom." It occurred to him just then how unique his proposition was: not only asking someone to move in with him just three dates in, but actually *wanting* her to.

Sophia smiled. "That's a very sweet offer," she said. "But I'd like to live apart until after we get married."

He felt the expression on his face freeze. "What is it?" she asked.

"It's nothing," he replied. "It's just...you said, 'after we get married.'"

"Oh," she said. "Yeah, I guess I did. Did that freak you out?"

He shook his head. "No," he said. "It was just...a little unexpected, that's all."

She frowned. "Well, that's the point of this, isn't it? If we like each other, it moves quickly. I mean, we could be married before the end of the year."

Arjun knew this was true, but hearing it said so plainly was like being hit by a brick. *This is what you want,* he told himself, staring into Sophia's eyes. The streetlights danced in her dark irises.

Standing there in the cool night, he tried to picture it again: him and Sophia, getting married and growing old together. The image was still fuzzy, as on an old TV. He tried to visualize it more clearly. *How does it make you feel?* he asked himself.

"Hey," Sophia said. "Are you still with me?"

Arjun nodded. "Yeah. Sorry. Do you want to go back inside? I'm sure Dan and Erica will be excited to hear the good news."

Sophia shook her head. "I need to call my parents and tell them first. Maybe my grandparents, too. But your friends were lovely, Arjun. I'm really glad I got to meet them."

He smiled. "Yeah, me too," he said—and, to his surprise, he really *was* glad. He stood on the curb with Sophia as she awaited her Uber, and he bade her goodbye with a promise to see her again the next day.

CHAPTER
Eighteen

Kelley Garcia returned from maternity leave on May eighteenth. Arjun was incredibly excited to have his assistant back, stringing a multicolored sign that read "WEL-COME BACK KELLEY" across the door of the basement office and even going so far as to pick up two dozen strawberry cupcakes from SusieCakes.

Kelley, on the other hand, was less than enthusiastic upon her return. "So, *this* is your new office?" she asked when she walked in and saw Arjun's new digs. There was a smear of dust across her midsection from rubbing up against one of the boxes piled in the hallway, and she rubbed her sweater to remove the stain. Arjun could almost smell her distaste, like a rotten egg scent permeating the entire basement.

Still, he tried to remain upbeat. "This is it," he said cheerily, sliding through the narrow gap between the desk and the wall. Kelley leaned against the door frame as though worried that the tiny office would explode if she entered, too. She craned her neck to look up at the posters plastered to the ceiling.

"Arjun—where am I supposed to work?" she asked. "This room won't fit two people."

"You'd be surprised," said Nisha, appearing in the doorway behind Kelley. "I'm Nisha, Arjun's office mate." Kelley moved aside to let her pass, and glanced at Arjun with a raised eyebrow and a look of knowing: *Ah, so* that's *why you're here.* He felt himself redden, and hoped that Nisha wouldn't notice.

"I love your earrings," Kelley said to Nisha, noting the little silver owls peeking through her hair. She sighed. "All right," she told Arjun resignedly. "I guess I'll take a desk out in the bullpen upstairs." She gestured for the tray of perfect pink cupcakes. "Oh, and I'll take those, too."

Usually, Arjun had the stamina to grind through endless busywork—but, more recently, he had found it increasingly intolerable. Perhaps this was an effect of his increased efforts on Raja's; he'd spent most nights cooking, buoyed by Emily Richter's interest in his idea.

Arjun had taken her up on her offer to meet, and they'd eaten lunch together at her restaurant, Portofino, in the Fillmore. Over seared branzino, Emily grilled Arjun about every detail of his restaurant: what he planned to serve, where he would buy ingredients, his plan to hire chefs and waiters, and even what kind of soap he would stock in the bathrooms. She seemed especially intrigued by Arjun's business plan and continued asking why Arjun had chosen that specific Hayes Valley storefront. He had answers to most of her questions, and he expected Emily to be as impressed as she'd seemed back at the PSI offices.

It hadn't worked out that way, though. At the end of that first meeting, Emily had stood, thanked him for his time, and told him to let her know if she could help him with anything. In the Uber back to his house, it occurred to Arjun that he didn't have Emily's contact information; they'd only communicated through her assistant. And, though he'd reached out to Emily's assistant a few times since that initial meeting, he hadn't received a word in response.

Nevertheless, he was undeterred in his idea. For such a person as Emily Richter to even be intrigued by his plan to open a restaurant was all the encouragement that Arjun needed. And so he'd continued developing the menu, dropping off deli containers full of food for Dan, Erica, and Kevin McPherson to sample and give feedback.

Back in the office, Arjun was thinking of a new recipe for lamb korma with mint chutney. He'd been experimenting with the recipe for nearly a week now—yet, every time he tasted it, he couldn't help but feel that *something* was missing. *Of course, it doesn't help that I don't even* like *lamb*, he thought.

He stood and shut his laptop. "I need a break," he said to Nisha. "Do you want to get lunch?"

She looked up from her computer. There was a brief questioning look in her eyes. Despite their promise not to make things awkward, there was still an unmistakable tension between her and Arjun, a sort of *What if?* that permeated their every interaction. Arjun and Nisha hadn't met outside the office again since their last visit to Buena Vista, and he wondered if asking her to lunch had been a mistake. *Don't be stupid*, he told himself. *You're friends. And, besides—you're with Sophia now.*

"So," he said. "Lunch?"

"Sure," she said, rising and slipping into her jacket.

Arjun found Kelley at her new desk, which sat between twin mountains of old newspapers. He cooed briefly at the pictures of Emmylou that she'd set up on the desk, then told her that he was taking a long lunch. "If you'd like, you can go home," he said. Kelley shot to her feet and bolted out of the office. If she'd been a cartoon character, she would have left her silhouette hanging in the air behind her.

· · ·

They set out for Dolores Park, which was a mile away on foot. "You know, you still haven't told me about this new match of yours," Nisha said as they passed beneath a row of pale purple jacarandas. "What's her name?"

"Sophia," Arjun replied. "We've met a few times now, actually. I like her."

"What do you like about her?"

He thought about it for a moment. "She's very…together," he said. "Like me, I think. Everything is in place for her, and it's like marriage is the one thing that's missing. I think she's a kindred spirit."

Nisha laughed.

"What?" he asked.

"It's nothing," she said. "So, what does she think of you?"

"She likes me, I think. She wants to get married."

That stopped Nisha in her tracks. "Really? She wants to get *married?*" she repeated. "You've only known her a month, Arjun. Less than a month. There's a gallon of milk in my fridge that's older than your relationship."

He chuckled. "You should probably throw it away, then. And that's the whole idea, isn't it? You meet someone, you hit it off, you get married. The love stuff comes after."

They continued on. It was a perfect cloudless day, the sky an unbroken expanse of blue. "So, are you?" Nisha asked. "Going to marry her, I mean."

Arjun shrugged. "I don't know," he said. "I can't think of a reason *not* to. Maybe that in itself is a reason to do it." He sensed that Nisha had some thoughts of her own on this idea —but, whatever they were, she kept them to herself.

Mission Dolores Park was a broad stretch of grass over-looking downtown San Francisco. Despite the fact that it was midday on a Monday, the park was packed: hundreds of people lounged on the grass, posted up in camping chairs or on picnic blankets. Vendors moved through the crowds, selling popsicles and pre-rolled joints. A circle of teenagers kicked around a hacky sack, and a group of elderly women did Tai Chi nearby. "That looks fun," Nisha said, pointing to a group playing beer pong (for which they'd set up a table in the center of the park).

"I think my beer pong days are behind me," Arjun replied with a smile.

She rolled her eyes. "Whatever you say, old man. Come on, then: let's eat."

There were a few food trucks lined up on one side of the park, and Arjun and Nisha split off. He got a Piri Piri chicken sandwich from a Portuguese truck that he recognized from an event at PSI; she returned with a plate of bright-orange tofu tikka masala.

"What do you think is happening over there?" asked Arjun, looking further down the field. A few dozen folding tables had been set up, piled with clothes and knickknacks.

Nisha squinted at the sandwich board sign standing near the table. "Looks like it's a flea market," she said. "Let's check it out!"

"Can we at least eat first?" he asked—but she was already striding across the grass. "Wait up!" he called over a bite of his sandwich.

A small band was playing nearby, and Arjun leaned over to drop a few dollars in their open guitar case. "Think they're any good?" he asked as the band launched into one of their songs.

"I'm a sucker for live music," Nisha said. "There's just something about it, you know? Honestly, it's better than sex."

Arjun laughed. "We should go to a concert together sometime."

She grinned mischievously. "We're at a concert now, aren't we?"

They made their way over to the flea market. The tables were bursting with all manner of odds and ends. Mountains of furniture stood on the grass: desks and dressers, beanbags and stools, and a complete dining set with chairs shaped like cupped hands. Mannequins in Victorian dress luxuriated in the aisles between the tables, with flowing capes and elegant jackets, tulip-shaped crinolines, and feather boas draped lazily around their necks. Nisha picked a flaming pink hat up off the nearest mannequin and placed it atop her head; the brim flopped over her eye. "What do you think?" she asked.

Arjun checked the tag. "Eight bucks. Not bad. I think we can do better, though."

Nisha pawed through a rack of jackets and took one off the hanger. She looked thoughtfully at it, then held it up for Arjun to inspect. The jacket had a tawny suede torso, with sleeves and shoulders made of weathered gray wool. "Try this on."

Arjun was generally opposed to the idea of wearing someone else's clothing, but he acceded to Nisha's request. "What do you think?"

"It looks great," Nisha said, grabbing his arms and looking him up and down. "Can I get it for you?"

"You like it that much?"

"I do. And, let's be honest: you need all the help you can get."

Arjun laughed. Nisha paid for the jacket (despite his protest), and he slung it over his shoulder. They circled around, closer to the band once more. "Do you know that song?" she asked him. "It sounds so familiar."

He nodded. "It's *San Francisco,* by Scott McKenzie," he said. "I think it came out in the sixties."

"Is it famous?"

"Well, for one thing, it's in every tourism advertisement for SF. Which, if you ask me, is where they should leave it."

Nisha grinned. "I never took you for a snob, Arjun."

"I'm not a snob," he protested. "I just have good taste."

She threw her head back with laughter. "That's *exactly* what a snob would say."

They stopped in front of one of the tables. A selection of clothing was laid across it—but that wasn't what had caught Nisha's eye. A snow-white electric guitar lay on the pile of clothes, as sleek and shiny as a sports car.

She picked up the guitar. "Watch this," she said, bounding back over to the band. *What is she doing?* Arjun wondered as Nisha leaned over to the singer and whispered a few words in his ear. From his vantage, Arjun could just barely make out the words the singer was saying: *Sure, you can do that.*

The guitarist reached into his vest and handed Nisha a pick. *She plays?* Arjun thought as she moved her fingers over the frets of the white electric guitar and mouthed a few words to the band. The drummer nodded and clicked his sticks together; the bass player strummed out a few notes. Then, the singer held the microphone close to his lips and began to sing.

The melody was instantly recognizable to Arjun; he'd just heard it, of course. It was the same old song: Scott McKenzie's *San Francisco.*

And yet…there was something different about it this time.

What is it? he wondered. The music pulsed forth from the speakers, enveloping him in a pocket of sound.

Before he knew it, the singer had crested the rise of the second chorus and stepped aside. Nisha approached the microphone and began to play.

Her solo did not follow the main melody of the song. She had reworked it, hanging an entirely new structure off of the old chords like a master seamstress, turning a worn-out garment into a dazzling new dress. The notes of the electric guitar sounded across the park, pure and bright and full of longing. A deep, wistful feeling filled Arjun's chest, as though he'd just discovered that something essential was missing from his life, something as vital as oxygen, or light, or love. He found himself putting words to the melody: *If you're going to San Francisco / Gentle people, with flowers in their hair.*

The solo ended, and the song finished. Arjun approached

the band, clapping wildly. He heard others applauding, as well; many of the shoppers at the flea market had stopped to watch the performance. *They're all clapping for Nisha*, he realized.

Standing with the band, Nisha beamed with delight and took her bow. As she straightened, she caught Arjun's eye and winked. *Was that the wind, or did my heart skip a beat?* he wondered.

She rushed up to him and threw herself into his arms. "Nisha, that was amazing," Arjun said breathlessly. "I mean, the guitar—and that *song!* My God, it was even better than the original. It was so…" he searched for the right word. "Romantic."

Nisha blushed. "How could you *not* be romantic about San Francisco?" she asked him—and, for a moment, Arjun could swear that she was looking right into his soul.

Arjun spent the rest of the day pondering that feeling he'd had at Dolores Park. Clearly, something was missing from his life—but what was it? Was it Raja's, the dream of a restaurant that was just a heartbeat away from being reality? Was it his father—the person who, ten years later, he still most wanted to see?

Or was it something else entirely?

He kept toying with the question that night at dinner with Sophia. Funnily enough, she'd suggested that they eat at Leather and Wood, having told Arjun that she'd "heard amazing things" and that the quail sous vide was "to *die* for." Arjun didn't let on that he'd been there before, only telling Sophia he was excited to go there with her.

"So, how did everything go at Stanford?" Arjun asked her once they had sat down and gotten their food. "Today was the first time you'd met all the econ department faculty at once, right?"

"That's right," Sophia said. "I told you how intimidated I was going into it. I mean, there are two Nobel winners on staff. But, honestly, it could not have gone better. Everyone was so incredibly nice. One of the Nobelists even asked if I'd be interested in writing a paper with him." She smiled and reached across the table. "I'm really excited to start, Arjun."

He stroked her fingers. "I'm happy for you," he said. "Who knows? Maybe there's a Nobel in your future, too."

She gasped. "Don't even joke about that. I would literally die."

She sliced open a square of summer squash ravioli and tucked it neatly into her mouth. "You know, there's another faculty meeting happening in a few weeks. The econ department throws a big party at the end of the school year. It's for professors...and their partners."

She looked pointedly at Arjun.

He nodded. He knew this could be the first of many such occasions with Sophia: accompanying her to faculty parties, conferences, commencements. There would be Thanksgivings and Christmases, birthdays and funerals. There would be weddings—maybe even *their* wedding. The very thought was like a rush of wind blowing through him.

He still didn't know if he wanted it with Sophia, not really. They hadn't known each other long enough to know. But he knew that he wanted to be married. He wanted it desperately —so desperately that he envisioned his future life with a fervor that made it seem real, as though he were not just envisioning it but *living* it. He was finally connected to another person, and he felt...

Complete.

And, suddenly, he realized what that feeling was, the one that had first stirred during Nisha Nandan's performance and had been gnawing at him since. It was a deep ache, a puzzle with a single missing piece—except he didn't know the shape of the piece, or even what the puzzle was supposed to look like in the first place.

But what if it's right here? he wondered. He'd been grasping at it like a blind man in the dark—but what if the key to his happiness was in front of him? What if *she* was in front of him?

Across the table, Sophia set her fork down. "Arjun," she said, looking up at him, her dark eyes like pools of water. "Are you doing okay?"

"Yes," he said. "I'm fine, really."

"You're still thinking about it, aren't you?" she asked, leaning back. "You know, a few days ago, when I told you how quickly this process can move—I sensed that I might have freaked you out a little."

She sighed. "I just need to get this out there: I want to be married. I know we're not 'in love' or anything like that, but…I can see it with you, all right? And I need to know: are *you* there yet? Can you see it with me? Because, if not, we're just wasting our time here."

He said nothing for a moment. His tongue probed the inside of his cheek as though it was searching for some answer carved into the delicate tissue. *This is it,* he told himself. *No turning back now.*

He nodded. "Yes," he said. "I can see it, Sophia." He reached across the table and clasped her hand in his.

She exhaled with relief. "I'm really happy," she said, smiling. "Let's get married."

CHAPTER
Nineteen

As it turned out, Arjun's engagement wasn't very official at all. After he called her with the good news, Dhanya the matchmaker had informed Arjun that he was not, in fact, engaged—despite the fact that he and Sophia had agreed to marry one another. "That is not how things work, *beta*," Dhanya had said patiently, as though talking to a small child. "You are not officially engaged until your *roka* ceremony."

"Right," Arjun had replied. He knew that he'd heard the term before—but, for whatever reason, it had suddenly lost all meaning.

Dhanya sensed his hesitance. "It's the Hindu engagement ceremony," she explained. "'*Roka*' means 'stop.' Your families will meet to agree to stop pursuing other people and to officially approve the match. There will be a *pandit*, who will conduct a traditional Hindu ritual. And, of course, you will exchange gifts. That's my favorite part. All other arrangements—most importantly, the date for the marriage itself—can be determined after the *roka* concludes."

All right, so Arjun wasn't really engaged. Still, when he told his mother, she had reacted in her characteristically melodramatic fashion: "Finally, Arjun—a daughter-in-law," she had proclaimed. "I can die at peace, now." Sarita had flown all the way from Iowa the very next day, and she declared the couple to be a perfect match within minutes of meeting Sophia.

With Sarita back in Des Moines on Sunday evening, Arjun was left to plan for the *roka* with Sophia. They'd agreed to hold the ceremony at a Hindu temple in San Ramon a few weeks later. Sarita would come, of course, and Sophia's parents would hop on a flight from Los Angeles. Arjun drew a blank when Sophia asked about his guest list. "Uh…Dan and Erica, of course," he'd said. He thought next about Nisha —would he invite her? *How would she even react to me being engaged?* he wondered as Sophia debated between burgundy and lilac color palettes.

He found out at work on Monday. "I have big news," he said, setting his bag down on their desk.

Nisha raised an eyebrow. "What is it?" she asked, lowering her laptop screen.

He sighed. *Time to rip off the band-aid*, he thought.

"I'm engaged," he said. "To Sophia. Well, pre-engaged, but…well, we're getting married."

He waited for some sort of response. Perhaps Nisha would be disappointed. Or maybe she'd be angry, hurling staplers and stationery across the desk at him while howling, "HOW COULD YOU?"

Instead, she said only: "Oh. Congratulations."

"Thanks," he replied, and a weighty silence hung in the air. For a moment, he wondered if he should say something else—but what?

He suddenly felt very stupid standing there. Nisha was still looking at him.

"Well, I should go," he said, gesturing to the door with his thumb. In truth, though, he had nowhere to be. He walked down the hallway and paused in the stairwell. It occurred to him that he had almost…*wanted* Nisha to be jealous.

Why? he wondered. *You're with Sophia now. You're getting married to* Sophia. And that statement was enough to shock his thoughts of Nisha Nandan into awed submission for a little while—before, inevitably, they surfaced once more.

The rest of the week flew by. Arjun and Sophia hammered out the details of the *roka* ceremony over FaceTime with her parents. Arjun realized that this was the first time he was meeting them; perhaps because they knew that he and Sophia had already agreed to marry, they went much easier on him. While they were both attorneys, they refrained from the cross-examination and warmly welcomed Arjun to the family. "We're so excited to meet you in person, Arjun," Sophia's mother said.

"And we're so sorry we haven't come up sooner," her father added. "There's this case—"

"—huge case," Sophia's mother cut in.

"Right, huge case. Anyway, we've both been terribly busy. But you know how it is, eh?"

Arjun nodded. "Of course," he said. He exchanged a look with Sophia. "You know, I could always come down to Los Angeles, if you'd like. It's just a short hop from SF."

"No need for all that!" Sophia's mother said, shaking her head vigorously. "We'll see you in two weeks, won't we? You know, that's how it was done in the past: the first time the bride and groom met was at the *roka*!"

Arjun smiled. "I suppose things are working out the way they're meant to, then," he said. He folded his hands in a farewell *namaste*. He was already imagining Thanksgiving with these new, very nice, very busy in-laws.

. . .

Arjun and Sophia had agreed to get dinner with Dan and Erica the following Friday at an upscale Italian restaurant called Scopa. "I hope this is one of many double dates," Erica had said.

To Arjun's knowledge, double dates involved only four people—so when he arrived at the restaurant with Sophia, he was very surprised to see Nisha Nandan sitting at the table right beside Erica.

He smiled awkwardly. Things with Nisha had steadily grown more stilted since he told her about his engagement to Sophia. Of course, they were still friendly, but Arjun felt like things weren't flowing as well as they used to, like a stream that was being slowly choked by pollution. Even being in the office with her was agonizing, and he'd ducked out early every day that week, opting instead to work from the coffee shop across the street.

"Hey, Nisha," he said. "This is Sophia Verma. Sophia, this is Nisha Nandan."

Sophia extended a hand. "It's a pleasure to meet you," she said. "And how do you two know each other?"

"We work together," Arjun said hastily.

"Arjun has told me all about you," Nisha said with a winning smile. "I'm looking forward to getting to know you better."

Arjun and Sophia took their seats. The women were on one side of the table, and Arjun sat between Dan and an empty chair. He pulled out his phone and texted Erica under the table: *You invited Nisha??*

Yeah, so? came the reply. *I thought you two were friends.*

We ARE friends.

So, what's your problem?

Arjun thought about this for a moment. *I thought this was going to be a double date,* he texted.

Well, now it's a triple date.

Arjun frowned. *Triple date?* he replied. He turned to the

empty chair to his right, and suddenly, it hit him like a semi-truck full of bricks.

As if on cue, Arjun heard footsteps behind him. He turned to see a tall, unfairly handsome man walking towards the table. The man had an easy, confident way about him, with jet-black hair and eyes as blue as a Caribbean sky. He smiled at Nisha, and Arjun felt his heart drop.

"Everyone, this is Patrick," Nisha said. Her eyes locked with Arjun's for a moment, as though she were introducing Patrick specifically to him.

"Patrick is one of my colleagues at the hospital," Erica said helpfully as he took the seat beside Arjun. "I thought he and Nisha would hit it off, and it looks like they have! Their first date was yesterday. What did you two do?"

"We went to Cal Sciences in Golden Gate Park," Patrick said. "Have you been? It's one of my favorite places in the city. Nisha liked it too, right?"

"It was fantastic," she said. "There was an incredible garden, with butterflies flying all around you. We must have spent hours there, just looking at all the different species."

Arjun imagined Nisha and this handsome stranger, arm in arm and surrounded by butterflies. It must have been steamy in that enclosure. Had they held hands? Had they kissed? Arjun felt his stomach clench into a knot of jealousy.

"It's nice to meet you," he told Patrick, extending his hand. The other man's grip was as firm as oak. *Why do I have such a problem with this?* Arjun asked himself angrily. *You're engaged to Sophia. Nisha is allowed to date other people.*

The waiter arrived with a bottle of wine, which he began pouring into glasses for everyone at the table. "So, Patrick," said Arjun, "what kind of doctor are you?"

Patrick sipped on his wine. "I'm a gynecologist," he said with a faint smile.

Arjun nodded. "Oh? That's quite the choice. Was there something about the female anatomy that appealed to you?"

Erica shot Arjun a withering glance, but Patrick only chuckled good-naturedly. "I know it seems weird," he admitted. "When I was doing my undergrad at Brown, I spent a summer in Uganda, helping to set up a hospital for a small village. While I was in Africa, I really got a sense of health disparities around the world, and how stark the picture can be for women and girls especially. That's what my foundation does, actually—four times a year, we spend a week in Uganda, conducting routine preventative screenings like mammograms and pap smears."

Nisha smiled at Patrick. "That's amazing," she said, resting her hand on his.

Arjun felt like he wanted to scream. "Brown, huh?" he said instead. "It's a fine school. I went to Yale, but who cares about things like college rankings—ow!" Something slammed into Arjun's shin under the table, and he looked up to see Erica staring daggers at him.

"Arjun," she said icily, "I think I dropped something by the bathrooms. Do you want to help me come find it?"

"I think I'm fine here," he said, rubbing his leg. The spot where she'd kicked him had already risen into a small lump.

Her eyes narrowed. "*Arjun.*"

"Fine," he said. He limped away from the table and followed her toward the bathrooms at the other end of the dining room. "What did you drop?"

Erica smacked him on the arm. "I didn't drop anything, you moron. Why are you acting like such an ass?"

"Stop hitting me!" he protested. "And I'm *not* acting like an ass. I'm having a great time, actually."

"No, you're being a child." She shook her head. "Is this about Nisha?"

Arjun leaned against the wall and crossed his arms. "What are you talking about?"

"Don't play dumb with me," she retorted. "I know something is going on between you two. And, if I'm being brutally honest, some part of me thinks you got on board with marrying Sophia so quickly because you have feelings for Nisha, and this is your way of pushing them away. But, Arjun, let me ask you this: if Nisha asked you to get together right now, would you drop everything and be with her?"

Arjun sighed. He thought once more of their kiss, of their moment on the bench. But those had just been mistakes. He and Nisha had said as much. *Just mistakes…*

Right?

You're engaged to Sophia now, he told himself, a phrase that was quickly becoming a refrain.

"I wouldn't be with her," he said. His voice was hushed, barely rising above the soft classical music playing over the speakers.

Erica stroked his arm. "In that case, you have to let Nisha move on. You decided—you *chose* Sophia. And you have no right to punish Nisha for your own decisions."

Arjun sighed. "You're right," he said. "As usual."

Erica smiled softly. "Now, if I take you back to the table with me, can you be civilized?"

He nodded. "Yes."

"Good," she said, and led him back to the table.

The main course had arrived when they sat down again. Sophia leaned over to Arjun. "Is everything all right with your friend? Did she find what she was looking for?"

"What?" Arjun had been forcing himself to focus on the delicious-smelling plate of pesto gnocchi that the server had placed in front of him, instead of whatever Patrick was whispering to Nisha that was making her laugh so much.

"The thing she's looking for," said Sophia. "She said she dropped something by the bathroom."

"Right," replied Arjun. "No, she didn't. Hopefully it turns up." His eyes flitted briefly to Nisha, then returned to his pasta.

Dan had begun telling Patrick about his wedding plans.

"We've just changed venues last minute," he said. "We had originally booked a small chapel in Loma Vista, but our first-choice location opened up, and we had to snap it up. So, we're getting married at the San Francisco Conservatory of Flowers."

Patrick nodded approvingly. "I would've done the same," he said. "The Conservatory is beautiful—especially this time of year. Still, I imagine getting a new venue adds to the stress."

Dan nodded. "No kidding."

"When's the wedding?" Sophia asked, covering her mouth with her hand as she chewed.

"May 31st," Erica replied.

"Shoot," Sophia said. "I'll be out of town."

Dan smiled at her. "Don't worry," he said. "We're live streaming it."

Dinner ended, and the evening wound down. Sophia and Patrick had both needed to use the restroom, so Arjun and Nisha found themselves standing alone on the curb, waiting for their partners to emerge. Arjun was staring into a streetlamp, trying to appear as nonchalant as possible—but he could sense Nisha's gaze boring into him. "So, what did you think of Patrick?" she asked.

Arjun thought back to his conversation with Erica, and his shin began to throb again. "He's great," he said, turning toward her. "I'm happy for you, Nisha."

She smiled. "I was afraid to put myself out there, believe it or not. But I'm writing again, aren't I? And, if I can embrace imperfection in that area of my life...well. I suppose, at the end of the day, I really *don't* want to be alone forever."

They stood silently for a moment, each unsure of the next thing to say—painfully aware of the lingering silence. "Any news on your restaurant, by the way?" Nisha asked. "It's been a while since you've told me anything about it."

He nodded. "I sent an email to the property owner, and he gave me a call the other day. He told me that he'd lower the price by a third if I signed the lease this week."

"That's incredible. Are you going to sign?"

"I still don't know," Arjun said, sighing. "I mean, am I really ready for this? To take the big leap?"

She chuckled softly.

"What?" he asked.

"You're ready," she said. "In fact, I'd bet that you've been ready for months now."

She was right, of course. Arjun had worked out every last detail regarding his restaurant, from the dishes he'd serve, to the décor, to the font that he'd use on the menus. He would never be more prepared than he was in that moment.

"I'm afraid," he admitted, his voice barely a whisper. "To put in an offer, I mean. All this time, it's just been an idea—actually buying the restaurant would make it real. What if it fails?"

Nisha shrugged. "Then at least you'll know," she said. "So, come on. Will you do it?"

What was it about Nisha that made him want to run *toward* his fears? What power did she have that she could short-circuit his instinct for self-protection? "I'll call him back tomorrow," he said. "Promise."

"*Today*," she insisted.

Arjun sighed. He pulled out his phone and punched in the owner's number. "Voicemail," he told Nisha.

"So? Leave one. He'll get back to you."

Arjun called back. "Bruce, it's Arjun Chowdhury," he said, his eyes never leaving Nisha's, the way that green looked different in the darkness: lush and deep, a jungle full of mystery and hope. "We'd spoken recently about the vacant restaurant on Hayes Street. I'm ready to submit a bid. Please call me back as soon as you can."

Arjun hung up the phone, his heart racing. His chest was full of a feeling somewhere between panic and exhilaration. "There," he said. "Are you satisfied?"

Nisha grinned. "Extremely."

They stood, not saying anything, for a few moments. "Thank you," he said. "I never would have pushed myself to do this without your help. I'm a cautious person—too cautious—but you…you make me want to take risks. So, thank you."

She stepped closer. "I care about you, Arjun," she said. "You're my favorite person in San Francisco. I don't want that to change, okay?"

He nodded. "Of course," he said. "I'm here for you." Without thinking, he opened his arms, and they embraced. It felt so good to hold her, to feel the warmth of her body against his.

"Arjun," said a voice emerging from the restaurant. It was Sophia. "Are you ready to go?"

He hastily pulled away from Nisha. "Yeah," he said. "Yeah, I'm ready. Good night, Nisha."

"Good night," she replied.

The Uber pulled to the curb, and Arjun opened the door for Sophia before getting in on the other side.

Sophia stared at Nisha through her window as they drove off. "I have a favor to ask you," she told Arjun as the restaurant faded from view. "I don't know if we're at the point where I can actually *ask* you favors—but we're getting married, so what the hell. I know Nisha is your friend, but is there…Can you stop hanging out with her?"

Arjun frowned. "What do you mean? Why would you ask me that?"

She sighed. "It's just…I noticed her acting kind of weird during dinner. Like she was trying to make you jealous with that Patrick guy or something. You know, rubbing him in your face like that? Anyway, just…can you not see her anymore, please?"

Arjun kept his eyes on the road. He nodded. "Of course, Sophia," he said, weaving his fingers through hers.

That was a lie, though. It was Friday, and Arjun would see Nisha at their office on Monday morning.

Twenty

"Rejected?" said Arjun, squeezing his eyes shut and pinching the spot between his eyebrows. "What do you mean, *rejected?*"

At least the voice on the other end of the phone attempted to sound apologetic. "I'm sorry," said Bruce, the owner of the vacant restaurant. "I know that you were excited to submit a bid for the space. But I received an offer this morning that was too good to pass up."

"Well, how much was the offer?" Arjun asked, sitting heavily on one of the barstools beside his kitchen island.

"A hundred thousand over market price. I really am sorry," he repeated. "But look on the bright side. It's San Francisco. There's opportunity everywhere."

Arjun jammed his finger into the red "END CALL" button on his phone. He wanted to scream in fury and disappointment. He walked over to the couch, pressed one of the pillows to his face, and did just that. It was a continuous burst of muffled sound, and he felt it shake his lungs, his vocal cords stretching to their breaking point.

He felt a paw on his leg. Sally had padded over, surely to comfort him. Arjun let her up onto the couch and stroked her fur. "What do I do now?" he asked her. Of course, Sally had no reply—she just licked his face.

The doorbell rang. Arjun ignored it, but then it rang again. He opened the door to find a mailman holding a gift-wrapped package. "Are you Arjun Chowdhury? I'll need a signature."

Arjun signed for the package and brought it inside. *What could it be?* he wondered, setting it on his kitchen island. He certainly hadn't been expecting anything. The package was the size of a shoebox, and it hadn't been heavy. He found a knife and slit open the wrapping paper.

He smelled the contents of the box even before he opened it. It was sweet, delicious—and familiar. Arjun opened the box's lid to find a cake waiting for him: the red velvet cake that was the signature dessert of the restaurant, Portofino. Arjun had eaten that cake half a dozen times, but there was something different about this one. Red icing letters looped atop the snow-white buttercream, perfect and taunting:

THANKS FOR LOCATION SCOUTING FOR ME!

Arjun didn't have to read the enclosed note to know who had sent this this cake. *How could I be so stupid?* he berated himself. He'd spilled his entire plan to Emily Richter, down to the smallest detail. She'd been only too happy to listen…and now he knew why.

Arjun picked up his phone and dialed a number. "Hey," he said. "Something's happened. I need you."

Nisha arrived at Arjun's apartment twenty minutes later, dressed in an oversized purple Northwestern hoodie, her hair in a messy bun. "And you're sure it was Emily Richter who snaked the location out from under you?" she asked, stepping inside and removing her shoes.

Arjun nodded. "Read the note," he said, handing her the envelope. She opened it and pulled out the sheet of paper inside. "She's opening up an Indian restaurant," Arjun said as Nisha scanned over the letter.

"Ouch," Nisha replied, setting the letter down on the kitchen island. "Talk about adding insult to injury."

Arjun began to pace. "I mean, what am I going to do, Nisha? I spent *months* planning this, assuming my restaurant would go in *that location*. All that work—just down the drain?"

She stepped towards him and grasped his forearms. Arjun stopped pacing. "You're spinning out," she said. "Close your eyes and just breathe. Do it with me, okay?"

Arjun nodded. "Inhale," said Nisha. "Good. Now, exhale."

He did as he was told: breathe in, breathe out, repeat. In, out, repeat. Repeat. Repeat. Repeat. He felt Nisha's hands on his forearms, anchoring him to the room. He could hear his heart beating against his eardrums—but, gradually, it slowed.

They pulled apart. Arjun slumped against the wall. "I've wanted this for so long," he said. "A way to honor my dad and my grandfather. A *legacy*. And I *had* it."

He closed his eyes. He took a deep breath in, then exhaled slowly. This time, it didn't help. "How am I supposed to just move on from this?" he asked, looking at Nisha.

She nodded sympathetically. "Come on," she said, extending her hand.

"Where are we going?" Arjun asked, remaining rooted to the wall.

"You'll see," she said, grabbing his hand. "Quickly, please."

Reluctantly, he followed her out of his kitchen and down the steps. She had parked her ancient Camaro on the street, and Arjun climbed into the passenger seat. He leaned against the window, watching the hills roll by. Thankfully, Nisha let him linger in the silence.

She hadn't told him where they were going, but it didn't take him long to figure it out. She parked the car on the side of a hill and engaged the emergency brake. "Let's go," she said.

"Do we have to?" Arjun asked. He wanted to stay inside the car—or, better yet, go home, crawl into bed, and disappear under the covers.

"Yes," she replied. She circled around, opened the passenger door from the outside, and pulled him out by the arm. She led the way up this time, guiding Arjun over the trails that wound through the forest.

It was a cruelly gorgeous day, with a slight breeze cooling their ascent. Above them, the branches began to clear, and the path grew wider until, at last, it opened up into that familiar meadow shaded by oak and elm. Nisha found the bench she'd been looking for, and Arjun followed.

"Our old spot, huh?" said Arjun, sitting beside her. The view was achingly beautiful today: the San Francisco Bay shone like a sheet of glass, with whitecaps surfacing and descending like dolphins as they raced towards the shore. "Do you remember the first time I brought you up here?"

Nisha smiled. "You wanted to show me how romantic SF could be," she said, sounding almost wistful. She turned to face him. "You're going to be fine, Arjun."

"How do you know that?"

She sighed. "I never told you about my divorce, did I?"

He shook his head.

"We met just after college," Nisha said. "It was…passionate. He was Indian, which my parents loved. And he was a doctor, which they loved even more. We dated for just six months before he asked me to marry him. And after that, I thought my life was all set. You know: the picket fence, two and a half kids, all of it. It was just a matter of time. And so, I dove into my writing, and he spent a lot of time at the hospital. We were building our lives, like bricklayers constructing a castle.

"We went on like this for two years. I published *The Kiss of*

Eternity and went on an extended book tour. He made Chief Resident and began spending even more time working. Our towers grew higher and higher. And we just kept building, not realizing that that's what was destroying us.

"You see, Arjun, eventually, we realized that the towers we were building weren't part of the same castle anymore. Sure, they had started from the same place—but they were different structures now, and once they grew apart, there was no putting them back together again."

He nodded. "I appreciate you being so honest with me," he said. "But why are you telling me this now?"

"My divorce wrecked me," Nisha said. "I know you saw some of that—but definitely not the worst of it. I thought I was done—that my whole *life* was over. But look at me now. I'm happy. For the first time in a long time…I'm happy."

She looked deep into his eyes and rested her hand on his. "Happiness isn't something that's given to us. It's something that we have to choose every day. It's something that we have to fight for. And you are a *fighter*, Arjun. You will figure this out. I promise."

Their fingers coiled together, her palm warm and soft against his. His heart pounded in his ears. He looked at Nisha, and an overwhelming urge swept over him, like a wave crashing into his body.

Why had he taken this to *her* first, instead of Dan, or Erica—or even Sophia? It was a stupid question to ask, because he already knew the answer.

He wanted Nisha's hand to stay in his forever. He wanted to turn towards her and put his arm around her. He wanted to caress her cheek and stare into those marvelous green eyes. He wanted to lean towards her and kiss her, to feel her breath in his mouth, hot and life-giving.

More than that, though, he wanted to open his lips and tell her the words that he'd known for some time now, had *known* he'd known, but had been too afraid to say.

An idea popped into his head. "I still have the recipes," he said. "My very own recipes. Can you help me with something?"

Arjun didn't sleep at all that night. The two of them stayed awake, hopped up on caffeine and adrenaline, as Arjun cooked his recipes, and Nisha tasted them. By the time 6 a.m. rolled around, there were fifteen dishes scattered on Arjun's kitchen island: mulligatawny soup, *malai kofta*, cherry-red tandoori paneer, and more. "All right," he said. "Last one."

He set a tureen on the table. "Birthday cake *kulfi*," he said. Inside the tureen were two perfect, round scoops of ice cream: cream-colored, flecked with multicolored sprinkles.

Nisha dug a spoon in and took a bite. She closed her eyes with pleasure. "That is so good. I think it's missing something, though. I can't quite put my finger on it."

Arjun nodded. He dug around in his cabinet and pulled out a tin of flaky Maldon salt. "Try this," he said, sprinkling some salt over the kulfi.

She tasted it again, her head arching back in pleasure. "That's the best *kulfi* I've ever had. Truly."

He smiled wearily. "I'm glad," he replied. "I'll get all of these recipes typed out and formatted. Can you help me compile them into a book?"

She nodded, yawning hugely. "Of course," she said. "I should probably head out, though. I haven't pulled an all-nighter since college."

"You don't need to go," Arjun said. "Crash here, if you want. I'm sure Sally would love the company."

Nisha smiled. "That's sweet. But I should probably move my car, anyway. Street sweeping today, right?"

She embraced Arjun. "This is a good step," she said. "I'm really proud of you."

"I couldn't have done this without you," he replied. "Nisha, I—"

He stopped himself just short of saying it.

She gave him a curious look. "What's that?"

"Nothing," he said, smiling wearily. "Get home safe."

Arjun had Dan and Erica over to his apartment that night for dinner. He hadn't seen them since the group date at Scopa—and, besides, he had a fridge full of leftovers from his marathon cooking session that morning (Sophia, industrious to a fault, had stayed behind to prepare the fall semester's syllabus). Arjun made fresh *lacchha parathas* in the kitchen with Erica while Dan sat on the couch drinking a beer and watching the Premier League.

Fragrant steam billowed from the various pots and pans on the stovetop, each heating up a different curry; the apartment was filled with intoxicating smells. *I wish Nisha were here*, Arjun thought, shaping one of the *parathas* into a neat triangle.

Stop it, he told himself. He was not supposed to be thinking of Nisha, despite the fact that she was the only thing he could think about since she'd left his apartment that morning. It had taken every fiber of his being not to sprint down the street and tell her how he really felt about her.

He turned to Erica. "I have something to tell you," he said. "But I need you to promise not to kick me again."

She laughed. "Why would I kick you?"

Arjun took a deep breath. "Because I think...I think that I'm in love with Nisha."

Silence followed. Then, quick as a striking mongoose, Erica's foot sped outward and collided with Arjun's shin. He yelped in pain. "What the hell!" he exclaimed. "I told you not to kick me!"

"Are you *fucking* kidding me right now?" Erica retorted,

practically yelling. Arjun saw Dan swivel his head toward the kitchen, evidently interested in whatever was happening. "You're in *love* with Nisha?"

That was enough to rouse Dan from his soccer game. "You're in love with Nisha?" he repeated, walking to the kitchen.

Arjun sighed. "Yes," he said. "I mean, I think I am."

Erica scoffed, throwing up her hands in exasperation. "Do you hear that, Dan? He *thinks*. Even better!"

"Hey, go easy on him," Dan said. He turned to Arjun. "What makes you think you're in love with Nisha?" he asked earnestly.

"It's just a feeling I have," Arjun said. "But I feel it so deeply—like it's a fundamental part of my existence. I think…I want to be with her."

Dan nodded. "All right," he said. "So, then, be with her. It's simple, isn't it?"

Arjun shook his head. "No, it isn't. I'm marrying Sophia, remember? We're engaged. Or pre-engaged. Or whatever the hell we are."

Dan raised his eyebrows. "So? If you really love Nisha, then you're doing a disservice to Sophia. Not only are you sacrificing your happiness by not being with Nisha, but you're also preventing Sophia from getting hers."

Erica shook her head. "You're so wrong," she said to Dan. She sighed. "Look, Arjun, I know you're going through a lot. But it's just pre-wedding jitters. Trust me, I had them after I got engaged to Dan. Big time."

A concerned expression dropped over Dan's face. "You did?"

"Not now, babe," said Erica, waving him off. "Anyway, Arjun—I thought the reason you wanted an arranged marriage in the first place was to build a relationship on a different foundation. Compatibility, not attraction or love.

Wouldn't you be undermining that if you were to suddenly dump Sophia and get with Nisha?"

Arjun struggled briefly for words. "I don't know," he admitted.

Erica pressed her advantage. "Look, Nisha is a great person. And maybe you really do have these strong feelings for her. But let me ask you: you had these strong feelings for all the other girls you've dated, didn't you? What if this thing with Nisha turns out the exact same way?"

Arjun's mind flashed to Vicky Chang. Erica was right: he'd felt the same about Vicky as he did with Nisha. *And you remember how that turned out, don't you?* he thought.

He nodded. "Maybe you're right," he said. "Maybe these feelings for Nisha are just jitters. Just temporary."

Dan clapped him on the shoulder. "Look: whatever you decide, we'll support you. Now, which one of these curries should I start with?"

CHAPTER
Twenty~One

The wedding took place on a Saturday, surrounded by flowers. The altar had been erected on the steps of the San Francisco Conservatory of Flowers, a beautiful glass building with a high central dome and wings that arched to either side, like a dove taking flight. Its delicate façade shimmered like a diamond in the warm light. The sky had taken on the colors of evening: blues and yellows and purples, more vibrant than even the flowers on the hillside below.

Arjun stood at the altar beside Dan, dressed in the navy suit that he'd had tailored specially for this occasion. He touched his fingertips to his lapel pocket, assuring himself that the rings were still there. They were light things, but they were weighted by significance, as though imbued by some spell. Arjun leaned over to Dan. "Are you ready?" he whispered.

Dan only smiled.

From the bottom of the steps, a string quartet began to play. The cellist plucked on his strings while the viola came in with the melody. The violins danced above it all, ornamenting the music with delicate harmonies. It was a song that Arjun knew well, and he couldn't help putting words to the music: *Come gather 'round, people, wherever you roam…*

The breeze whispered to life, sending the smells of hibiscus and rose drifting toward the altar. The aisle was lined with pink linen, and it was edged with blooms. To either side of the aisle, people stood from their white folding chairs. Arjun could feel their anticipation: a frisson that lingered in the air, like a collective bated breath.

There was a red brick archway at the other end of the aisle, and the opening was strung with garlands of pink peonies that hung down like a veil. A hand emerged and parted the flowers gently, as though caressing a lover's face. Erica stepped through the curtain, her arm threaded through her father's. Her face was covered with a lace veil, and she wore a pearlescent white dress that reflected the brilliant sunset above. She held a bouquet of crimson roses closely to her chest, and she stepped in time to the music, treading lightly over the flower petals that the flower girl, her niece, had so carefully laid just a few minutes earlier.

Arjun glanced over at Dan. His friend's eyes were luminous, glazed over with tears. It looked like he was seeing Erica for the very first time—as though he was falling in love all over again.

A lump was forming in Arjun's own throat, as well. *Changing times, indeed*, he thought, reaching into his jacket for a handkerchief.

Erica reached the end of the aisle, and Dan climbed down the steps to receive her. He took Erica by the hand and led her under the altar. He leaned over to her and whispered something that not even Arjun could hear, words meant only for the two of them.

Dan lifted the veil covering her face. His movements were delicate, as though he were uncovering a priceless work of art. Erica smiled up at him, only him. They were together adrift on a great river, all alone, even among all these people.

The music faded, leaving only the sound of the birds in the trees.

Dan's father was the officiant. "You may be seated," he said to the audience. "We are here today to join two souls in love, under the witness of family, friends, and God." He beamed at the couple. "I know how long both of you have waited for this. I won't delay you any further. You have each prepared vows; it is traditional for the groom to go first."

Dan nodded and cleared his throat. "Erica," he said, his voice muffled with tears. "I've loved you since the tenth grade. I've loved you through college transfers and new jobs, through earthquakes and blizzards, through broken arms and kept promises. I've loved you before I even knew who *I* was. I've loved you so long that I don't know how to do anything else.

"I don't know what the future holds for us—no one does. But when I look into my future, I only see one thing for certain: you. You've been here through everything. And I promise you that I will be here through everything else."

Dan's father looked to Erica. She was already crying; Dan reached out and wiped her tears away with his thumb. "Do you remember when we moved to Chicago?" she asked. "We were twenty-two, bright-eyed, and enthusiastic about taking on the world. After a few short weeks, reality set in. I broke down crying on our couch—just a complete mess. I was done, I told you. My job was a dead end, and I didn't know anyone in the city. Do you remember what you said to me?"

Dan smiled.

"You said, 'But, Erica, you know *me*.' And I burst out laughing. It didn't solve my problem—but it was enough for me. *You* have always been everything I needed. You are kind, and you're steady, and you can make me laugh when all I want to do is cry. Dan, you are my soulmate. I love you, and I cannot wait to be married to you."

Arjun looked out at the audience. The sun was setting, and faces glistened with tears.

Dan's father smiled. "Well," he said. "I won't be one to go against the wishes of my soon-to-be daughter-in-law. Does the best man have the rings?"

Arjun reached into his jacket and drew the rings from his pocket. He handed them to Dan.

"Dan," asked his father, "do you take Erica to be your wife?"

He nodded. "I do," he said. He slipped the ring onto Erica's finger.

Dan's father smiled. "Erica, do you take Dan to be your husband?"

"I do," she replied immediately. Dan's wedding band was a simple gold loop, and it slid easily into place, as though it was always meant to be there. Dan's father placed his hand on his chest.

"Then, by the power vested in me by the great state of California, I now pronounce you husband and wife. You may now kiss the bride!"

Dan and Erica stepped closer and kissed. The crowd cheered and hooted, a cacophony of joy and jubilation. Arjun looked out into the audience, and somehow, his gaze fell upon Nisha Nandan, sitting near the back. She caught him looking and smiled.

The reception took place indoors, under the great glass dome of the Conservatory's orchid gallery. Arjun sat at the head table with Dan, Erica, their parents, and the rest of the wedding party. Dinner was served; Arjun had chicken medallions with a savory pan sauce, along with a few spears of asparagus. The wait staff came around with champagne flutes, which they distributed to the guests.

Erica's parents gave the first toast, followed by Dan's

parents. Erica's sister was the Maid of Honor. That turned out to be a bad move; she was already drunk, and her innuendo-laden speech didn't make matters any better.

Arjun's speech was last, and he stood and buttoned his coat jacket.

"Good evening," he began. "For those of you who don't know me, my name is Arjun Chowdhury, and I have the privilege of being the best man at this wedding.

"I met Dan in AP English sophomore year of high school. I had never met anyone so like me, and we got along quickly. Within a week of knowing him, I was spending nearly every day after school at his house." Arjun glanced into the audience. His mother had flown in for the wedding, and she was chuckling softly at the memory of the two then-teenagers.

"So, naturally," Arjun continued, "I was disappointed beyond words when Dan started spending all of his time with this girl in our English class—a girl I hated because, for the first time in my life, *she* was the teacher's favorite instead of me. Can you guess who she was?"

The crowd laughed; Arjun forged on. "Gradually, though, I began to look forward to hanging out with Erica just as much as I did Dan. And, eventually, I felt that I *couldn't* hang out with one without the other. See, they were a package deal —like two perfectly matched socks.

"In the old days, newlyweds used to plant sycamores on either side of the walkway leading to their front door. As the years passed, the trees would reach toward one another— and, eventually, their boughs would knit together and become one. Over the last fourteen years, I've watched Dan's and Erica's love blossom: the kind of complementary love where she is strong when he is weak, he is funny when she is serious—he hates olives, and she loves them. A sycamore tree kind of love."

He paused. He found himself looking at Nisha again, and in the brief moment when their eyes met, Arjun wondered if she knew what he was thinking. "That's the kind of love I'm still looking for," he said. "And, in these two, I have an amazing example to which to aspire." He raised his glass. "To the newlyweds. May you continue to grow together for the rest of your lives."

There was a round of applause, a symphony of silverware against glass. The caterers wheeled out an enormous cake, three feet tall and draped in vanilla buttercream and colorful fondant flowers. Dan and Erica fed one another, and Arjun laughed with everyone else when Erica smeared cake all over Dan's lips and chin. The lights darkened, and the couple shared their first dance to the Knife's "Heartbeats", played on the acoustic guitar. When the music ended, Dan threw up his arms. "Everyone!" he called, and then the night really began.

Arjun wasn't a natural dancer, so he decided to wait until he'd gotten a buzz to partake. He snagged an extra slice of cake and found Sarita conversing with some other middle-aged people at her table. Arjun paused for a moment before approaching her. He was suddenly struck by how *unfair* it was that his mother was at this wedding all alone. After all, hadn't his father had known Dan and Erica just the same as she did? *What would he be doing if he were here right now?* he wondered—a question that had made his throat tighten at every major life event.

"Hey, Mom," he said, sitting beside Sarita. "I brought you some cake."

She smiled at him and laid her hand on his. "Just think," she said, "this will be you and Sophia in a few months. Can you imagine it?"

Arjun closed his eyes. An image came to mind: a groom leading a bride around the ceremonial fire. The groom wore a crimson *kurta,* and the bride was resplendent in a red *sari*—

but, when they turned to look at Arjun, he saw that they had no faces.

Sarita seemed to know what he was thinking. "Don't worry, Arjun," she said. "It will come."

Nisha was on the dance floor, shimmying her shoulders in a flowing blue dress. Sarita caught him looking. "*Beta*, are you alright?"

"Yeah," Arjun said. "Hey, Mom? Can I ask you something?"

She nodded.

"When Revathi *bhua* and Manju *bhua* came to our house, they mentioned something about Vicky not being suited for me. That our relationship was wrong because it wasn't arranged. But you stuck up for me."

She smiled. "Of course I did. That's a mother's job."

"Did you mean it?"

Sarita sighed. "You deserve to be happy. That's all I want. I trust you to make the right decision—and, whatever you choose, I will always support you."

Arjun squeezed his mother's hand. "I love you, Mom."

He felt someone tap him on the shoulder. "Nisha," said Arjun, looking up at her. "This is my mom."

"A pleasure," said Sarita, extending her hand and examining Nisha with that appraising gaze of hers. She smiled. "Well. I'd better get my dancing in while I can, eh? I'm afraid that, no matter how hard I try, I simply *cannot* stay up past ten o'clock." She rose. "It was nice to meet you, Nisha."

Nisha took Sarita's seat. "That was a beautiful speech you gave," she said, slicing off a bite of cake with the side of a fork. "You certainly upstaged the Maid of Honor."

Arjun laughed. "Thanks," he said, cutting off his own corner of the cake. "It took me a while to write. Like, days."

She smiled. "So, where's Sophia tonight?"

Arjun shrugged. "Some economics conference in Austin. What about Patrick?"

She shook her head. "He's here somewhere, but not with me. I don't think we really connected romantically, you know?"

He had to keep himself from smiling. "I'm sorry to hear that."

She leaned back and draped one of her arms over the back of her chair. She looked out at the dance floor, at everyone grooving to "Proud Mary."

"You know, this reminds me a lot of my wedding," she said. "My first wedding, I mean. All these people, all so happy."

She turned suddenly toward Arjun. "Do you love her?" she asked. "Sophia."

He sighed. "No," he said. "But I will."

Nisha smiled wistfully. "I hope so, Arjun. I really do."

The music slowed, and Arjun recognized the song as Fleetwood Mac's "Landslide." Nisha stood and stuck out her hand. "Come on," she said. "Dance with me."

He balked. "I'm a terrible dancer."

"So am I," she replied. "But that's not about to stop me. Now, are you coming, or what?"

He smiled. "Sure," he said, and he took her hand.

She led him out to the dance floor, weaving between the groups of people. His hands moved to her hips, and she put her arms around his shoulders. She stepped closer, and he moved, as well, until he could feel her breath against his cheeks. "I think this is my favorite song," he said.

"Why?"

"It always makes me sad," he replied.

He looked down at her. "I just noticed: there are little flecks of gold in your eyes."

Nisha smiled. She leaned her head against his chest, and Arjun thought that his heart was pounding just a little bit louder, only for her. They moved with the music, swaying back and forth like sea grass.

They danced for a long while after that. There were fast songs and slow songs, happy songs and wistful songs. Holding Nisha against his heart, Arjun's memory flashed back to that day in Dolores Park, when she'd played the electric guitar with the wind in her hair.

Gradually, the ballroom began to empty. As the older folks shuffled out, Arjun found himself sitting alone with Nisha at one of the circular tables on the periphery of the dance floor. "It's getting late," she said. Her voice was terribly soft.

"Do you want to go home?" he asked.

She shook her head. "No."

"I booked a hotel room for the night," he said. "It's only a few blocks away. Do you want to come up for a drink?"

She nodded. They gathered their things and stepped out into the night. It was the last day of May, but the air had chilled. Nisha took Arjun's arm and walked close by, warming herself against his body.

They arrived at the hotel and took the elevator up to his room on the second floor with a view of the park. Arjun slung his jacket over the desk chair, crouched by the minibar, and peered inside. "Anything good?" Nisha asked.

"Nothing," he replied, shutting the fridge.

"So," she said. "What now?"

Arjun looked at her. She was sitting on the edge of the bed, her head slightly angled. She sat upright, expectant. There was a spark in her eyes.

An idea occurred to him. A wonderful, terrible idea. He knew what both of them wanted. All he had to do was step towards her. One move, and it would begin. *Would it be so bad?* he wondered.

"There's a TV here," he said instead. "Do you want to watch something?"

Nisha raised an eyebrow, as though she'd known what he'd been thinking just a moment ago. She shrugged. "Sure."

It was the usual after-midnight dreck: The Real Housewives of Wherever, Rick Steves' Europe, a documentary about Gettysburg playing on PBS. Arjun clicked through rapidly, then stopped. "Oh, my God," he said. "It's fate."

"What is it?" Nisha asked.

Arjun smiled. "It's *When Harry Met Sally*," he said, settling into the bed next to her.

He could not have said when they fell asleep—whether she drifted off first or he did. But, when morning came, Arjun woke to find Nisha Nandan under the blankets beside him, their bodies woven together like marriage trees.

CHAPTER

Twenty~Two

For a moment, Arjun felt immensely content. He watched the slow rise and fall of Nisha's chest, the way her nostrils flared ever so slightly when she exhaled. He felt the weight of her arm flung across his chest. He leaned over and brushed the hair out of her eyes. Then, he got up and went to make himself a cup of coffee.

Halfway to the machine, he turned around. That really *was* Nisha Nandan lying in the bed. And, last night…*Oh, no*, he thought, his heart dropping into his stomach.

Nisha stirred and propped herself up on one elbow. Her hair was messy, and she was dressed in the fluffy white hotel bathrobe. "Hey," she said, stretching.

"Hey," he replied, unsure how to phrase his next question. "Did we…?"

She laughed softly. "No," she said. "We just slept. I didn't drool on you, did I?"

Despite himself, he smiled. "I don't think so," he said. He felt immensely relieved that he and Nisha hadn't actually been intimate—but there was also a twinge of regret, followed by a flood of shame. *Oh, my God*, thought Arjun. *What am I going to tell Sophia?*

He rubbed his temple. "Listen, Nisha—"

"Wait," she said, holding up a hand. "I need to tell you something."

He frowned. "What is it?"

She paused, and her eyes found his. Arjun knew that something big was coming, a few words that would bowl him over like a thunderclap. "What is it?" he asked once more, his voice so quiet that he thought Nisha might not hear.

But she had heard.

She took a breath. She was still half under the covers. "I love you, Arjun," she said, her green eyes sparkling. "I'm in love with you."

There was a howling sound in his ears. It was as though he were ten thousand feet above the ground, soaring through the clouds. Nisha's simple statement echoed in his brain, three words more beautiful than the finest song ever written: *I love you.*

"You…you love me?" he repeated.

She nodded. "Yes," she said, her voice barely a whisper.

"Why?" he asked, incredulous that a woman like this could have made such a proclamation about *him,* of all people.

She laughed. "Because only you would ask a question like that," she said. "Because you're my best friend. Because you moved my book back. Because, when I felt broken, *you* were the one who made me realize that I wasn't—that I never was." She sighed. "So, yeah. I love you."

She looked at him expectantly. "Say something," she said. "Please."

His throat felt like it was made of sandpaper. "I can't," he said, the words grinding like knives against his throat as he forced them from his mouth. "I'm really sorry, Nisha. I'm really, really sorry."

She shook her head. "Why not?" she asked, as if this were a debate.

"Nisha, I'm with *Sophia*," said Arjun. He sat heavily on the floor, leaning his back against the wall. "My engagement ceremony is in a few weeks," he said. "This is what I'm supposed to do."

She got out of bed. "Supposed to…according to whom? You? Your family?" She crouched in front of him and stared into his eyes. "You don't love her, Arjun. You told me as much last night."

He shook his head, then stood. "Sophia and I are getting married," he said, telling himself just as much as he was telling Nisha.

Still, she would not relent. "Why?" she asked, standing with him. "You don't even know why, do you?"

"Because I've tried it before!" he exclaimed, surprised at the loudness of his outburst. "I told you about Vicky Chang, didn't I? And I know you think it shouldn't matter—but it matters to *me*, Nisha. I got my heart shattered. If we got together, could you tell me with *complete certainty* that it wouldn't happen again? That I would never get my heart broken?"

Nisha said nothing. She sat down on the edge of the bed. "Can you?" Arjun repeated, his gaze hard as granite.

Finally, she spoke. "Someone once asked me whether I would still marry my ex-husband if I knew how it would turn out." She sighed, and Arjun could hear the tears in her voice. "And the truth is that I would. Because I was doing what I thought would make me happy. And, yeah, it didn't work out. But if it had, it would have been the best thing in my life."

She sighed. "No one can predict the future. But you can't let fear and uncertainty stop you from pursuing your own happiness. Don't you see how happy you would be with me?"

And, suddenly, he *did* see it, more clearly than he'd seen it before with anyone. The future wasn't hazy like it was with

Sophia. It was like watching a movie, the picture clear as crystal: him and Nisha curled up in bed, buying an old Victorian in San Francisco, raising their kids, and spending their lives together.

But it wasn't enough.

He looked at Nisha and saw the tears shimmering on her cheeks. He wanted to hold her, comfort her—instead, he turned away. "I'm sorry, Nisha," he said. "I really am."

He walked out of the room before she could say anything else. He headed down the stairs and stepped out into the harsh morning light.

It was the first of June, and summer had arrived.

Twenty~Three

When Monday morning came, Arjun did not return to the basement office. Instead, he found Adam D'Antonio and asked if he could have his old office back.

His boss gave him a curious look. "You want to come back to PSI?" he asked hesitantly, as though he hadn't heard correctly the first time.

"I mean, I never really left PSI, did I?" said Arjun, trying to make light of it. "I still work here, you know."

Adam guffawed. "You've got me there," he said. "But, after all this time, why come back upstairs? Did things go south with you and that girl?"

Arjun feigned a smile. *Was it that obvious?* he wondered. "Nothing like that," he replied. "It's just time for me to return to where I belong."

His boss grinned. "I like the sound of that," he said, clapping Arjun on the shoulder with one of his gigantic hands. "Welcome back to the land of the living!"

Kelley was equally enthused when Arjun broke the news to her. "Finally," she said, kicking her feet up on her old desk just outside his office. "This is *much* better than that bullpen at the *Current*. I mean, honestly, Arjun—what were you thinking?"

He shrugged. "I don't know."

The truth was, there was only one thing on his mind: Nisha Nandan. Since their fight in the hotel room, Nisha had drifted through his thoughts like a ghost. When he closed his eyes, he saw her: typing away at her computer, her face screwed up in concentration; playing the guitar, her fingers moving deftly over the frets; leaning in to kiss him, her eyes closing just before their lips met.

Arjun tried to distract himself with work, but even the crushing monotony was not enough to tear his thoughts away from her. Half of him wanted desperately to rise from his desk and sprint down to the basement, to fling open the door and see if Nisha was still there. He could have texted her, of course, but he hadn't spoken to her since the previous morning. In fact, he hadn't told anyone about their night together, not even Dan or Erica (who, by this time, must have been on their honeymoon flight to Tokyo).

There was a knock at his office door. It was Kevin McPherson, dressed as usual in one of his flamboyant Hawaiian shirts. "Hey, Kevin," said Arjun, turning away from his desktop. "What's up?"

"Nothing much," said Kevin, sitting as Arjun gestured to one of the chairs across his desk. "We haven't talked much since…you know."

Arjun smiled. "Since Emily Richter stole my storefront from under me? It's okay to say it."

"What are you going to do now? Are you going to find a new restaurant?" Kevin pulled a folded sheet of paper out of his pocket. "I took the liberty of finding some other buildings for lease across the city. I know it's not the location you wanted, but…"

Arjun took the paper as Kevin slid it across the desk,

genuinely touched by the other man's thoughtfulness. "I really appreciate this," he said, scanning the list. "But I don't know if that's the move I want to make now. A friend actually helped me to turn the recipes I developed for the restaurant into a book, *Raja's Kitchen*. I put it up on Amazon a few days ago."

Kevin raised an eyebrow. "That's great news. How many copies have you sold?"

Arjun laughed mirthlessly. "Two," he said. Dan and Erica had bought one copy; Kelley had bought another.

Arjun sighed. "Maybe this is a sign," he said. "I mean, nobody seems to care about the recipes. And the food in the book is the food I was going to serve at the restaurant. So perhaps this is the universe's way of saving me from a very expensive mistake."

Kevin frowned. "So, what does this mean for Raja's?"

Arjun shrugged. "It's dead, Kev." Until now, he hadn't actually *heard* those words aloud. But there was a finality to them, a weight that attached itself to his soul and nearly dragged him through the floorboards.

"Thanks for stopping by," he said. "And thanks for the list. But I should probably get back to work."

Arjun was still in a depressive slump that night during dinner with Sophia. She'd returned from her conference in Austin with a new haircut: she'd trimmed off the ends of her hair that had been dyed blonde, leaving her with a sleek black mane that fell just past her shoulders.

Arjun listened distractedly as she told him about the various lectures she'd attended. His mind was elsewhere: *How do I get more book sales?* he wondered.

I could throw a couple thousand dollars at a marketing firm, he thought. *But who knows if that would work.*

I could beg bookstores to stock it and hold a reading…but who would show up?

I could get some restaurant critic to write a glowing profile on the book.

That last one was the most promising…but Arjun didn't know any restaurant critics. He stared down at his food; his appetite was nonexistent.

Across the table, Sophia perked up. "I almost forgot!" she said, rummaging in her purse. "These arrived today from the printer."

She drew out a white envelope and slid it across the table. Inside was a card: gold lettering embossed onto thick maroon cardstock. "What do you think?"

"It's nice," he said. His mind flashed back to that night in the hotel room with Nisha, and he felt a sudden pang of guilt. He'd been agonizing over whether or not to tell Sophia, but he'd eventually decided against it. He and Nisha hadn't slept together—well, technically they had, but nothing more. *But, if it's no big deal, why not tell Sophia?* he thought.

Arjun picked up the card and read aloud: "You are cordially invited to the engagement ceremony for Mr. Arjun Rishi Chowdhury and Dr. Nandita Sophia Verma at the Sri Datta Sai Mandir in San Ramon, CA." There was a date inscribed below the invitation: June thirteenth, less than two weeks away.

"I was thinking we'd keep it small," said Sophia. "Just our families and close friends."

Arjun nodded. "That sounds good to me." While Sarita had told most of his relatives about Sophia, he still hadn't told most of his friends and acquaintances that he was getting an arranged marriage. He doubted they'd have the patience to sit through a *roka* ceremony, anyway. Besides: "fiancée" was easier to explain than whatever nebulous term defined the status between the first meeting and the engagement.

"Of course, the wedding itself will be much bigger," Sophia continued. "Actually, I wanted to know: what would you think of getting married in India?"

"India?" repeated Arjun.

"That's what I said," she replied, a note of irritation rising in her voice. "It's much cheaper than getting married in the US, let alone San Francisco. I don't know if you've saved anything for a wedding, but I've basically been a poor graduate student for the past decade, and I don't want my parents to shell out too much."

Arjun nodded. "I'll think about it," he said—though, in truth, he'd always envisioned his wedding in San Francisco.

"Please do," said Sophia, blowing on a spoonful of hot soup.

Arjun wondered again if he should tell her about Nisha. *You have to,* he decided. *It's impossible to keep a secret this big. You owe it to Sophia to be honest.*

He looked up from his food. "Sophia, there's something I need to tell you…"

"What is it?"

His mouth went dry. "Nothing," he said. "Let's get married in India."

She smiled. "You come around quick."

They walked back to Arjun's apartment after dinner. Now that it was June, evenings had become warmer, and the air hummed with the songs of grasshoppers and cicadas. "It's still early," said Arjun, climbing the steps to his front door. "Do you want to come inside for a drink?"

The implications of what he'd just asked suddenly occurred to him. *Do you really want this?* he wondered. Or was it some way of assuaging his shame? Sleeping with Sophia would move their relationship further than his relationship with Nisha—and perhaps, his guilty conscience would quiet down once again.

But Sophia shook her head. "I'm old-fashioned about that

kind of thing," she said, lingering on the sidewalk. "I think I'll just head home."

Arjun nodded. "All right." He waited with her on the curb until her Uber came, hugged her goodbye, and headed inside for the night.

Sitting on his couch and cuddling with his dog, Arjun found the episode strange. After all, he and Sophia would be engaged in less than three weeks—and they hadn't so much as kissed. *What will it be like when we get married?* he wondered. He tried to picture their first coupling: the demurely averted eyes, the first furtive movements, his hand moving uncertainly over her waist and drawing her in to kiss. Would the first time be awkward? *It always is*, he acknowledged—but, usually, the first time occurred *before* a couple walked down the aisle.

Arjun's phone buzzed. It was a text from Sophia: *Dinner again tomorrow? I've heard good things about Quince.*

Let's do it, he replied without thinking. He sunk back into the couch. Sally found a spot by his feet and was asleep in seconds. His laptop was on the coffee table, and he opened it and checked on his book again. The numbers were no more encouraging than they'd been that morning: despite everything he'd put into it, it had still only sold three measly copies (Kevin McPherson had purchased the third).

He sighed. He was closer than ever to his goal of marriage, but he felt like a dish towel with all of the water wrung out. He picked up his phone again and, without thinking, fired off a text to Nisha. *Hey,* he typed. *Hope you're doing well.*

A few dots appeared at the bottom of the screen, indicating that Nisha had read his message and was typing her response. Then, suddenly, the dots faded away. Nisha was ignoring him…and could he blame her? *I love you,* she'd told him, and what had he done? *I left her all alone,* he thought bitterly.

His mother called a few hours later, after Arjun had become fully entrapped by some terrible B-movie on Showtime. "Hey, Mom," Arjun said, pausing the movie. "Did you call to talk to Sally?"

"Very funny," Sarita replied. "How is my grandpuppy doing?"

Arjun laughed. "She's great. Getting some nice shut-eye. What's up?"

"Nothing," said Sarita. "I just wanted to call and tell you…I'm proud of you, Arjun."

He sat up. "What did you say?" In his thirty years on Earth, his mother had hinted around it—but she'd never outright said those words to him, not even when he got into Yale and Stanford.

"I'm proud of you," she repeated. "I was worried about you for the longest time, *beta.* These past few years, it's like you've been…unmoored. Having a girl will be good for you. And you found a good one, Arjun. Sophia is perfect."

Arjun stood up. His mother was right about Sophia—much as it chagrined him, she was always right. But, still, his mind was not on Sophia. It was still back in that hotel room, with Nisha's words echoing through his mind:

I love you.

CHAPTER
Twenty~Four

Kiki's was busy for a Thursday night.

Dan slid into the booth, wielding twin tiki tumblers in each hand. "One for you," he said, handing one to Arjun, "and one for me."

The tumbler contained some sort of blue slushie that reminded Arjun of the Icees from the SuperAmerica in Iowa. It was delicious.

"So," he said, with a satisfied exhale, "how was Japan?"

Dan grinned. "Amazing," he said. "We had to have a short honeymoon because of Erica's residency, but we made the most of it." He leaned in and whispered to Arjun: "*We did it in a capsule hotel.*"

Arjun snickered as Erica arrived from the restroom. "What are you laughing about?" she asked, sitting down.

"Nothing," said Arjun, giggling into his drink.

Erica's head whipped towards Dan. "You told him about the capsule hotel, didn't you?"

Dan shrugged. "I thought he should know."

Erica shook her head. "I'm married to a child."

Dan grinned. "Aw, babe. You said 'married.'"

She smiled indulgently, then turned her attention back to Arjun. "So, what's new with you?"

"Nothing," said Arjun, which was unconvincing even to himself. Erica noticed his tone immediately, like a bloodhound on a fresh scent.

"You have something juicy," she said, her eyes widening. "What is it?"

"It's nothing," said Arjun, trying to put more conviction into his voice.

Still, Erica wasn't having it. "You know about the capsule hotel," she said. "It's only fair that you tell us your secret."

"It's not a secret," said Arjun. "Really, guys, it's nothing."

Dan glanced over at Erica. "I know what it is," he said with a sly smile. He turned to Arjun. "You slept with Sophia. It's about time."

Arjun felt the color rush to his cheeks. "No," he said. "I didn't sleep with Sophia."

"…but you slept with someone," said Dan.

Erica's eyes widened even further. "What? Who?"

Arjun shook his head. "You guys aren't going to drop this, are you?"

Dan and Erica replied in unison this time: "Nope."

Arjun sighed. He looked down at the table and scratched at the vinyl edging around the tabletop. "It was Nisha," he said finally. "I slept with Nisha."

It was as though a bomb had gone off. "You *didn't*," gasped Erica. "Where?"

"At the hotel, after your wedding," Arjun said. "But I didn't have sex with her. We literally slept together—like, in the same bed."

Erica shook her head. "I can't *believe* you!" Arjun braced for one of her lectures—or, worse, another kick. "I mean, what did I tell you last time?" she continued. "This was a *bad idea*, Arjun. But did you listen? No, of course not." She seemed to realize something. "How did Sophia take the news? Are you two still together?"

Arjun avoided her gaze. "I didn't tell her." Before Erica could protest, he continued: "And I'm not going to. It's not like we meant to fall asleep together. We were just sitting, and it was late…we drifted off. Is that so bad?"

Erica was incredulous. "Are you serious?" she asked. She took a deep breath, preparing for the torrent of profanity she was about to unleash across the table. "Arjun," she began, "you and Sophia are getting *married*. I mean, honestly—"

There was a shrill beeping noise underneath the table. Erica unclipped her pager from her belt and checked the message on the tiny display. "*Shit*," she groaned. "I have to go to the hospital. But this isn't over, Arjun."

She moved to leave, and Dan stood, as well. He hung back for a moment as Erica made her way to the door. He drummed his knuckles on the table and sighed. He looked down at Arjun. "You're my best friend," he said, "so I have to give it to you straight. This is a bad look. I'm not going to debate whether or not you crossed a boundary with Nisha. But it's not fair to string Sophia along if you have feelings for someone else. You need to make a decision."

Arjun shook his head. "That's the thing," he said miserably, tracing his fingers over the ridges of his tiki cup. "I have."

Dan nodded. "Okay," he said. "Call me if you need to talk to someone." He squeezed Arjun's shoulder and followed Erica out of the bar.

Arjun decided to stay at Kiki's for a bit longer. He sat at the bar, hoping the alcohol would dull his racing thoughts enough for the walk back home. He knew he needed to take a hard look at himself—but there was no better way to procrastinate than with a stiff drink.

Halfway through his second scotch, he heard a voice that made his heart go cold. "I think it's ridiculous," a woman was saying to her friend, just down the bar. "The VCs in Menlo Park are children. Dumping a hundred million into that company is the same as setting it on fire."

The woman's back was turned to Arjun. She had shiny black hair that fell just past her shoulder blades, and she wore a thin beige trench coat. Arjun stood. The other end of the bar was on the way to the exit. *If I'm quiet, I can sneak right by her,* he thought. He treaded silently, keeping his head down and moving as quickly as possible. Finally, he slipped past her. The door was only a few feet away…

He felt a hand on his shoulder, and his stomach did a backflip. "Arjun?" came a voice. *Her* voice.

He turned to face the woman. She looked completely different but exactly the same. "Vicky Chang," he said, forcing a smile. "How nice to see you again."

She smiled back at him. The corners of her eyes crinkled, just like they had all those years ago. Arjun used to love that about her. "I thought I recognized you," she said. "But I didn't want to accidentally mistake you for the wrong Indian guy."

He chuckled, then hated himself for chuckling. "Well, tonight's your lucky night," he said.

Her smile disappeared when she saw his jacket under his arm. "Wait, you're not leaving, are you?" she asked.

He nodded as casually as he could. "I was going to," he said. "I need to take the dog out."

She raised an eyebrow. "You have a dog? I thought you were allergic."

Arjun shrugged. "I got a hypoallergenic breed." He pulled out his phone and showed Vicky the screensaver: a picture of Sally wearing a onesie (Nisha's idea). "Her name is Sally."

Vicky took his phone and practically melted. "What a *cute*

name," she gushed. She glanced over her shoulder at her friend. "Can we meet her?"

Against his better judgment, Arjun piled into an Uber with Vicky and her friend, a cherubic blonde woman named Callie. "So, how do you two know each other?" Callie asked. Arjun was sitting in the passenger seat, and he exchanged the quickest of glances with Vicky through the rearview mirror.

"It's a long story," Vicky said, her cheeks reddening. Callie nodded smugly, and Arjun knew what she was thinking: he was an old flame of Vicky's, a one-night stand, maybe. *If only you knew...* he thought.

They arrived at his apartment, and Arjun climbed the steps and let them inside. He heard the patter of little paws on the hardwood floor, and he kneeled to receive Sally, who, as usual, leaped up on her hind legs and started licking his face as though it were covered in peanut butter. "Hey, girl," he cooed, rubbing her soft yellow ears. He stood. "This is Sally," he said as his dog padded over to the two women, sniffing inquisitively at their trouser cuffs. Then, Sally laid down, rolled over, and permitted the women to lavish her with belly rubs.

"What a sweetie," said Vicky, standing up again.

"Yeah, she's the best," said Arjun, smiling despite himself. That evening's series of events was almost unbelievable: that he would see Vicky Chang again. That he would invite her to his home. That they were now bonding over his dog. *Maybe next time, we'll go ice-fishing,* he mused. "Can I get you two something to drink?" he asked.

"I have some work to do, actually," said Callie. "Vicky?"

She shook her head. "I'm fine to stay here." She turned to Arjun. "If that's all right with you?"

"Sure," he said, his Midwestern manners programmed so deeply that he couldn't have refused even if he'd wanted to.

Callie gave Vicky a sideways look, but she only shook her head. *I'll be fine*, she seemed to communicate. Callie gave a terse nod and went outside to call her ride.

Vicky sat on the couch while Arjun got them a couple of Perriers from the fridge. Sally slinked off to her crate and began wrestling with her favorite toy, the Gumby that Nisha had purchased for her. The sight of the toy was a bit painful for Arjun; he'd called and texted Nisha several more times over the past few days, but he'd still received no response.

"It's nice to see you again, Arjun," said Vicky, unscrewing the cap on her bottle. "I'm glad you're doing so well."

He looked down at his lap and smiled softly. "Yeah," he said, trying not to betray his inner turmoil. He glanced at Vicky's hand and noticed a thin silver band across her ring finger, studded with a small diamond. "Congratulations," he said.

"Thanks," she replied, working the ring around her finger with her other hand. "It's new. We only met six months ago, actually. I was still in New York, and he proposed right before I got on the plane to San Francisco. We've been doing long-distance ever since then."

"Is that difficult for you two?" he asked—and, to his surprise, he wanted her to say, *No, we're actually very happy together*.

She shrugged. "I guess I never had the sense of really *being* with him, you know? We were only together—like, in the same place—for two months, and we didn't ever cohabitate. So, yeah, the FaceTime dates are weird, but not as weird as they could be."

Arjun considered this for a moment. "You'll get through it," he said, and Vicky chuckled. "What?" he asked.

"Nothing," she said. "It's just...me freaking out about something, and you coming in and being all reassuring. It's like old times, huh?"

Arjun said nothing. To acknowledge their relationship, his greatest disappointment, would be like a knife to the heart.

It seemed, though, that Vicky did not want to let it lie. "Did you ever get my voicemail?" she asked.

He debated whether to answer truthfully. "I did," he replied finally.

She nodded. "I'm sorry for contacting you out of the blue like that. Sometimes five years feels like so long ago that I forget how painful everything was for us."

Painful for us? Arjun thought incredulously. Vicky had been the one to leave *him*, to tell him that she loved him but did not want to marry him, to cause him to sabotage all of his subsequent relationships...and *she* was telling him how difficult it was for *both* of them?

"Anyway, I know I probably made you feel very awkward just now," she continued. "But maybe it was all for the best. I mean, I'm engaged now, and you're doing so well here in SF."

He nodded. He felt the anger building up in his chest, the *hurt*, five years of repressed emotion bubbling over like boiling milk.

"I'm not doing well, Vicky," he said. *Stop it*, he told himself, wanting desperately to put on a stoic face, for her not to know how deeply she'd wounded him. But the dam had broken, and he did not know how to stop the flow. In an unbroken stream, Arjun spilled everything to her: his string of failed relationships, his decision to pursue an arranged marriage, meeting Nisha and then agreeing to marry Sophia. He told her about his night in the hotel room with Nisha, how she had told him that she loved him...and how he'd replied that he would marry Sophia, anyway.

By the end of this recounting, Arjun felt raw with emotion. He couldn't believe he'd said all of this to Vicky—and, more than that, he couldn't believe that she was still here beside him.

He sank into the couch and closed his eyes. Vicky put her

hand on his shoulder. "What's wrong with me, Vic?" he asked, leaning back and gazing at the ceiling.

She sighed and took his hand. "Look at me. I want to tell you something, Arjun." She stared deep into his eyes. "To be honest, I probably should have told you this a long time ago. Our breakup: it wasn't about you. You didn't do anything wrong. I just…I wasn't in the right place for it at that time." She paused. "You're a romantic, Arjun. You can try to deny it, but you've always been one. So, I'm betting that this difficult decision of yours…well, it probably isn't so difficult, after all."

"What do you mean?" he asked.

She only smiled. It was a wistful expression, mysterious and wise. "Only you know the answer to that," she said, standing. She embraced him, and as quickly as she'd reappeared in his life, she disappeared once more.

Arjun came into work the next day with a wicked hangover, which was not at all helped by Kevin McPherson, who burst into his office with a zeal that Arjun had never seen before. "I'm a little busy, Kev," Arjun groaned, rubbing his temples.

Kelley appeared in the doorway. "If you'd like a meeting, you can schedule one," she scolded.

"Too bad," said Kevin, pushing past her and taking a seat unprompted. Kelley began to protest, but Kevin quickly opened his laptop and showed it to Arjun. "Look," he said, jabbing at the screen with his stubby pointer finger. "*Look!*"

Arjun leaned in closer to the screen. He rubbed his eyes. "I'm not dreaming, am I?" he asked. The effects of the hangover were ebbing away, as though someone had stuck a syringe into his arm and was draining all of the alcohol out of his bloodstream.

"You are not dreaming," confirmed Kevin. His computer was open to the Amazon page for *Raja's Kitchen,* Arjun's cookbook. "You've gotten almost a hundred reviews. How many sales do you think you got?"

Arjun shook his head. His heart felt like it was about to

vibrate out of his chest. "My phone," he said. It had died overnight, and it rested face down on his desk, hooked up to the charger. He turned it over and logged into his seller page.

"Holy shit," he said. "Can that be right?" He turned his phone over to Kevin. "I've sold almost two thousand copies." A notification pinged on his screen. "Two thousand and five, now."

He shot to his feet and began pacing behind his desk. He looked at Kevin's laptop screen again, then refreshed the Amazon seller page to make sure that this wasn't some fantasy. He opened his email and saw at least a dozen messages waiting in his inbox, all from bookstores around the Bay Area. "We loved Ravi's Kitchen, and we'd love to stock it," said one of the emails—along with a request to buy one hundred copies. Arjun felt the sudden urge to begin running, or to drop down and count off fifty push-ups. "How…how this happened?" he managed, too hopped up on adrenaline to form a coherent sentence.

"You got a review from a critic," Kevin said. "It was published last night, and it looks like it got a ton of engagement. The article was really well-written, too. Hell, it almost made me want to go and buy another copy!"

Arjun's fingers were shaking violently, and the string of words he typed into the search bar came out as gibberish. "Do you have the article?" he asked.

"Right here," said Kevin, pulling his phone out of his back pocket. "I'm surprised you didn't know about it. It was published in the *San Francisco Current*."

Arjun raised an eyebrow. "The *Current?*" he asked. His heart began to pound in his ears, as insistent as the tide. "Who wrote it?"

Kevin squinted at his screen. "Uh…someone named Nisha Nandan."

Arjun's adrenaline rush came to an abrupt halt. "What did you say?" he asked, feeling the color draining from his face.

"Nisha Nandan," repeated Kevin. "Do you know her?"

Arjun could not say anything. He turned his chair away from Kevin as he felt hot tears welling behind his eyes. "Yes," he said, staring out the window. "I know her."

Arjun met Sophia for lunch at a restaurant in Palo Alto, but he only had thoughts for Nisha. He had rejected her—so why had she done this monumental thing for him? At the bottom of her article, she'd written a short disclaimer: *The author has a personal relationship with Arjun Chowdhury, the author of* Raja's Kitchen.

He was tempted to call her and ask: what *was* their relationship now? *Not that she would answer,* he thought with a sinking feeling. Still, as much as he knew that he could not be with her, he did not want to lose her from his life. *But is that even possible anymore?* he wondered. He'd noticed that Nisha had used the present tense—*has* a relationship—and he clung to that fact like a shipwrecked sailor might cling to a piece of floating debris.

"What's the matter?" asked Sophia, noticing that Arjun had barely touched his salad. "You seem kind of distant."

"I'm just tired," said Arjun, absentmindedly spearing a cabbage leaf with his fork. "My book had a big day today."

Sophia furrowed her brow. "Your book? What do you mean?"

"*Raja's Kitchen,*" said Arjun, a bit surprised that she was asking. "I told you about it, didn't I? It's a cookbook that I've been working on for the past few months."

She nodded. "That's right. I'm sorry; it must have slipped my mind. What's going on with the book, then?"

"I published it a week ago and had nothing to show for it. For a while, I thought it would die…but, overnight, it sold two thousand copies." He checked his phone. "And it's almost up to three thousand now. Honestly, I think it could even hit four thousand by the end of the day."

Sophia smiled. "How impressive," she said. "So, this book…is it just a hobby for you?"

He shrugged. "It was, before. My real goal was to open a restaurant, and the book was just a way of testing the water. But, honestly, given the growth I've seen today alone, I think I should just go for it. You know, leave PSI and devote all my time to starting my own restaurant."

Sophia looked as though she had smelled something unpleasant. "What is it?" Arjun asked.

She sighed. "Look—I don't mean to sound overbearing, but you're not serious, are you? You wouldn't really quit your job, right?"

He frowned. "Why not?"

"It's not exactly very sensible," said Sophia. "You make good money at PSI. Great money, actually. And, sure, your book is doing well—but that doesn't mean your restaurant will. What happens when you open the restaurant and it fails?"

And there it is, thought Arjun. Not *"if"* — *"when."* As though the collapse of his dream was a certainty. He felt indignation rising in his chest, and he turned away from Sophia before he could say something he would regret.

She reached across the table and squeezed his hand. "As an economist, I can tell you that restaurants are the riskiest type of business to open. You can't pursue something that uncertain as a newlywed. Promise me you won't let this distract you from your real job."

Arjun looked into those deep brown eyes of hers. He nodded. "Okay," he said. "I promise."

In a way, he was almost relieved when he dropped Sophia back off at the apartment she was renting in Mission Bay. He felt aggrieved that she'd extracted this promise out of him, had tried to pry him away from something that was so clearly important to him. The bitterness only built as he recalled that Sophia hadn't even *remembered* that he had written a book, despite them having discussed it half a dozen times.

He took a deep breath when he entered the PSI offices around three. It would do no good to start resenting Sophia now. After all, he decided, there was plenty to like about her. Indeed, from her perspective, her request was probably quite reasonable.

Without thinking, he opened the door leading to the basement and descended. He hoped he would see Nisha, so that he could thank her and explain to her that he still needed her in his life, needed her like grass needs the sun. When he opened the door, though, the office was dark and empty.

He climbed the stairs back up to the offices of the *San Francisco Current*. There was a secretary typing away near the front of the bullpen. Arjun walked up to her desk and tapped his fingers on the wood. "Hi," he said. "Can you tell me where I can find Nisha Nandan?"

"She's not in today," the secretary replied. "In fact, she hasn't been in all week."

"Is she okay?" asked Arjun, immediately concerned.

"I think so; she took vacation, not sick leave. Maybe she's in Fiji."

He nodded, though this seemed to him to be an absurd notion. "Can you do me a favor?" he asked. He reached into his pocket for a business card and slid it across the desk. "When you see her, please give me a call."

"What do you think?" Arjun asked, panting. "Honestly, Sophia, it doesn't get much better than this."

She looked around. "It's nice," she said, not sounding fully convinced by even this small declaration. The smell of humus hung deep and rich in the air, as fragrant as fine wine. Even though it was Saturday afternoon, Buena Vista Park was deserted, except for the few squirrels that chased each other through the trees.

Arjun led Sophia over to the benches on the hillside. Using the bench he and Nisha had shared felt strange, so he sat on the adjacent one. "Come on, take a seat," he called to her, gesturing to the spot beside him. "This right here is the best way to look at San Francisco."

She looked dubious. "Really? The best?" She put her hands on her hips. "What about Coit Tower? Twin Peaks? Or even Bernal Heights?"

He shook his head. "Okay, this is *my* favorite way to look at San Francisco," he sighed, trying not to betray his annoyance. "At least check it out."

"The bench looks kind of dirty," Sophia told him, looking distastefully at the chipping green paint.

Arjun shook his head. "All right. Is there another place you'd like to sit?"

She checked her watch. "I have to leave soon, actually," she said. "Not that this wasn't fun—I just have a bunch of pre-work for the professorship that I need to get done."

"Can it wait?" he asked. "We just got here."

"You can stay," said Sophia. "Really, it's fine. I'll take an Uber back to my place." She leaned over and kissed him on the cheek. "I'll see you tonight for dinner, right?"

"Of course."

He watched Sophia climb down the slope once more, take a turn down the path, and disappear into the trees. A feeling bubbled up in his chest, a feeling that he understood but couldn't quite name—like trying to describe a vague pain to your doctor. It wasn't that he didn't like Sophia; on the contrary, he liked her very much. On paper, she was the perfect partner.

But that's just it, he thought. *"On paper." But what about in real life?*

He shook his head. There was no point in asking questions like that. After all, that was the strange bargain he'd made by pursuing an arranged marriage: he was not in love with Sophia, and he wasn't meant to be. They would marry, and they would build a love together.

There was a rustling noise behind him. Arjun turned around to see a woman moving up the trail. She was wearing black leggings and a baggy green hoodie—the same color as her eyes.

His heart began to beat very quickly. "Nisha?" he asked.

She looked unsurprised to see him, as if she'd expected him to be there. "Hey, Arjun," she said, and there was a kind of tiredness in her voice, as though she'd been walking for a long while. She remained where she stood, ten feet away from him, her back to a thicket of wildflowers.

"I can't believe it," he said. "What are you doing here?"

"You know this park is for everyone, right?"

He laughed, felt how *good* it was to laugh. "It's great to see you, Nisha. That article you wrote…" He was momentarily lost for words. "Thank you," he said at last. Thank you so much."

She gave the smallest of nods.

"I'm sorry," Arjun told her, stepping closer. "I really am, Nisha. I mean, running off like that, when you were so honest and vulnerable with me. I was…I was too afraid to face myself." He paused. "Why did you do it? Why did you write that article?

She shook her head. "When you care about someone, you don't just turn it off."

"I care about you, Nisha," he said immediately. "I care about you a lot. More than anyone, I think. I just…I want us to be okay. I miss—"

"Arjun?" came a voice.

It was Sophia. He saw her walking back up the hill, a thin line of sweat trickling down her forehead.

"Sophia," he said, trying to appear nonchalant. "What are you doing back here?"

"I dropped my phone," she replied. "Have you seen it?"

He shook his head. "I'll help you look," he said, bending over. He glanced off into the trees where Nisha Nandan had been standing just a moment ago. Now, she was gone.

"Who were you talking to?" Sophia asked. "I heard voices."

"No one," replied Arjun, his brain in a sudden fog. "Just a hiker who got lost on the way up."

As he squatted near the ground and searched for Sophia's missing phone, Arjun wondered what he would have said to Nisha if Sophia hadn't shown up when she did.

Twenty~Seven

Arjun's new outfit itched.

His mother had bought it for him, all the way from India by way of one of her cousins in Ahmedabad. It was a dark blue *kurta* with golden embroidery: swirling patterns began on the chest and worked their way down the front. Even though the garment was made of fine silk, it was inexplicably heavy, and the stiff collar scratched at Arjun's neck. He walked over to the bathroom mirror and looked for a rash.

It was June thirteenth, the day of his *roka* ceremony, and he was back in Iowa. Originally, his engagement ceremony was set to take place at the Sri Datta Sai Mandir in San Ramon, but his mother had called him and Sophia a week ago insisting that she'd seen something in a dream, which told her that the ceremony should take place at the Hindu Temple of Iowa, instead. That was not enough to convince Arjun (after all, this wasn't the first conveniently timed dream that Sarita had had)—but when his mother offered to pay for the whole ceremony, Sophia had jumped at the opportunity.

Arjun sat on the couch in his old living room and thumbed through the book on the coffee table, a thick tome filled with black-and-white photos of Des Moines. Sarita was in the kitchen. "You know, one of my friends sent me an article about you," she said. "Some magazine called *Edible San Francisco*?"

"That's right," he said. It had been nearly two weeks since Nisha's original article in the *San Francisco Current*, and a reporter from *Edible* had called a few days ago to profile him and *Raja's Kitchen*. Book sales had grown exponentially, and the customer reviews that had rolled in were highly positive. Arjun had already ordered a second printing of his book, and he'd sold copies to nearly one hundred bookstores across northern California. In fact, just three days previously, Arjun had taken a call from a New York City publishing house; the publisher wanted the rights to distribute *Raja's Kitchen*, promising to put Arjun into Barnes and Noble nationwide. "I tried a few recipes myself," the publisher said. "Honestly, I wouldn't be surprised if *Raja's Kitchen* was in every home in America."

Sarita returned to the living room, a bottle of pomegranate-flavored sparkling water in hand. "How are you feeling?" she asked.

"About what?" replied Arjun, staring absentmindedly at a picture of the stars outside First Avenue.

"About your *roka, beta*," she sighed, shaking her head. "Honestly, sometimes I think you're not even paying attention to your own life."

He nodded. "Right," he said. "That."

The truth was, he was nervous. His Great Love Story was thirty years in the making—and today, it would be over. Sophia was the One.

Part of him felt relieved. Another part of him was incredibly nervous. *What if you're making a mistake?* he wondered, not for the first time that day.

Of course, he couldn't say any of that to his mother. Instead, he said: "I'm feeling fine. Sophia is perfect."

Sarita gave him a knowing look. "I'm happy for you," she

said. "And, remember: once you're officially married, I expect grandchildren within the year. I've been waiting for far too long for that."

Arjun chuckled.

"I almost forgot," she said. "I have something for you." She walked over to the bookcase and found a thick, black-spined photo album weathered by age. She opened the book and pulled a thin envelope from one of the clear folders within.

"This is for you," she said, handing Arjun the envelope. It felt flimsy in his hands, as though he might crumple it up just by staring at it. "Be careful," she warned, reading his thoughts as usual. "That piece of paper in your hand is one of my most valuable possessions."

"What is it?" he asked. Gingerly, he lifted the flap of the envelope and drew out a yellowed piece of paper. His eyes fell upon the text: small, messy handwriting in black fountain pen.

His heart thumped against his ribs. "Dad wrote this?" he asked, his voice almost a whisper.

Sarita nodded. "Ever since he died, you've had to be the elder in this family. Yes, you have me, and your aunts—but none of us could ever understand you the way he could." She paused, her voice thick with emotion. "I wish your father were here today. And, in a way, he is. I told you that he used to write me love letters, didn't I?"

She placed her hand on his shoulder, and Arjun felt the weight of her, this small woman who, for years, had been the axis of his entire universe. He rested his hand atop hers and was surprised to feel that hers was not a young hand anymore. The skin was thinner and rougher, and he could feel the veins beneath the surface like the roots of trees.

His mother cleared her throat. "I'd better get going," she said. "The *pujari* will have work for me to do, surely."

"Let me go with you," said Arjun, and, for the first time

since he was a child, he did not want to let go of his mother's hand.

She smiled. "Stay here a while. Commune with your father. And, when you're ready, meet me at the temple." She kissed him atop the head. "I love you, *beta.*"

"I love you, too, Mom," said Arjun, and he watched her amble down the hallway, slip on her sandals, and walk out the front door.

He sat on the couch, unable to summon the strength to open the letter. The last time he'd spoken to his father was almost ten years ago. In the decade since, Arjun had gone through every voicemail, every grainy VHS tape, even his father's tax ledger. He thought he'd seen it all, that the well had run dry—but, as it turned out, his dad had more to say to him.

He looked up at the portrait on the wall, at those deep-set eyes and that contented smile, which seemed to say: "It's all right. I'm here now."

Arjun took a deep, shuddering breath. He lifted the paper from the couch and began to read:

My Beloved Sarita,

It's raining in Amsterdam, and I am thinking of you. Do you remember the day we met? It was raining then, too. I am embarrassed to admit that I scarcely remember more than that—not because you were not arresting, but because I was as nervous as a leaf caught in a monsoon.

Why was I nervous? I knew so little about you. Of course, from the moment I laid eyes on you, I knew that you were beautiful—*But, I wondered, is that anything upon which to base the Great Love Story of my life?*

Then, I had a realization. All great love stories begin that way: briefly, unremarkably. All great loves are, at first, strangers. This was the beauty of our arrangement, was it not? Our love built slowly, in the margins, until it lit a fire in my soul—a fire that warms me even on this cold and rainy day.

I miss you, my darling. I miss our son. I hope to be home soon.

Ravi

Arjun read the letter again, and twice more after that. His eyes scanned the page ravenously; he was like a man in the desert dying of thirst, trying to suck the last few drops of water from his pouch. He looked once more at the portrait hung on the wall, stood, and walked over to it. He traced his fingers gently over his father's face as though he could feel the cheeks and whiskers, the moles and wrinkles, and all the bones underneath. His father's absence hit him, then, like a gaping void opening right in the center of him, a black hole that threatened to consume him from the inside out. "I wish you were here, Dad," he said softly. Then, he tucked the letter back into its envelope, found the black-spined book on the shelf, and replaced it once more.

His phone buzzed. He didn't recognize the number; it was probably Sarita, calling from the temple's phone to tell him she needed him to pick something up for the *roka*. He picked up. "Hello?"

The voice on the other end was not his mother's. "Is this Arjun Chowdhury?" a woman asked.

"Yes, this is Arjun," he replied. "I'm sorry, who is this?"

"It's Katie," said the woman. "From the *San Francisco Current*."

Arjun recalled the blonde secretary he'd spoken to a week ago. "Hey, Katie," he said, wondering why she was calling him now. "What's up?"

"Well, you told me to call you if I heard from Nisha Nandan."

He nodded. "Right," he said, though he knew that this was the absolute worst time to be thinking of Nisha. Still, he hadn't spoken to her, let alone seen her, since their chance encounter at Buena Vista. Some part of him still desperately needed to know where she was, and that she was okay.

"I just wanted to let you know that she just put in her two weeks' notice," Katie said.

Arjun sat down heavily on the couch's arm. "She's leaving the *Current*?" he replied, feeling like the wind had been knocked out of his lungs. "Did she say why?"

"She told me that she was moving to New York City. Something about getting over her writer's block. Did you know that she was a novelist?"

"Yeah," he replied softly. "Yeah, I did."

"Anyway," said Katie. "You told me to call, so…"

"Right," said Arjun, his mind a million miles away. "Thanks, Katie."

He hung up. Then, he took a deep breath and stood up again. *It doesn't matter,* he told himself, even though he knew this wasn't true. If Nisha really did leave, it would be like losing an organ: an eye, a lung—a heart.

Then again, in a way, it could be a good thing that Nisha was leaving. He knew that he still had unresolved feelings toward her. But it was like his father had said: real love was built slowly, intentionally. That was what he was building with Sophia. *That* was his real ticket to happiness, to the life he'd always wanted.

He checked his watch. It was time to leave for the ceremony. He examined his reflection in the mirror again, combed his hair, and brushed his teeth again for good measure. "Today is a good day," he told himself. "You're getting engaged. You should be very happy."

His car was parked in the driveway, the old Corolla still marked with the dents and scars of his teenage recklessness. He unlocked the front door and climbed inside. It was a warm day in Iowa, and he rolled down the windows, eager to feel the wind in his face. He turned on the ignition and began to drive.

The route from his house to the temple was one that he knew well. Arjun viewed this kind of driving almost as a meditative activity, and he turned on the radio and let his mind drift into autopilot. Mercifully, the roads were empty, and he drove with ease, the music playing softly in the fringes of his attention.

He thought more about his father's letter. It was like a cosmic reassurance, his father counseling him even beyond death itself. Arjun's father had married his mother only a month after meeting her; his letter proved how deeply he'd loved her, how fiercely.

Arjun gripped the steering wheel a little tighter. *That's what I want with Sophia,* he told himself. *That's what I will have with Sophia.*

He stopped at a red light. A man was walking his dog across the intersection. Arjun heard a song playing faintly on the radio, and he turned the dial up. The song was soft, plaintive—and Arjun knew it immediately.

If you're going to San Francisco…

He felt the hairs on the back of his neck rise. Why was this song playing *here*, two thousand miles from California? And why now, just before the most important moment of his life?

Arjun's mind flashed back to that day at Dolores Park, with Nisha stroking chords on the white electric guitar. He remembered the wind in her hair, the way her body moved and swayed in the clear afternoon light.

The light turned green, but he didn't move. Cars were honking behind him, but that didn't matter. It was only Arjun, and the song: the past and the present and the future swirling around him like an ocean wave.

The song took on a new dimension, and as Scott McKenzie faded out, Arjun heard music like he'd never heard before, a melody that contained within its notes and measures the world entire: rushing rivers and night winds, the call of sparrows at dawn, the excited chitter of the city. It was San Francisco: the hills and the valleys, the smell of fog and sea, magnolia and pine. It was his first kiss and his last, and it was Dan's smile and Erica's embrace. It was his mother, and it was his father, too. It was all of Arjun's experiences, all of his joys and defeats, all of his love and pleasure and pain, and it plucked him up like a child plucks a flower, and it held him tightly and would not let go.

And suddenly Arjun was driving, and as he drove he heard the symphony: the soaring violins and the earnest cello, the fiery horns and the booming timpani, and the bass so resonant that he felt it in his chest as his own heartbeat. And in the center of it all was Nisha Nandan, flying on the melody, her laughing eyes sparkling with delight.

He could not have said what happened next. He didn't remember driving to the airport and purchasing a one-way ticket. He didn't notice the silver clouds wheeling outside the plane windows, the *thump* of the plane against the tarmac. He didn't notice the driving rain, the heavens rending apart to drench the world below. All he knew was the music: the thundering, brilliant music, like life itself distilled into notes and chords. He sprinted to the taxi line and gave the driver an address. *307*, he remembered, chanting it like a mantra as the taxi sped past the streetlights of San Francisco. He arrived at the apartment building and sprinted inside. He did not have time for the elevator. He leaped up the stairs, two at a time, three at a time, faster and faster, *faster* until he reached the landing, and he turned and raced down the hallway until he found the door.

The song was coming to a boil now, the violins racing toward the heavens. Arjun knocked on the door, and there was no answer. He knocked again, louder this time, an insistent drumming as unstoppable as the rain outside.

The lock turned.

Nisha Nandan stood in the doorway, a vision in an oversized t-shirt and men's basketball shorts. She'd been sleeping; her brown hair was unruly, and she wore clunky black glasses instead of her usual contact lenses.

The sight of her made Arjun's heart skip a beat.

"Arjun?" she asked slowly, as though she was unsure whether she was still dreaming. She crossed her arms. "What are you doing here?"

"I was wrong," he panted, the rain dripping down his face and puddling on the floor. "My idea of love…it was all wrong. I thought a lightning strike kind of encounter would never work for me. That building a relationship on what I *wanted* meant that I could never really get to something that I *needed*."

He paused, searching her green eyes. "I have wanted so many things in my life, Nisha Nandan. But you're the first thing I've ever needed. You're the only thing I need."

He took a breath. "I love you," he said. "And that's the only thing that matters."

He said no more. He stood in her doorway, silently, waiting for her to say something, anything.

She shook her head. "Screw you, Arjun," she said.

She stepped closer and kissed him.

Epilogue

TWO YEARS LATER

San Francisco's Financial District is a triangle sketched out by Washington Street, Kearney Street, and the Embarcadero. It is a vibrant area, a forest of skyscrapers that rises above the people and the smaller buildings below. If you were to have been on the corner of Washington and Kearney streets at 4:22 p.m. on June twenty-third, in a year not too far removed from this one, you might have seen a man in a dark blue suit rushing by with a white bag tucked under his arm. This man's name was Arjun Chowdhury, and he was really, *really* late.

He held his cell phone to his ear, talking as rapidly as he walked. "Can we move anything around?" he asked, slightly out of breath.

Gordon, his new assistant, sighed on the other end. "Not really," he said. "A lot of this was set months ago."

"What about Green Apple Books?" he asked. "The signing at three."

"That's tough," Gordon replied. "I mean, you've re-scheduled three times already."

Arjun groaned. "Move it. Tell them I'll even do a recipe demonstration next time."

Gordon knew better than to protest; by now, he was more than used to Arjun's busy and ever-shifting schedule. "Whatever you say, boss."

Arjun passed a bookstore as he walked, and he paused when he noticed the display in the window. The sign on the top of the shelf said LOCAL AUTHOR, and he saw a picture of himself beside it. The lower shelves were packed with cookbooks, including copies of *Raja's Kitchen*, Arjun's perennial bestseller, and the four other cookbooks he'd developed and published over the last two years. He smiled and snapped a picture before moving along.

He caught the Muni and rode the six stops to Cole Valley. Arjun had always liked this part of the city. It was close to Golden Gate Park, and its mix of shops and restaurants was as bustling and eclectic as anywhere else. He walked briskly up the street, past a dog park and a Mediterranean restaurant, before arriving at a storefront with boarded-up windows.

Arjun drew his keys from his pocket and let himself into the building. It was a large space and was still in the process of being constructed. Light seeped through the cracks in the wood where the windows hadn't been completely covered. This was the site of Arjun's new restaurant, at long last. He'd designed it himself: the dark wooden floor, the golden wallpaper striped with jade, and the tables and the chairs that were being custom-built by a carpenter nearby. He'd left the kitchen design to Kevin McPherson, whom he'd just hired as his executive chef. But he'd insisted on choosing the restaurant's name, and the sign was propped against one of the walls: NISHA'S, it said, in looping green letters.

Gordon was in the back, deep in conversation with Kevin. Kevin still preferred to wear Hawaiian shirts in the workplace, but he'd traded his Birkenstocks for a pair of comfortable sneakers.

"No, no," Kevin was saying, pointing to a spot on the walls. "The ovens need to go *here*. Putting them elsewhere would disrupt the flow of the kitchen. Or do I need to explain it to you again?"

Gordon saw Arjun approaching. "I'm sorry about this," he said. "As I've explained to Kevin, the ovens need to be near the venting system. Failing to do so would put us in violation of San Francisco city code."

Kevin's eyes widened. "Screw the code!" he exclaimed.

Arjun laughed. "I agree with the sentiment, Kev. But I still think we should listen to Gordon on this one. Hey, we're still on for dinner on Friday, right?"

"At your place? Yes, I'll be there."

"By the way," said Arjun, "Nisha invited her friend, Daniel. She thinks you two will hit it off…so maybe dress up a bit?"

Kevin laughed. "Is he worth dressing up for?"

"That's for you to decide," said Arjun. "But he was Mr. December on last year's 'Gentlemen of San Francisco Fire' calendar."

Kevin grinned. "I'll buy a blazer."

Gordon checked his phone. "Arjun, your one o'clock is here."

"Ah," said Arjun. "If you gentlemen will excuse me."

He went to the door and opened it. "Kelley," he said, smiling broadly and embracing his former assistant. "It's so good to see you." A little girl bounded past him, and Arjun caught her and scooped her up in his arms before she could run into anything. "And Miss Emmy is here, too. My, you're getting so big."

Kelley smiled indulgently. "I told her I was going to see you, and she insisted on coming with. Sorry for the short notice."

"Don't worry about it," said Arjun, leading them to one of the few tables that had been completed and delivered to the restaurant. They sat, and he held Emmylou in his lap. "So, how's the life of a full-time artist?"

"Tiring," Kelley replied. "Though maybe that's just that girl you've got there. I mean, they're called the 'terrible twos'—but that is a *dramatic* understatement."

He laughed. "What do you think, Emmy? Do you feel terrible?"

She looked quizzically up at him, then erupted into a shriek of laughter before burying her face in his chest. "So, what brings you by?" he asked Kelley.

She reached into her black tote bag and pulled out a roll of canvas, which she unfurled across the table. It was a painting of Arjun and Nisha sitting on a bench—*their* bench—in Buena Vista Park. His arm was around her shoulders, and they looked at one another, laughing at some unheard joke.

"It's a little rough right now," said Kelley. "I've just done some basic blocking. I'm probably going to take another run at it for the final painting because I'm not sure I like the lighting here." She pointed to a patch of trees; Arjun could not discern that there even was an issue. "And I definitely need to practice painting Nisha's hair because it's kind of kinky here, but in real life, it's more wavy than kinky, right?"

"While you're at it, can you make me look like Superman?" asked Arjun. He leaned in and spoke in a low voice. "Between you and me, though: maybe sit on this and come do another outline in a few months. Like, six months."

Kelley leaned back, and her eyes widened. "No!" she exclaimed. "Are you saying—Nisha's…?" Kelley made a curving motion towards her stomach.

He put a finger to his lips. "No one knows," he said. "I only found out last week."

"Last week?" blurted Kelley. "How are you feeling?"

"Good," said Arjun contentedly. "This is what I've wanted for a long time. I'm happy."

Kelley laughed and beckoned for her daughter. "Give it a few years."

It was a quarter past seven when Arjun finally got home, having settled the argument between Kevin and Gordon for now. Thankfully, the commute was easy: his new house was the Victorian just across the street from the restaurant. Arjun bounded up the steps, the white package in hand.

He opened the front door. "Honey, I'm home!" he called, grinning as Sally bounded up to greet him. He'd always wanted to be a man who said that sort of thing when he arrived from work; now, most days, he did.

"I'm upstairs!" called Nisha. Arjun ascended and found her in the large, sun-filled room that served as their shared office. There was a bay window with a sitting area just underneath, and bookshelves ringed the walls. A large desk occupied the center of the room, and Nisha sat at one end, surrounded by stacks of papers.

Arjun went over and kissed her. "Did you have a good day?" she asked him as they pulled apart.

He nodded. "And I got the cake you wanted, too." He set the white paper bag on the table and removed the cake inside. It was chocolate buttercream on chocolate cake, velvety and delicious. "Chocolate cake is kind of an odd pregnancy craving, don't you think?"

Nisha groaned. "*You* try growing a baby inside you, and then you can tell me what's weird. By the way, did you decide what to do about that invitation we got?"

He shook his head. "I know Sophia and I are friends now. And Patrick is a good guy…but don't you think going to your ex-fiancée's wedding is a little weird? Besides, her parents will be there—and they *hate* me."

Nisha laughed. "Well, you did set Sophia and Patrick up. That has to count for something."

Arjun shrugged. "I'll think about it."

He heard a light moan, and he turned around. "Hey, Neesh," he said, pointing to the bassinet in the corner, "is that—"

"A baby? Yeah, it is. I'm sorry, I didn't tell you, but Dan's in Seattle, and Erica had some emergency at work, and long story short, we're babysitting Teddy tonight."

Arjun walked over to the crib just beside the couch and peered inside. The baby was sleeping peacefully, his eyes darting from side to side under his little eyelids. Arjun stroked the baby's cheek and drew the shade on the crib. He returned to Nisha and kneeled in front of her. He pressed his ear against her stomach.

"And how's our girl doing?" he asked, wrapping his arms around Nisha's midsection.

"No complaints yet," said Nisha good-naturedly. "I'll let you know if she starts talking in there."

"And your other baby?"

Nisha laughed. "I think I'm mostly finished with this draft," she said. "Though I still can't decide on a title. Did you have any ideas?"

He stroked his chin. "What about *The Arranged Marriage*?" he asked. "Nice and simple."

She shook her head. "It needs to be a bit punchier," she said. She waved her hand. "It'll come to me."

Arjun stood. He looked at the clock on the wall. "Our guest will be here any minute," he said. Nisha took his hand in hers.

"It'll be fine," she said. "It's not like she's a monster. In fact, I find her lovely."

He laughed. "Trust me, Nisha: my mother is Machiavelli in Gucci pumps. And she's going to freak out when she finds out—"

"It will be fine," she said. "I think she'll be glad to have a granddaughter, don't you?"

"It's not that," Arjun replied. "Knowing my mother—she'll want to move in!"

The doorbell rang, and he looked at Nisha. She smiled reassuringly and squeezed his hand. "I'm right here," she said.

He wrapped her in a hug. "You promise?"

"Promise," said Nisha, and together they went to open the door.

About the Publisher

Harbor Lane Books, LLC is a US-based independent, digital publisher of commercial fiction, non-fiction, and poetry.

Connect with Harbor Lane Books on their website www.harborlanebooks.com and on social media.

www.ingramcontent.com/pod-product-compliance
Lightning Source LLC
Chambersburg PA
CBHW030002010826
48973CB00007B/2124